seventeen

seventeen

Per Nilsson

TRANSLATED BY

Tara Chace

Front Street
Asheville, North Carolina

Front Street
An Imprint of Boyds Mills Press, Inc.
815 Church Street
Honesdale, Pennsylvania 18431

seventeen

the father

1

Here. Here's where we ended up. The roads were long and winding, the roads that led us here. For a while we traveled together, we followed the same path for a brief time. And now we're here. We ended up here. You and me. You lying there on the floor, me sitting here looking at you. Your eyes are closed, but you're breathing.

2

I was the first person to see you. In the whole world, I was the first person to see you. No, the second. At the same hospital, at this hospital, but in a different room. Seventeen years ago. When you came into the world.

I was there. I saw you. I was the second person to see you. The third was your mom, the woman who bore you in her body for nine months, the woman who bore what would become you. And you were on your way into the world, and I was sitting next to her. We would breathe together when the contractions came, we'd been practicing—deep, cleansing breaths and panting, blowing breaths and various other breathing techniques—that's how it was back then. We brought a baby into the world together, not just a mom without a dad. We practiced, I helped with the breathing. The baby was you.

Maybe you'd say that that was when everything began. Maybe that's where a human being begins, a life.

You were almost bald and helpless, and they laid you at your mother's breast and you sucked in the first sweet, yellow milk and I sat on the edge of the bed and watched and was filled with love. It was a miracle. A love like never before and never again.

You were so helpless. Just as pitifully helpless as all tiny newborn human babies. Like we all were. Just as dependent. A nothing, a living lump that doesn't know anything and can't do anything besides nurse and poop and pee and scream, and who depends on the presence of warmth and food and love out here in the world. Miraculous. It's a miraculous system.

I held your head in my hand, your heavy head. I tried to get you to look at me.

Father. I was your father, you were my son.

You're still my son.

You're almost bald now, too. And you look completely helpless lying there in front of me on the mattress in the bright light. Your eyes are closed.

3

But maybe that's not where a person begins, at birth, maybe it's more correct to say that your life began before that. You were already someone when you were born. You were more than an empty vessel, you were more than a lump of clay waiting to be formed. You brought something with you. You were already you from the beginning.

So, in other words, everything started at conception when one of my sperm won the race to your mom's egg and penetrated it, where the chromosomes combined, gave instructions: This will be a person. This will be you, yes, you.

Even that first cell, even that little gelatinous clump embedded in the lining of your mom's uterus was you. That little embryo was you. The fetus was you. All of the instructions had been given. In other words, you started nine months before you peeked out at the world.

You started in a cabin on the ferry between Copenhagen and Oslo. Yes, it's true. It had to be then; we figured it out, your mom and I. That's where you were created. Your parents were not sober, your parents had had drinks in the bar, your parents had danced to a bad cover band called the Pink Panthers that played Creedence Clearwater Revival songs and other old hits from the sixties and seventies. Your parents had danced passionately, closely, and loudly sung along with the chorus of the songs, your parents had stumbled, giggling, their legs wobbly, through the long corridors back to their cabin, your parents were happy and horny, your parents screwed. Bang.

That was where you started.

That doesn't mean that you were a mistake. No, we wanted to have you. We were trying. We'd stopped using birth control. I was twenty-eight, your mom was twenty-seven. There was a time when we'd said, "A child? Never." Having children means giving up your own life, having children means you stop living, stop fighting, make yourself weak and vulnerable and cowardly and dependent. Plus, there are way too many children in the world already. But now we wanted to. Your mom had heard her biological clock ticking. As they say. She wanted to first, but I was right behind her. We wanted to have a child. And you were the one we wanted.

And you were the one we wanted. Now I'm being silly. As if you get to pick. As if you could even imagine that your child would be someone else. A famous soccer player. A young rock star. A great pro golfer. That you could be someone other than who you are. Now I'm being silly. *You were the one we wanted.* How do I know?

Anyway, you're the one who came. You came and you were loved.

4

Now we've come to this point. From here we can go any direction. We can leave all our baggage by the side of the road, fling the heavy backpack into the ditch.

We don't need to bring anything with us. We can leave everything behind. Free! Without all the stuff that ties us down, that chafes against us and burdens and limits us. Free as children, like being born again. We can forget it all, we can leave it all behind.

No. That's not true. We can never forget anything, we always have to carry everything with us.

A person can't be reformatted. Everything leaves traces on the hard disk.

5

Yes, well, you have a lot to carry. Not just the things that happened during the seventeen years of your life. No, you carry a much longer history with you, you carry human history.

A person starts way before birth. Before fertilization. There's chemistry, too, there's DNA molecules. Dad's sperm brought something with it, something was waiting in Mom's egg.

Generations shaped you. You carry experiences, memories, traits from many generations back. Ten, twenty, a hundred generations stretch out behind you. An unbroken chain, a backward relay race through history.

A man meets a woman. A conception. A child.

A meeting, a conception.

A meeting, a conception.

A meeting, a conception.

Already we're back in the 1800s. A different time, a different world to live in. You carry something in you from that time and that world.

And much further back: a meeting, a conception; a meeting, a conception; a meeting, a conception; a meeting, a conception …

Let's hope the meetings were filled with love. Let's hope that the man and the woman loved each other. We don't know. Maybe you're a love child, maybe you carry not only your mother's and your father's love for you but also the loving meetings of a hundred men and a hundred women.

Maybe that's not the case. Probably that's not the case. At some of those meetings that led up to a conception and a child, love was probably missing. Instead: Force. Violence. Habit. Dependency. Lust. Intoxication. Or chance. And some of those children grew up alone, afraid, and cold. Maybe you carry this within you, too.

Hmm. Are you noticing that I sound a little solemn? Like a minister almost. But I didn't come here to preach, I promise.

6

You smelled so good when you were a newborn. You smelled like life. Now you smell bad. Now you smell like vomit and alcohol and sweat and tobacco. Your stench fills this bare little room.

But you're breathing, I see that you're breathing. That's what's important.

I could hold you in the palm of my hand when you were a newborn. Your whole little body in my hand, a whole tiny life in my hand.

Now a young man is lying on the floor in front of me. A boy, a young man. Tall. Almost six foot three, I'd guess. Very skinny. Not a lot of muscle definition, not fat. How much do you weigh? A hundred and fifty pounds? Shiny, sickly skin under the glare of these fluorescent lights. A few acne scars on the one cheek. Not much of a beard, huh? Just a little bit of fluff.

A boy or a young man? I don't know. Have you had sex? I don't know. There's so much I don't know about you.

I don't know what kind of person you are. It doesn't show from your appearance, at least I can't see it. Your hair's short, but you're not a skinhead, it's more of a crew cut. No, you can't be one of those beer-guzzling racist pigs, no, that's impossible, that would be way too ironic, even if having an absent father can cause a bunch of shit. I mean, you hear that and read that, but no, not a racist, no. Maybe you're into hip-hop. Maybe you listen to rap music and have a lot of friends with weird last names, I mean not the usual Swedish ones like Svensson and Andersson and Persson and things like that, I mean friends whose parents came to Sweden from Bosnia or Chile or Somalia or Iran or Kosovo. Although usually you can tell that, can't you? Baggy pants and baggy clothes, right? Sheesh, I know way too little about all the different youth subcultures.

What other kind of person could you be? There's vegans and animal-rights activists. You're thin enough at any rate. Maybe an antifascist activist, demonstrating against globalization and police brutality, smashing storefronts, wearing ski masks and wanting to take back the streets. You could be like that, you could be one of those, one of those types.

But maybe not at all, maybe you're someone who doesn't care. Only about yourself. Someone who sits at his computer. Someone who wants to get the best grades, and trade stocks and bonds and earn the most money. Someone who has the latest cell phone.

Anyhow, I don't think you're one of those soccer fanatics, practicing every single evening and playing home games and away games on the weekends and belonging to the soccer team's fan club and screaming from the bleachers. No, that would be weird with the parents you have.

I don't know what type of guy you are, I know nothing about you. I know nothing about how you live. I don't know what's important to you. I don't know you. I intended to participate in your life, you know. To be one of the people who shaped you, who showed you different paths. My intention was to accompany you on your journey. It didn't turn out that way.

But you managed to grow quite a bit in seventeen years. I can't hold you in my hand anymore.

•

Now the door opens. The nurse is back now, the same one as before, the short, chubby one with the curly hair. Now she's checking your pulse, she opens your eye and looks at your pupil. Then she turns to me and smiles a sad nighttime smile.

"Everything OK."

I can't decide if it's a question or a statement, I don't know if she means how you're doing or how I'm doing, so I just nod and clear my throat.

"Ahem."

"He seems stable now," she whispers. "I'll be back in an hour or so and we can fill out some paperwork."

I nod and clear my throat again. I haven't told her yet, but I suspect I'm going to have to soon.

The nurse stands there with her hand on the door handle and looks at me with an expression I can't quite interpret. "The police want to talk to him when he wakes up," she says. "It sounds as if ... more ... happened than just this. But that's up to him, of course. We won't release his name ... but, well ..."

She nods toward you, then she opens the door and leaves me.

7

Seventeen years old. A person's never so smart and never so dumb. And a person never gets any older, I've often thought that, that I'm still such a seventeen-year-old even though I'm almost fifty. Just as smart and just as dumb. Just as sure and just as unsure. Just as proud and just as cowardly.

No, in many ways I've failed to grow up. I don't know if it's the same for other people, if it's the same for everybody. But I don't think so. Lots of people seem so confident and stable in their grown-up roles, lots of people look so natural dressed in their grown-up clothes. On TV I see twenty-five-year-olds who seem like self-assured adults in a way I never was.

Now I'm sitting here sighing, a sentimental old man.

Well, I get like that easily. I mean, normally, too. You should be prepared for that.

And I remember. I haven't forgotten anything. I still carry such a jumble of memories from that time with me, although there are periods of my life that are a total blank.

Country Joe & the Fish. For example.

Have you ever heard of Country Joe & the Fish? No, probably not. A lot of bands from the sixties and seventies have become popular again, I've seen and heard that, but not them. Still, they were big, in the early seventies and before. An American West-Coast band. The singer's name was Joe McDonald. The guitarist was Barry Melton. They were big even though they only had one hit song, just one chart-topper: "I Feel Like I'm Fixin' to Die Rag," one of the most vocal songs about the Vietnam War. They played at all the festivals, and they were some of the heroes in the hippie world. But listen up: the group was called Country Joe & the Fish. They took their name from a Stalin quote, something about how the revolutionaries will live among the people like a fish out of water. So, Country Joe is Joseph Stalin. Joe. Joseph. That's exactly how it was, the times we were living in. The same group that did a song called "Acid Commercial," an ad for LSD, could pay tribute to one of the century's biggest dictators and mass murderers. So typical for our time. We were so dumb, so naïve.

And I remember that, that thing about the name.

I carry tons of completely useless trivia like that around with me in the world, although I later heard that it was a quote from Mao.

And the Doors, speaking of group names. The Doors were another one of the most popular groups. I'm sure you know them, right? Jim Morrison was the lead singer. He was one of the biggest heroes in the sixties. A sex symbol who starred in the girls' wet dreams and a poet in the boys' hashish-clouded heads. He was one of the people who died young in the sixties, too, along with Jimi and Janis and a lot of others. But anyway, the group the Doors took its name from the title of a book, *The Doors of Perception*. It's a thin little book by Aldous Huxley, and it's about his experiences on mescaline, it's about what happened when he took the hallucinogenic drug mescaline, a natural relative of the synthetically manufactured LSD, although Aldous Huxley had in turn taken the title of his book from a poem by the eighteenth-century English poet William Blake: "When the doors of perception are cleansed, everything will appear to man as it is, infinite."

I remember stuff like that. This is what I carry with me from my time as a seventeen-year-old. Strange, isn't it? I've forgotten so much else, I've forgotten so much else. And these days everything is slipping away, nothing seems to stick, I forget names and facts and get things all mixed up in my head.

I forget a lot of important stuff. But I'll remember Barry Melton. And that Aldous Huxley died the same day President Kennedy was shot in Dallas.

8

It was a long and windy road that led here.

You're lying there on the floor in front of me in the harsh light, I'm sitting here on this uncomfortable stainless-steel stool looking at you. There you lie. Here I sit. We ended up here. It was a long and winding road. That's what I think.

It is not quiet here. A fan is whirring, there's a persistent buzzing tone crackling from the fluorescent lights, rattling and clattering from out in the corridor, the sound of footsteps, sometimes running and sometimes walking quickly, the sound of doors closing and opening. You can hear voices, but no words.

I shut out the world. We ended up here, I think.

We're still alive, I think. You and me. Despite everything.

And I know why I'm here. I'm here to tell you the story.

9

Seventeen years old.

Well, so you're seventeen.

Seventeen, that's ... let me see ... seventeen times three hundred and sixty-five days, which is about twenty times three hundred, or six thousand days. Plus a little. A seventeen-year-old has lived for six thousand plus a few hundred days. How have you spent your days, how have your six thousand days shaped you?

I don't know you, I don't know who you are.

And I don't know what you're like.

If someone were going to describe you, if someone got to choose two words to describe you, which words should they pick?

Happy & Funny.

Weak & Cowardly.

Sad & Boring.

Kindhearted & Dumb.

Lonely & Brooding.

Self-centered & Stingy.

Proud & Self-confident.

Considerate & Generous.

Which would you pick? What two words would best describe you? What two adjectives best capture your character? Ugh, who can you sum up in two words? No one, of course.

You're my seventeen-year-old son, you're lying here on the floor in front of me, but I don't know you.

Seventeen.

A person is never wiser than when he's seventeen. Never wiser and never dumber. Never as honest.

What am I saying? *A person is never wiser than when he's seventeen.* What kind of bullshit is that? Seventeen-year-olds suck. Self-absorbed and chicken and fake, they just live to be seen, desperately searching for different masks to wear, different roles to play. Proud and self-confident, the seventeen-year-old stands there like he's the center of the world. Scared and insecure, the seventeen-year-old is trying to find himself, always keeping his eye on everyone else, not to be too much like them, not to be too different, always this pathetic balancing act.

Always governed by everyone else in his desire to be himself. That's what a seventeen-year-old is like.

But sure. Sure. There's more. A ... strength, yes. A curiosity. Maybe even a kind of honesty, too. I don't know, I'm sure it varies.

Maybe we never get any older than seventeen. I mean ... there are a few years when we are formed. Sure, you can say that there are periods in our childhoods that form us, but ... but when I think about myself, it's like I can never really escape the way I looked at the world when I was seventeen. When I knew everything, when I had all the answers. No matter how lost I feel now, some of those answers still hold true for me. Even though I can see how I was obviously part of an era, how I was part of a generation. And yet ... I'll never be any older or wiser.

Do you get what I mean? Ugh, I can't explain it.

I just know that there's a seventeen-year-old in me, the seventeen-year-old I once was. I was seventeen in 1972. I'm not going to get any more grown-up. Well. Well sure, of course I've gotten more grown-up. But I'll always carry something from that time and that life within me.

And I'm here to tell the story and that's where I'm going to start. Here comes my first picture. Listen and try to see.

10

Four seventeen-year-old boys are sitting on the floor of an apartment in an old apartment building near Värnhem Square in Malmö, Sweden. It's a Friday in early May 1972. Listen to their conversation:

"Time to pack a bowl?" one asks.

"Time to pack a bowl!" the second echoes.

"What've we got?" the third one asks.

"Primo Afghani black, the best I've smoked since that Lebanese gold last winter. You know, we should invest in a little party. There's this dude Kjellgren knows who went and brought some shit back. They say he has two kilos. We ought to ...," the first one says.

"I heard he was a spongy bum," the second one says.

"Less talking, more packing," the third one says.

"Seriously, dude, for three hundred bucks we could probably score three hundred grams. We'd be set for the whole summer," the first one says.

"Seriously, dude, we don't have three hundred bucks," the second one reminds them.

"Seriously, dude, we could get it," the first one says.

"Has anyone seen my bong?" the third one asks.

"Seriously, dude, three hundred bucks is no problem. We just shoplift some shirts and some expensive pants and a couple of art books," the first one persists.

"Seriously, dude, we're so not welcome in any of the big department stores here in Malmö anymore—like NK or Domus—we're totally gonna have to send someone else," the second one says, passing the bong to the third.

"Seriously, dude, there's too much talking in this apartment. Do you know what the Swedish title of *Do It!* is? I saw the translation at Lundgren's Bookstore yesterday. *Don't Just Talk.* That's what it's called in Swedish, of all the fuckin' ridiculous ...," says the fourth.

"Dude, you want to translate stuff? How about *Turn on, tune in, drop out* ... in Swedish that would be ... uh ... *tänd på* ... that can mean 'turn on' or 'get high,' uh, and ...," says the third.

"*Stäm in?*" the fourth suggests.

"*Stäm in!* Heeheehee, that makes it sound like some kind of sing-along, like some cheesy Swedish Lawrence Welk wannabe, like Carl Anton, 'Now everyone *stäm in* and we'll sing that old favorite, "Dandelion and the Scent of Tar," a one, and a two, and a one two three ...,'" teased the third.

"*Tänd på, stäm in, droppa ut* ...," the fourth one says, giggling.

"*Droppa ut*? That's more like 'dribble out.' Hey, speaking of which, have you fixed the faucet yet, Guran? You said you'd take care of that," the first one says.

"That's Timothy Leary, right?" the second one asks.

"What do you mean? What's Timothy Leary?" the fourth one asks.

"Dude, he was the one who said it. Or wrote it. Turn on, tune in, drop out. Well, it certainly wasn't Jerry Rubin," the second one insists.

"*Hoppa av*, damn it. It should be *hoppa av*, not *droppa ut*. *Hoppa av* means more like 'opt out' or 'drop out.' Idiot! *Tänd på*, uh ... *kom med, hoppa av*," the first one says.

"*Kom med?* Hello world, here's a song that we're singing, *kom med* get happy ...," the third one sings confrontationally.

"Don't just talk! Pass the bong!" the first one says.

Four seventeen-year-old boys are sitting there on the floor, one of them lights a bong, takes a long drag and then passes it to the next guy. It's a nice spring day, and the sun's slanted rays are making their way into the room through the grimy windows and illuminating the pool of smoke rising like a mushroom cloud over the four heads, the sweet scent of the hash smoke mixing with the scent of incense and herbs. The conversation is over. Only a few coughing fits and some giggling disturb the music from the stereo. A scratchy record spins around on the phonograph playing

17

the Grateful Dead or Jefferson Airplane. Other records are stacked in crates along the walls, books are strewn around in piles, and a few daffodils in a wine bottle on the windowsill provide a splash of yellow.

Can you see the picture?

Do you even understand what we're saying, do you understand what we're talking about?

"Pack a bowl" means "get the bong ready." Warm the little clump of hash, crush it up, mix it with tobacco from a half a Prince cigarette, and fill the bowl on the bong or chillum with the mixture.

"Spongy" is a funny old word from back then. I'd forgotten the word, but a friend reminded me. If someone is "spongy," it means he's a freeloader. A bum. In other words, a drag.

So. A very brief lesson in early seventies slang. I'm sure you understood the rest.

Jerry Rubin was a crazy hippie-yippie guy from America who wrote two books that became bibles to a lot of people at the time. Timothy Leary was an LSD prophet.

That picture is so clear for me. The sunlight through the smoke, the dust swirling and dancing in the light, the music, the hushed voices. And those wilting daffodils by the window. The weekend before I had spent three hours on an LSD trip sitting and staring at them and thinking: Yellow. The color yellow. This is the color *yellow*. Now I know the color yellow.

They're friends, those four boys. Three of them live there in that apartment. Mattsson is the one who lives there officially. His father rented the apartment for him because he felt guilty about being such an absent father. Mattsson is an anarchist. Before the last election Mattsson put up four thousand posters that said "Vote for Yourself." Mattsson knows absolutely everything there is to know about what happened at the Democratic Convention in Chicago in 1968 and about the trial afterward. Mattsson knows a lot, he reads a lot. Mattsson wears round Lennon glasses. And Mattsson wants to see the world.

The second guy's name is Per-Inge. He's the big guy with the long, curly hair. Six foot six and broad shoulders and big and strong, he lumbers around like an enormous, friendly grouch dressed in a big white Afghan coat, and all the girls fall in love with his beautiful smile and friendly eyes. "I'm a poet and I know it, hope I don't blow it," it says on a little slip of paper that's nailed to the wall over his mattress. It's a Dylan quote, but Per-Inge knows he's a poet, too. He won't take a step without a black notebook. He was my best friend. It brings tears to my eyes when I think of him.

Jonny is the third one. Jonny has curly hair and gingerbread eyes and he's always staring off into the distance, as if he's looking for something. I'm looking for the Truth, he says, and you can hear the capital T. That's my mission here on earth, he says. He often does his looking by sitting still in the lotus position for large parts of the day, he's tried every meditation technique there is, and he tells us funny Zen stories or teaches us about different bodhisattvas and Krishna and Meister Eckhart and the Tibetan yogi Milarepa who ate so much spinach he turned green. And other spiritual stuff.

The fourth one is me. I'm the one they call Guran. I don't live there in that apartment, but I'm always there. Well, almost always.

And who am I? Who was I? Even then I'd already found my

shtick. Even then I was Guran-with-the-camera. I was on my third camera that spring, an almost new Minolta that I bought off a guy who was fencing some stolen goods on Strøget in Copenhagen. The guy threw in three lenses, a normal one, a 210 mm telephoto and a 28 mm wide-angle.

"I was so lucky," I said when my mom asked. "There was this collector in a camera store who was looking for exactly the kind of camera I had before, so he gave me this nice one in exchange. What luck, huh?"

And she believed me. She always believed me, and it was so easy for me to lie to her. Even then, it was easy for me to lie, to anyone. And, you know, it was easiest to lie to the people who trusted me the most, and lies come so easily to me, as easily as the truth. But tonight I'm going to be honest.

I always had a camera with me. That's how you could recognize me.

I was Guran-with-the-camera. Always a camera bag hanging by its strap over my shoulder. I had a little darkroom in a closet at home, and a real darkroom with a good duplicator at school. I stole the photo paper and developing fluids from photography supply shops. The film, too. Always black-and-white, always Tri-X. The walls of Mattsson's apartment were covered with my pictures.

I had my thing. I'd found my shtick. Per-Inge wrote poetry, Jonny meditated, and Mattsson did crazy stuff. I took pictures. I saw the world in pictures, everywhere I went I saw pictures.

I'd found my thing. Everyone has to find their thing.

Four boys, four friends. We get together every day. We smoke hash every day. Every once in a while we take stronger psychedelic drugs. We've tried most things, but we don't inject. Speed kills. And never H. We're interested in living, not dying. We're interested in living more.

We get the money for the illegal drugs we stuff ourselves with by stealing. Or shoplifting. We go to department stores and shoplift things and then return them for a refund:

"My grandmother gave me this shirt for my birthday, but I'd like to exchange it."

Or, "My parents bought me this nice art book, but I already have it."

We're always considerate and polite and proper when we stand there at Customer Service and talk about exchanging our goods for cash. We're professional, both when we do the stealing and when we do the exchanging.

"Stealing," Mattsson giggles. "Ha! We're redistributing the wealth, that's all. I mean, the whole capitalist system is based on stealing: They steal our time, they steal our lives, those fuckers, they say we only have value as dumb beasts of burden or dumb consumers. Ha! We'll show those fuckers. He who laughs last laughs longest. He who laughs last laughs best. Ha!"

Why am I telling you this? Should a father tell his son this stuff? I'm telling you because my mission tonight is to be honest. My mission here tonight is not to lie and make up exciting adventure stories, my mission is not to raise you or teach you right from wrong.

And why am I remembering that specific Friday in May when the motes of dust were dancing in the sunlight? It was just a day like all the others. We sat there on the floor and smoked hash the way we usually did.

It's the daffodils, of course. But there's another reason, a much more important reason: I remember that Friday because of what happened on Saturday. That Friday was the last day in a chapter of my life. A new one was about to begin, but of course I didn't know it yet.

11

I want to give you two pictures from the day my life changed. Two pictures from a Saturday in May 1972.

One of the pictures is the clearest picture of my life. A picture that will never be erased, a picture I'll carry with me until I die, and then that picture will die, too, because it exists only in my head. I had my camera with me, but I never picked it up. I couldn't, and I didn't need to.

I already explained that I'd made it my life to see the world in pictures. I'd done that already by the age of seventeen. And maybe that's why this picture appeared before me that Saturday in May. It was as if the whole world had stopped. It was as if God raised his fat index finger and pointed and said, "Behold!"

That's how it felt. And if it had happened any other way, you wouldn't be lying in front of me now. If it had happened any other way, you wouldn't exist.

So, I'll tell you: It was a pro-bike demonstration. As I recall, there'd been bike demonstrations in downtown Malmö for a couple Saturdays in a row. There were about a hundred protesters, mostly young people, who biked from the Triangle down to Stortorget and then back along Södergatan to Gustav Adolf Square. We biked slowly and tried to block traffic as much as we could and so, of course, the drivers were irritated and they honked and we shouted, "No cars on city streets!" We shouted, "Environmental stickers don't mean shit when they're stuck to cars!" We shouted, "Power to the people!" We shouted, "Pollution solution revolution!" And we shouted, "Down with all your beep beep beep! Let freedom ring: ding ding ding!" And then we would all start ringing the bells on our handlebars and laughing and hollering.

I don't know who organized it. Maybe it was the Allhusgruppen, this sort of loose coalition of young people who were trying to get the city to open up a community center where everyone could come together and hang out. As they put it, a noncommercial meeting place. As they put it.

There were some grown-ups there, too. This eccentric old guy with a gray beard that everyone called Biker Bengtsson used to ride at the head of the group, and this really famous actress from Malmö City Theater always came along. She had red hair and she'd starred in some TV show that was really popular and people considered her a radical and a communist, but Mattsson liked to provoke her. He would ride next to her and hiss: "Stalinist, sure you are," until she ran into the bike in front of her, crashed, and ripped big gashes in her fancy, silky Mah-Jong–brand outfit—the "clothing with a political conscience." So Mattsson apologized, but the famous actress just swore at him furiously in a Stockholm accent.

Am I talking too much? Do you want me to show you that picture? Of course. I'm getting to it. I just wanted to set the scene for you first.

And so here we are: A sunny Saturday in May, and we're

17

biking from Stortorget back to Gustav Adolf Square. No, it wasn't a pedestrian-only street back then. And Södergatan was a big parking lot, the whole street—bumper-to-bumper honking cars that we were zigzagging in between. We would slap the blazing hot roofs of the cars with the palms of our hands as we biked by, and a trail of angry voices would follow us as we made our way through traffic. And there were so many of us. We were young and strong.

I'm feeling good. I remember that. Even before I discover her, I'm feeling good. The sun is shining and together we can change the world. That's how it feels.

We're young, we believe in love and peace and understanding. We understand, we see the world and we understand it. We're fighting the fight our parents can't or won't fight, our parents who dozed off in front of their TVs, our parents who sold their souls for gadgets and money and the welfare state and convenience and security and an extra week-long package vacation every year. That's the situation.

But what's going on? What's going on over there by the crosswalk?

There's some kind of disturbance. Angry shouting and hollering can be heard above the slogans and the honking. I see how Mattsson flings down his bike and rushes ahead. Whenever something happens, he wants to be part of it. I see some signs and banners fluttering and billowing in the air up ahead. The air is thick with car exhaust. There's no room to squeeze between the cars, so I pick my bike up and carry it over my head with all the ticked-off drivers screaming. I manage to get through on the sidewalk, leave my bike outside Tempo, run up ahead and, there, in the crosswalk by Stora Nygatan, I see her.

She's standing there.

There's a commotion over there, almost a fight. A group of demonstrators has stopped traffic, and of course Mattsson is part of it. Some of them are holding up a banner that says "When You Commute, Don't Pollute." And three drivers are standing there in white shirts with sweaty, red faces, screaming and trying to shove the protesters out of their way. And two well-dressed young men from the Democratic Alliance come over with their sign that says "Help America Stop the Spread of Communism" and they try to help the drivers, and the angry voices and shouting cause an even bigger crowd to form, and soon the pushing and shoving and yelling are going to turn into violence and fisticuffs. Everyone senses that. And there she is.

Rebel Girl.

She's standing there, and I see her.

This is the picture: A sunny Saturday in May 1972. Downtown Malmö. Demonstration. Commotion at the intersection. Cars, cars, cars. Exhaust. Angry voices. Sweaty drivers. And she's standing there. She comes into focus, everything else fades blurrily into the background.

She's standing there, the most glorious rebel girl. Facing the cars, she stands there with one arm raised, making a fist, dressed in a faded green U.S. Army jacket and worn blue jeans and kaffiyeh. She's standing there. Strong and proud, she stands there stopping traffic and doesn't seem to notice the chaos around her. She's shouting something I can't hear. Behind her and next to her, people are starting to fight, but she keeps standing there with her arm raised as if she were a soldier in an army, as if she were a saint on a mission from God, as if she were the Struggle incarnate.

And I'll carry that picture with me until I die. It exists only in my head; I never picked up the camera.

It was as if I'd been turned to stone. I was captivated. I was enchanted. I was in love. Who is she? I don't recognize her … A very petite girl with straight dark hair and bangs, and even from where I'm standing I can see the resolve in her eyes.

We can change the world. That's what her eyes say.

Yes, I think. Yes!

And then I see it happen. I see how one of the guys from the Democratic Alliance gets his eyeglasses broken and gets angry and scared, and now he's thrashing around like crazy with a wooden stake broken off one of the signs. And I see it hit her. It catches her completely off guard, and I see the blood on her forehead and I see her fall and I rush forward.

I'm courageous. It may be the only time in my life that I've exhibited courage. Cowardice and indecision and running away, lots of times, sure, but now, on this very Saturday in May, I'm courageous. I push and elbow my way through the crowd. I don't hesitate for a second, and I'm filled with a single desire: to help that girl. To save her, to take care of her, to protect her.

My desire is so strong and my courage is so great that I succeed. If I hadn't done what I did, you wouldn't be lying here now. If I hadn't done what I did, you wouldn't be you.

Next picture: She's lying there on the ground. Real fighting has broken out all around her now, feet are stomping near her head, almost tripping over her, I hear shouting and punching, but I see only her. Her pale, bloody face. Eyes open. Not scared but ... confused. A small child who doesn't get what's going on.

Now her eyes find mine. Yes, a tiny bit of fear, yes, I see it now, and I kneel down beside her, I whisper in her ear that I'm going to help her, I whisper that she has to get out of there, I ask if she can stand up, I pull her up, I dry off her face with the sleeve of my shirt and discover that she has a deep gash on her forehead and that blood is spurting out of it and I pull off my shirt and tie it tight around her head.

She supports herself on me, hanging heavily at my side. She stumbles along, she's very pale, her face is white like the moon and her brown eyes look at me with such bewilderment: What happened? What's going on? She's turned into a small, helpless girl, that proud revolutionary.

No, not helpless of course. Of course I would put it that way. I want to be the hero who, bare-chested, snatches her away from catastrophe, the hero who saves her. And, actually, that's what I do. In a way. I'm sure she wouldn't have died, wouldn't have bled to death on the street there, but she could have been seriously trampled or injured even worse. Certainly. Let me be a little bit of a hero. For once in my life.

So, I get her out of there. I curse the bikers who've turned the whole downtown area into gridlock, but I manage to get her down to the NK building, and traffic is moving on Amiralsgatan and I hail a taxi. "To the hospital! To the emergency room! Hurry!"

The taxi driver hesitates for a few seconds, wondering if there's a risk that his cab will wind up getting all bloody, but then he opens the rear door and lets us in.

I sit next to her on the back seat, my shirt has turned red, but still the bleeding seems to have stopped. She leans her head against my shoulder and I carefully stroke her cheek. She smells good.

"It's going to be OK," I whisper. "Everything's going to be OK."

Everything is going to be OK. But not right away. When we get to the emergency room at Malmö General Hospital and get out of the cab, the girl's legs won't support her. The shock and blood loss have turned her into a rag doll. But the taxi driver rushes over and rings the bell, and personnel dressed in white immediately come and look after the girl with experienced hands, placing her on a gurney. I have to answer a few quick questions, and then they wheel her off.

"What happened to the broad?" the taxi driver asks as he walks back over to his cab.

"Some idiot hit her with a stick," I say, pulling my wallet out of my back pocket.

"Shit, man, there's a lot of meatheads out there. Makes you wonder where we're headed," he says, wiping the sweat off his forehead with an enormous handkerchief. "Ah, what the fuck. It's on me, dude. Hurry up and get on in there so you can hold your doll's hand while they stitch her up."

And then he hops into his cab and drives away. Solidarity, I think. Or at least good old-fashioned kindness.

I have to answer several questions at the admissions desk, and then I wait in a waiting room that smells like emergencies and blood and tears, I'm given a blanket to wrap around my shoulders, and I close my eyes and doze off.

I don't know how long I've been sitting there, but after sitting there in a kind of trance for a while, I notice how the hospital smell mixes with the smell of money, and how someone is blocking the light from the window.

I open my eyes, squinting. Yup, it's true. He smells like money, the elegant, well-dressed, gray-haired man standing in front of me. Aftershave. Cologne. Tailored clothes. The smell of wealth. Well, you know.

"Ahem," he says, extending his hand. "I assume you're the young man who looked after my daughter. It's still not quite clear to me what happened, but I understand that I owe you a big thank-you. My wife and I. Yes, and Karin, too, of course."

Karin, I think as I shake his hairy hand.

Now I see her, too. She's standing a few yards behind her father, pale, with a bandage on her head. A woman is supporting her, an upper-class woman wearing makeup and a gray dress. Yes, her mother of course, and daughter Karin smiles a weak smile and makes a face. I understand. Rich man's daughter turned Rebel Queen. Nice girl turned revolutionary. She's ashamed of her parents.

But her smile warms my heart. Like never before, like never ever before.

"To reimburse you for the shirt. And the taxi ride. And a little thank-you."

I turn toward Rich Father again and take the bills he's holding out. I stuff them in my pocket without counting them.

"Thanks. But ... thanks."

"We're the ones who should be thanking you. As I said before."

And his wife nods earnestly in agreement. She stands there in the shadow of her husband, a few steps behind him.

"Well. Now we have to go home so Karin can rest and

recover from today's mishap."

But before they leave the emergency-room waiting room, Karin comes over to me, rebel daughter Karin, injured in battle, she sinks down next to me on the bench and her parents discreetly take a few steps toward the exit.

"How does it feel?" I whisper.

"Four stitches," she whispers. "Nothing to worry about. I'll have a little scar to remember the day by."

I nod. We sit there in silence and look straight into each other's eyes while we sense her father's presence behind us. And her mother's.

"I'm Karin," she whispers.

"I'm Göran," I whisper. "But people call me Guran."

"I'm going to call you Göran," she says.

She looks steadily and confidently into my eyes, and her words make my cheeks glow as if I were sitting way too close to a campfire.

"Call me," she whispers, and slips a piece of paper into my hand.

I nod. She leans forward and gives me a soft kiss on the cheek and then she's gone.

And I sit there with a yellow government-issue blanket wrapped around my shoulders and a slip of paper in my hand, and suddenly I shiver as if from cold, and I know what it is, it's loneliness and longing, and I know that just like her I'll have a scar to remember the day by, a scar in my heart and I'm yearning, already I'm yearning to see her again, and I know that I will.

Her name is Karin.

She kissed me on the cheek.

She's going to be your mother.

That's how it was. Those were my two pictures.

The picture of her standing there with her arm held high in the crosswalk.

Then the picture of her on the ground when our eyes meet.

One scar on her forehead and one scar in my heart.

I was seventeen, she was sixteen. My life changed that Saturday in May, a new life started. Not instantaneously, like if you flip a switch or snap your fingers, not like that. I didn't leave my old life just like that in a second, but I had already been changed, I had already found a new path to follow in life, and I knew it when I left Malmö General Hospital and strolled toward home, bare-chested in the blazing sunshine that Saturday afternoon.

A love that starts like that ought to last a lifetime. That's what people think.

12

Seventeen.

I was seventeen when I met her.

And we lived together for seventeen years, for seventeen years we were never apart for more than a few days here and there. For seventeen years we shared a life.

And now ... now it's ... let me think ... more than eleven years since we separated, since I moved out. I saw her a few years ago in Göteborg. She turned away. Of course she turned away. But it hurt me, even though I know that what I did after the catastrophe can't be forgiven. She will never be able to forgive me.

I haven't seen her since I came back to Malmö, strangely enough. And I haven't talked to her since then. Then, in that other life.

And now you're lying here, and you're seventeen like I was, and I don't know you and you don't know me, but I'm telling you the story because I want to give you … your story. I want you to know a little about the road that led here.

I don't know you, I don't know anything about the life you're living. I don't know why you're lying here. I don't know what happened.

But our paths crossed here tonight, you're here and so am I, and I'm telling you the story even though I don't know if you can hear. Well, I think you can hear me, I think what I'm saying is sinking into you, lying there on the floor below me.

I should have told you the story sooner. But I never managed to do it, suddenly everything was too late. I know I had the thought even when you were a newborn, I thought: I want you to get to know me, your dad. You have a bit of me in you, if you get to know me for who I was as a child and teenager, you'll learn something about yourself, too. Someday I'll tell you the story. That's what I thought.

It was a good thought, but I never managed to get started.

Now I'm telling you. I know that you hear me.

13

About my childhood. Very briefly. Just a couple pictures.

I was born in 1955. My mother and father were middle-aged, middle-class, middle-of-the-road Swedish people. Regular people. Your grandma and grandpa. My dad worked at the post office and my mom was a secretary, although she quit working when my big brother Krister was born, and then she was a housewife until I started school. Made cabbage pudding and cleaned the house and washed dishes and went shopping and collected grocery store receipts from Konsum.

An average small Swedish family with two children and a row house and a Volvo Amazon. I was six years old when we bought our first black-and-white TV. That was the same year I told the barber down by the outdoor market that I wanted a "Kennedy cut," and I remember the barber's annoyed sneer as he said, "You'd need a little more hair for that, boy."

Then he gave me a crew cut instead. A year later I saw Yuri Gagarin when he made an appearance at that same outdoor market.

Maybe you don't know who Gagarin was? The Soviet Union and the United States were in the middle of what was called the Space Race and the Soviets were triumphant, sending first the space dog Laika and then the cosmonaut Yuri Gagarin into space, thus demonstrating that communism was superior to capitalism as a societal system. According to the propaganda.

Poor Laika had to die up there in cold, black space, but Gagarin came back to Earth and toured all over Europe making appearances, and he smiled and was charming and he said that "now atheism is finally proven, because I've been up in space and didn't see any trace of God anywhere."

Well, I don't remember him saying that, of course. I heard that later. But sure enough, Yuri Gagarin even came to our little marketplace. I was there. I saw him.

I'd built a plastic model of a three-stage rocket. I was never that good at building models, they were always sticky with glue and there were always a few pieces left over.

That's how it was. It was a different time. We bought milk in glass bottles. From Konsum, or Solidar as it's called now, the co-op grocery store. Never from ICA or Pålsson's or any of those other corporate grocery stores. My dad was a Social Democrat from the soles of his feet to the top of his head, and for him solidarity meant buying his groceries from the co-ops. And buying gas from OK, the oil co-op. And going to study circles at the Workers' Educational Association. And getting his insurance from Folksam, the mutual insurance company. And driving a Volvo. And letting his sons join the Young Eagles, the Swedish branch of the International Falcon Movement of Socialist Education International.

He was duped, from top to toe.

I read comic books about Captain Mickey and Davy Crockett and Allan Kämpe. I went to school on Saturdays, too. Then we would get rice pudding with fresh fruit on top or sago soup before we broke for lunch. My classmates had names like Britt-Marie and Kjell-Åke and Pia and Ronny and Lars-Göran and normal Swedish names like that. I started working on my swimming because I had big feet. I'd read a book about the Swedish world-champion swimmer Arne Borg, and in the book it said that he had big feet.

Ugh, why am I telling you all this? Just sentimental mumbo jumbo, the kind of thing men and women my age start talking about at parties when they're sitting around the kitchen table over the last bottle of wine: "Do you remember *Rekord,* that sports and entertainment magazine? Do you remember when you could buy salty rabbit-dropping candies for a penny apiece? Do you remember those amazing stickers we got at Sunday school? Do you remember when IFK Malmö played Rapid Wien in the quarterfinals for the Europe Cup? Do you remember Småstad? Do you remember *The Breakfast Club* every Saturday morning on TV? Do you remember Andy Pandy? Do you remember the pop sensation Tages? Do you remember arch supports and Raket cheese?"

Sentimental old-person mumbo jumbo. We never learn anything from it, never. And you, especially not you. You don't learn anything about yourself or about your dad from my slogging around in Memory Swamp.

No, I wanted to tell you something else. Another way.

I'll start over. I'll try again.

I was a kid who thought a lot. I was a kid who did a lot of day-dreaming. I was a kid who created worlds in my head. I talked to myself. I talked to God. I was a chosen child, I knew that. I wasn't like the others.

Does that sound familiar to you? Have you felt special?

But I wasn't lonely. It's strange. I should've been lonely, I was the kind of boy who should've been left out. But it was the opposite of that. I was popular. I was picked early or, to be honest, I was often one of the two people picking the teams. Other people wanted to be on my team. I wonder why. I wasn't strong or cool. It must've had something to do with my ingenuity. I've thought about that many times.

Does that sound familiar to you? Have you been a leader?

I was afraid of the big guys who drank beer and gossiped and laughed in their loud, booming voices. I was afraid of the kids from Persborg—big gangs of them would rove around on summer evenings looking for a fight. I was afraid of having nightmares. There were periods in my childhood when I woke up every night drenched in sweat, shaking because of some dream, and I wouldn't dare go back to sleep. I would sit up in bed so as not to have to return to those horrors.

What are you afraid of? What were you afraid of?

Another thing I was afraid of was getting a hard-on in the sauna. I used to go to the sauna with Kjell-Åke and his dad every Friday night in the sauna that was in the basement of their apartment building, and as we sat there I was always thinking, "Do not get a hard-on, do not get a hard-on, do not start thinking about naked girls, do not start thinking about naked girls …" And of course then I would start thinking about naked girls and dirty thoughts. But I never did get a hard-on in the sauna.

Incidentally, my first sexual fantasies were so bizarre. Ha! I remember them. Even though I was the nicest, most harmless nine-year-old you could imagine, I connected sex with violence. I remember that so well. I would fantasize about how Ulla-Britt or Helen in my class would be sitting naked, tied to a chair, with evil villains threatening them. I might fantasize about how evil villains would come into the gym when we were having P.E. and force all the girls to take off their clothes, and then they would have to poop and pee on each other and stuff like that.

Ha! Strange. I've wondered many times if that's how it is for other boys, if that's how it is for everybody. Because those images and fantasies came from inside myself. I'd never read any pornographic magazines or seen any X-rated movies. Sure, I played doctor with the girls sometimes with some of the older guys on my street, but I still didn't really understand what it was all about. I didn't understand the giggling and the meaningful looks. I hadn't gotten that far yet.

Do you remember your first sexual fantasies? Before you really knew what all that was about, I mean?

Ha! I remember one time when ...

"Ahem ..."

14

Oh! I feel how my cheeks start burning and I avert my gaze. It's the nurse. She came back. How long has she been standing there? I never heard her open the door. How much did she hear? It must've sounded like child pornography. She must think I'm some kind of perverse pedophile or something.

I sit there blushing like a pimply teenage boy, caught by his mom with his hands under the covers.

That's right. I'm forty-six years old, and still I can be turned into a thirteen-year-old in a second. That's what I mean.

"He can't hear what you're saying."

I look up and our eyes meet. She smiles a cautious madonna smile, and my childish nervousness disappears as if by magic. There's something about her eyes. She has girlish eyes, actually, a girlish face. She is considerably overweight, two substantial arms with wobbly, pinkish skin, an ample roll of fat around her middle, bloated cheeks, and still her face is that of a little girl. She reminds me of a picture in some picture book we read when you were little.

"Actually, I think he can," I say, trying to return her smile.

"There are so many things I want to tell him, so many things I had planned to tell him but haven't yet. So now I'm doing it. And, actually, I think he can hear me."

I detect a friendly, slightly melancholy curiosity in her eyes as she tilts her head to the side and looks at me.

She stands there in silence, waiting. She still hasn't said why she's here.

"I'm ... I'm telling him about myself," I continue. "My son. I'm telling him about myself as a child. And a teenager. That's the kind of stuff I've never told him. Actually, that's the kind of stuff I've never ... never told anyone."

I don't know why I'm explaining this to her, a strange emergency-room nurse, and the instant I do, I regret it. What's happening tonight is just between you and me. It doesn't have to do with anyone else.

But she takes me seriously, completely seriously. She nods thoughtfully, and I catch a glimpse of a little gleam in her gray eyes.

"Funny ...," she says. "Strange."

Now she's gleaming like a whole lake at sunset.

"Remarkable," she says.

"Extraordinary," she says.

She's turned into some kind of living thesaurus, and she takes a step back and leans against the wall. She's off in her own world. I have to wait a few long minutes before she snaps back out of it and starts to explain:

"It's funny," she says then, looking almost a little ashamed. "It's funny because just last night I was sitting there talking to my daughter, and we were talking about ... stuff like this. Yes, she ...

she asked about my earliest memories, and then she told me that she remembered things from when she was one year old in the toddler group at day care, and I told her my earliest memories, and then I got to thinking that people ought to tell their stories. All parents should tell their stories. Just like you were saying. Although … as I said before, maybe you should tell your son when he can hear you better …"

She falls silent. I wait. She's thinking. Finally, of course, I can't help asking, "What's your first memory, your earliest memory?"

A small wrinkle appears between her eyebrows. She hesitates, but just for a few seconds, then she tells the story: "The sandbox. I was playing in the sandbox at a playground in the courtyard by the buildings where I lived, and a girl was mean to me. She took my pail and shovel, she stomped on my sandcastles, and I felt so … miserable, and … surprised. I didn't get it, and I didn't know what to do. And my mom wasn't there and I just screamed and ran away and then … there was a grown-up who looked after me. I think … I think what I discovered that day was that evil exists … ugh, that sounds so stupid …"

A self-conscious laugh, then silence again.

"Not at all," I say. "That doesn't sound stupid at all."

She sighs and doesn't say anything, and my little reply hangs there in the room like a deflated balloon on a tree branch. Finally, she sighs again and says, "But I was three years old then. My first three years are a blank. I've looked at the photo album, I've heard my parents tell the stories, but I can't come up with any memories."

"That's how it is for me, too," I say quickly. "Walking in the woods in a beech forest is my first memory. A Sunday memory. My dad is carrying me on his shoulders. My mom is wearing a suede jacket. It's a bright memory, the sun is shining through the leaves, so bright and so green that it almost hurts your eyes. And my mom is happy, she's laughing. There's a brightness in her face, too. That's how I remember it. I think I was three years old, too. I think I've also lost my first couple years, but it's clear that I carry within me everything that happened. I believe that. And, of course, some people ... some people claim that you can access it all, some people claim that we never forget anything, just hide it away ...,"

I stop talking, feeling dumb.

While I'm talking I see how she has lost interest; her interest in me and my memories and my amateur psychological speculations has dipped below zero. Her eyes are northern wintry seas now, frozen solid. She regrets telling me her story and the fact that for a brief instant I tricked her into taking off her professional uniform and turning into both a mother and a sobbing three-year-old girl. I tricked her into becoming a human being instead of a nurse for a few minutes.

I feel dumb, ugly, silly, and above all: old. Way too old.

So I sigh and grin idiotically and say, "Sorry."

She waves away my apology, casts a quick glance at you, and leaves the room.

15

Where was I? What was I saying? What was the last thing I told you?

Too many balls in the air now, too many loose threads, how are you ever going to be able to discern any pattern in this tapestry?

In a very disorganized way I'm talking about the first time I met the woman who would become your mother. When I was seventeen.

And my prepubescent sexual fantasies as a nine-year-old. And my memory of bright green and bright joyfulness as a three-year-old. My life is bubbling out of me. I'm a pot that's boiling over. Yes, but I know what's most important to me, what I really want to tell you.

I want to tell you about my life and my world as a seventeen-year-old.

I want to tell you about my life with Karin, your mom.

I want to tell you about my life as a father, about you and me together.

I want to tell you about the catastrophe and about what happened then. Yes, well, you have to give me a chance to explain. I'm not expecting you to be able to understand, let alone forgive me, but you have to let me explain.

I've never done that.

Now I want to. I'm going to tell you now.

Do you remember?

I'd met Karin on that Saturday at that demonstration and brought her to the emergency room. I'd met her father and he'd given me money. I counted the bills I'd stuffed down into my pocket on my way from the hospital back into town. Three hundred dollars. You probably don't get how much money that was in 1972. Three hundred dollars!

It took me a few hours of wheeling and dealing to turn the crumpled bills into just over three hundred grams of primo hashish from Afghanistan, then I trotted over to Mattsson's apartment, happy and high, as high as a kite.

"It's party time!"

My friends stared at me when I unwrapped my three aluminum-

17

foil packets on the kitchen table.

"You're shitting me."

"Where'd you get the dough for this?"

"From God," I giggled.

Nobody asked any more questions. We were accustomed to not asking too much.

And then we sailed away.

But I didn't forget her. No illegal drugs in the world could make me forget her, the slip of paper with some numbers on it burned like fire in my pants pocket all night and when it was almost midnight I ran down to a phone booth, fished out the slip of paper, and dialed her number.

As I waited with the receiver pressed against my ear I started to sweat. Shit. This was not a very good idea, calling in the middle of the night, stoned, with a case of the giggles, with a mouth as dry as a desert after several hours of uninterrupted smoking. What if ... what if the rich father answers? No, I'll never finagle my way out of this one ... I was just about to hang up when she answered.

"Hello?"

"It's me!" I shouted into the receiver. "I mean, hi. I mean ..."

I stopped talking. What did I want with her anyway? Again I was ready to hang the receiver back in the cradle when I heard her voice:

"Hi. I'm glad you called. I was hoping you would."

Then something remarkable happened. For the first time in my life I felt the power of love. The power of Love. In a phone booth at Värnhemstorget on a Saturday night at the end of May

1972, I felt the power of love for the first time. Or at least of falling in love. It was stronger, oh, so much stronger than a hash rush, and I was filled with a longing, a joy, a desire I had never even come close to.

Being in love. The most powerful drug of them all.

Yes. That's how it is. Or how it was.

"I want to see you," I said. "Soon. Now. Right away. Immediately."

"Good," she said. "Because I want to see you, too. Now, right away, immediately. Can you come over here?"

"Where do you live?"

"In Bellevue. Where the rich people live."

She gave me her address.

"That's far," I sighed. "And the streetcars don't run at this hour."

"Take a taxi, then," she said. "The old geezer must've given you some money, right?"

I sighed again. The money was all gone, invested in burned brain cells and consciousness expansion. Traveling by taxi just wasn't part of my worldview. And I'd flung down my bike on Södergatan an eternity ago. It must surely be long gone.

"No, I'll ride my bike." I sighed. "But it'll take me a little while."

"I'll check the gate," she said. "Don't try to get in. That'll trigger the alarm. Just wait and I'll come."

"OK," I said and rushed back to the apartment and borrowed Per-Inge's bike and set off on my long trek through Malmö.

Despite being filled with the Power of Love, it was a grueling late-night ride on a hard-to-pedal old-lady bike with soft tires, and

I was drenched with sweat a half hour later as I finally stood outside a locked gate in a high wall that surrounded one of those palatial old upper-class homes in a neighborhood that I had previously only ever biked through on my way to the Limhamn ferry or Sibbarp. I stood there gazing in at a garden as big as a park while a security camera stared at me, and after only a minute I heard footsteps on the gravel, and then she was there and let me in.

"Hi," she whispered.

"Hi," I whispered.

"You don't need to whisper," she whispered.

"Why are you whispering then?" I whispered.

Then she took a step forward, coming right up to me, put her arms around me, and pressed herself against me. Her hair tickled my nose. She smelled good, she smelled freshly showered.

"I was so happy you called," she whispered.

That's also a picture I'll remember forever. This picture is also part of the Greatest Hits of My Life, although it's a picture I will see from the outside. It's a picture that requires another cameraman: We're standing there pressed up tight against each other, Karin and I, in the mild pastel May night, tall trees tower up behind her like we're standing in the overgrown garden of a castle, a small pool with a fountain reflects the full moon, and there's a thin stream of burbling water, and there's a white statue standing in some boxwood shrubs, a naked Greek discus thrower about to heave his discus down toward Limhamn Field and the Sound. Click.

"I got sweaty on the ride," I whispered.

"I can feel that," she whispered. "Come on."

I glanced nervously up at the enormous house, like a gloomy, cheerless stone castle. I could just make it out through the trees, but she took me in the other direction, her warm hand in mine as we walked along the neatly raked gravel walkways down to the corner of the garden.

"This is where I live. Welcome to my house."

She opened the door to a little caretaker's cottage, took a step to the side, and let me in. I stepped cautiously inside, peering curiously around. The first thing I saw was Lenin, a gigantic Lenin poster was staring at me strictly in the flickering gleam of the candlelight. There were tons of other communist posters pinned up on the walls around him and communist books crammed into a small bookshelf. There were a few ottomans and a low table, and in one corner a wide foam rubber mattress, neatly made with the bedspread on. Everywhere there were candles burning in wine bottles.

"You have your own house?" I asked, surprised.

"Sure. It's just this one room and a kitchen. And a bathroom," she responded, smiling.

"How's your forehead?" I asked.

"Fine. It feels a little tight. I've been asleep all evening. But it doesn't hurt," she answered, still smiling.

She opened a cupboard and pulled out a large, red terry-cloth bath towel.

"If you want to shower there's a shower over there," she said, holding it out.

"That would be great," I said, taking the bath towel.

She kind of didn't give me any choice.

When I emerged from the shower, wrapped in the soft bath towel,

17

she was gone. I walked over and scrutinized the bookshelf. Not just Marx and Lenin. Would you look at that? The spines of a few familiar books, *Steppenwolf* and *Catch 22* and even *The Lord of the Rings*, a three-volume paperback set in English, aha, so then Tolkien wasn't counterrevolutionary …

She was there then, standing behind me. Suddenly she was there, without my having heard her come in. That's when she pulled the towel off me. That's when I stood there naked while she embraced me from behind, pressed herself against me, she was also naked, I felt her soft breasts on my back, I felt her lips on the back of my neck. Yes. Her breasts. Her lips. Her breath on my spine like the gentlest little summer breeze, her hands on my chest and my stomach like the softest kittens on a voyage of discovery in the grass. I closed my eyes. My heart was pounding. My cock was about to explode. It was pointing, proud and stiff, straight at a little plaster bust of Mao Tse-Tung.

We stood there for a long time, silent and naked. Then she whispered:

"Come on."

I'm sorry. Are you embarrassed? Your own father, your own mother, such a long time ago. But you don't need to worry, I'm not going to get any more intimate. Those aren't the sort of revelations I want to make. Besides, I wouldn't be able to do that anyway: I get embarrassed myself. If your eyes were open, you'd see how I'm blushing.

No, I'll fast-forward over those hours on her mattress. I'll just say: Never before, never anytime since in my life have I been so … so what? Fulfilled. Present. Delighted. Happy. Yes, I suppose happy is the word if I'm going to be honest. Yes. Never before, never anytime since.

If I got to choose to live one hour of my life over again, I would choose an hour from that night. Well, or the instant when you were born, of course.

Indeed, it's strange how things come full circle. That sixteen-year-old girl's breasts on my back. And eleven years later you sucked the first sweet yellow drops of milk from those breasts, your little mouth found its way, and you knew from the beginning that mama means food, that mama means safety, that mama means warmth, you were a newcomer to the world and already you knew so much.

Now I've lost track of where I was again. I've lost my train of thought. But it sure is strange. Life sure is a strange puzzle.

16

I was a novice at sex when I met Karin, but not a virgin. Two drunken sexual encounters were the sum total of my experiences, plus a little bit of normal teenage making out at dance clubs and parties with my classmates.

The first time was on the beach after a summer dance at Höllviken. I don't even know what the girl's name was, but it wasn't her first time, I knew that. It went very quickly. I felt like a fool afterward.

The second time was at a party with everyone from my class. I was drunk then, too, and ended up in a bedroom with Bitte from my class.

"I've always liked you," she said. "You're not like the others."

"Hmm," I said, and kept struggling with the hooks on her bra.

I knew that I was giving myself away as a beginner. But she

probably was, too. At any rate we left bloodstains on the bedspread on Lars-Göran's parents' double bed.

Several weeks went by at school before we talked to each other again. Even when we ran into each other, we avoided eye contact. I guess we both felt ashamed, although I don't really know why. Maybe just because we'd shown that we were novices.

So, I'd done it twice. I was a novice at sex and a novice at falling in love, too. A junior-high romance with a girl in the other homeroom, and a summer infatuation with a redhead the summer before. That was it.

And you? You who are lying here on the floor in front of me. Have you experienced love?

It's different now, I would think. We were young during the era of sexual freedom. Before AIDS and HIV. Sex was a nice recreational activity that everyone should have the right to engage in, without faithfulness or jealousy having to be involved, and …

But now I'm lying. I mean, that's what people say about that era. The truth is that I don't know if that's how it was. The truth is that I wasn't particularly interested in sex when I met Karin.

Oh, yes, that's the truth. I wasn't looking for sex or love or girls. It was totally other things that were important to me. Then. You could definitely say that she taught me something, that she opened a door, that she showed me another world. You could say that I grew. Or maybe it was just the opposite.

And at dawn, when we said good-bye, I learned that there's a price to be paid. All this delightful, damp, soft, giddy happiness has a price, and that price is spelled p-a-i-n.

She said, "You have to go before my mom and dad wake up.

It'll be so complicated otherwise ..."

I said, "I don't want to."

She said that she didn't want me to, either, but that I had to, and obediently I left the warm, soft mattress and her warm, soft close-ness, and got up into the damp morning cold and got dressed while she lay there with the covers pulled up to her chin and watched me with a meditative smile, and when I was ready I knelt down next to the mattress and said, "When will we see each other?"

"Actually ...," she began, and paused before she continued, but then she said it: "Actually, I already have a boyfriend."

I thought she was joking. Obviously, she was joking. Funny. Haha.

"Had," I said. "You mean that you had a boyfriend. You said it wrong. Wrong tense. You're grammar's a little weak. Must've gotten a C in Swedish."

"An A," she said.

Four seconds went by before I got that she wasn't joking. An ice-cold morning shower, thank you so much, I hate you, you little whore, you bitch ... And that boyfriend of yours? I'm going to castrate him with a dull knife.

Sexual freedom lost its appeal in that second.

"Just wait," she said.

She sat up and placed her hand on my cheek. "Don't be mad," she said. "Don't be sad. You're so ... amazing. I just need a little time. You have to let me have a little time. I'll call you."

I nodded. I loved her like I'd never loved anyone before. And that slimy boyfriend of hers was about to be an ex-boyfriend, I was sure of that now.

"When are you going to call?" I asked. "If you don't call, I'm

53

17

going to jump out the window."

"I'll call," she promised, caressing my cheek. "Tonight. Or tomorrow. Are you going to be home?"

"I'll be sitting by the phone waiting," I said. "All evening. And if you don't call tonight, I'll sit there all day tomorrow. And if you don't call then, I'll jump out the window."

"I'll call," she said, and leaned over and kissed my forehead.

I left her, walked through that overgrown park garden in the gray early dawn. The dew shimmered on the grass, the birds were singing their morning songs, outside the gate my bike was resting against the wall. I biked down to the ocean, walked along the empty beach at Ribersborg, soft swells rolled in, the sun slowly started to warm things up, and I was happy like never before.

Into the salty wind I sang, "For you've touched her perfect body with your mind," and I tried to get my pubescent voice to sound like Leonard Cohen's mellow, grown-up bass.

Happy and unhappy like never before. Wise and confused like never before.

I'd become so grown up since yesterday, and so childish. So free, and so constrained.

I'd learned so much.

I knew so little.

I knew one thing for sure as I stood there gazing out over the sound while seagulls and shorebirds cried out above my head: A new era has begun. A new era in my life.

17

Very lovey-dovey, no doubt about it. An early morning after a night I'll never forget and a new era of my life and birdsong and blah blah blah. And it's true, every single word.

I left out one thing that happened that morning, one thing that was not at all lovey-dovey, just ridiculously embarrassing. Something I've never ever told anyone. The kind of thing no one should tell anyone.

But I'm going to tell it. I'll tell it to you, because Chance or Fate brought us together here tonight, because I want to be honest, because I've waited for so long, and … and so that my story won't be too much mushy romance. Or gritty realism.

Here's what happened: I went to the bathroom that morning. Before I sat there by Karin's bed, before she told me about her boyfriend, I went to the bathroom.

I sat there for quite a while thinking about everything that had happened since I'd showered there a few hours earlier, and those thoughts made me feel good, of course. I was a little constipated, that's why I was sitting there so long. Then I finished and wiped and flushed and washed my hands and was right about to leave the bathroom when I discovered a big, fat turd sausage swimming around down there in the water.

Phew, how lucky, I thought, that I discovered it. And I flushed again, and … nothing happened. Just a little gurgle. No water, no flushing. My big, shiny turd sausage spun halfway around like a drowsy whale out in the ocean.

I waited a bit for the water to fill the tank, then I tried again. Gurgle. Nothing happened.

Do you get how ridiculous, how embarrassing that was?

What should I do? If Karin went into her bathroom and discovered that I'd left behind this greeting, she'd never want to see me again. She wouldn't even be able to think about me. I would be Göran Turd Sausage forever.

Do you get how awful it was? My hands were sweating, my cheeks were burning, my heart was pounding. What should I do?

I tried to flush. Nothing. Not even a little gurgle.

And it was so big. Gigantic.

"He was so full of shit," Karin would say when she told her girlfriends about me, and then she would giggle, and then she would tell the story and all of Malmö would be filled with girls giggling. Göran Turd Sausage.

Although really I didn't care about all of Malmö or about my reputation, it was Karin I cared about. I didn't want to lose her, having just found her.

I must've stood in there in Karin's bathroom for half an hour before I finally decided what I would do. There was a little window there, out onto the big garden, and I carefully opened it and using a little toilet paper I picked the turd sausage up out of the water and flung it out. Then I washed my hands carefully and went back in to Karin.

When I sat down by her mattress I'd already forgotten my troubles in the bathroom. The love I felt was so enormous and so strong, everything else became so small. And then we talked and she told me about her boyfriend and said that she would call me and blah blah blah. And when I left her and shut the door to her little house behind me, I found a big turd sausage lying on the gravel walkway beneath the bathroom window wrapped in a bit of wet toilet paper. I picked it up and took it with me as I left the yard.

Outside the gate I stopped, contemplating it with curiosity. Now it wasn't my enemy anymore. It was more like a friend now. Firm and fine, almost pretty. My lucky turd sausage. Ha. I started giggling to myself, standing there early in the morning outside a luxurious home in Bellevue with a turd sausage in my hand.

Then I remembered the security camera. Oh no! Was it on? Would her family sit there and watch this on tape tonight? "Ahem, it seems like your new boyfriend has kind of a weird hobby, Karin," her rich father would chuckle, and her mother would turn up her nose and … I giggled again and turned to face the camera and smiled proudly and held up the turd sausage as if it were a record-setting fish I'd just hauled out of the sound. Nothing could hurt me now.

Then I hopped onto Per-Inge's bike and rode down toward the ocean. I left the turd sausage on the wide gravel walkway leading up to the neighbor's mansion. Capitalist pig, I thought. Here's a little greeting from the working classes. Watch out, you bastards.

18

We ended up here, we're here now. I'm sitting here, you're lying there. The fan is humming, the triple-glazed windows hold the city's night noises at bay. You could well say that that's where our shared road began, one weekend in May 1972, the weekend I met Karin, the woman who would become your mother. One of the roads that led here started there. Over eleven years would go by before you were born, but one could certainly say that from that weekend on you were a possibility. If I hadn't met her, if I hadn't loved her, then you wouldn't be here. Or you would've been somebody else.

17

Can you think like that? Well ... you can think however you want. Is there any point in thinking like that? No.

But you do exist, you are who you are, you're lying here now and I'm going to give you your story now. Both the beautiful and the ugly, both the serious and the silly.

19

We're all children of our time. Many of us don't want to admit it. But of course we're a part of the pattern, of course we're shaped by the spirit of the times, by currents and ideas that are grounded in a specific time. Some of them are planned and planted by people who want to make money or win us over to some ideology, but some of the thoughts and ideals that shape a generation of young people seem completely unpredictable, seem to just suddenly waft through the air like seeds from thousands of dandelions and then suddenly catch on and take root.

Those of us who were young at the beginning of the seventies were children of our time. Everyone in Malmö didn't live or think the way we did, of course, the way my friends and I did. Some people went to supper clubs and danced, some wore suits, some listened to the Swedish Top 10, some drove around in big American cars, some didn't care about politics or the world beyond Malmö. Actually, most of them didn't care about that stuff. But even so, the image people have of that time has always been one of young people rebelling in different ways. All the same, I never really see myself when I see some fifty-year-old on TV talking about the sixties and seventies and the student movement or the antiwar movement and the Swedish music movement. It turns into a bunch of Determination and Righteousness. It turns into a bunch of, "We were so involved back then." Unlike young people today, who only think about their cell phones.

"We were involved in important issues like international justice and the fight against American imperialism." Unlike now, when young people are only involved in promoting free-range chicken farming and the right to party in the streets.

"The only violence we ever resorted to was that one egg someone threw at the American ambassador." Unlike now, when you can't tell the demonstrators apart from the rioters.

"... and we were so wise and determined and pure of heart and genuine and blah blah blah ..." Unlike now. Unlike young people today.

Maybe it's because those student-movement veterans are often five or ten years older than me. We were sort of at the end of the era, my friends and I. But I still don't think all that stuff is right. I mean, I don't know that much about young people today apart from what I see on TV or read in the paper, but it doesn't match the pictures and memories I carry with me from my own youth.

I mean, sure, we demonstrated. Whenever we had the chance. Against the United States and commuting by car and nuclear power and capitalism and commercialism and for the people of Vietnam and the people of Chile and the Greeks and black people in South Africa and peace and the environment and love. And other stuff. Of course we thought we had the answers to every question. Of course we considered ourselves left-wing, of course we were part of a movement. But all of the communists were just academic snobs pledging allegiance to Lenin or Mao or some other dictator and mass murderer. We understood that. We were anarchists. Or libertarian socialists. Thoreau and Bakunin and Kropotkin were our political household gods.

It was about a revolution inside your head, too.

It was about living the revolution, not just talking about it.

It was also about an artificial paradise. It was about hash, it was about lysergic acid diethylamide, it was about little white happy pills.

It was about opening closed doors.

It was about finding keys.

It was about being cool.

How different is it now? I don't know, and you can't know either, of course. Now Malmö has computers and cell phones and skinheads and gangs and new synthetic drugs and new music, and whole parts of town full of people from the Balkans or Africa or Asia or South America. We didn't have that then.

And the world is so different. Communism is dead, I think. The marketplace and capitalism have triumphed. Everyone in Sweden owns stocks. The new enemy wears a full beard and worships Allah. Never in our wildest or worst dreams could we have imagined that development when we were seventeen. How will your world look in thirty years? And how different is it to be seventeen now?

I feel like I'm lecturing now. Sorry. I'll try to quit doing that. But it's because I've thought about these things so much, I've thought about the times that formed me.

I'll try to tell the story instead. More action and less reflection.

20

Now I remember something. Now I remember something I'd forgotten. Weird.

Now I remember that we were sitting on a grassy hillside in Slottsparken on a sunny spring day, Per-Inge and I. We were high and happy, we were throwing rocks into the canal and the different plopping sounds were making us happy and making us giggle like madmen, and we were watching the ripples in the water form patterns of concentric circles and intersection points.

Then we lay on our backs in the grass and talked about the student movement, about the war between the generations.

"Imagine if we have kids, imagine if we become parents, imagine if our children want to rebel in the worst way they can think of."

"Why would they want to do that? They're going to have awesome parents. We're going to be awesome fathers, we're going to live with lots of other people, we're not going to shut ourselves off in some apartment in some neighborhood full of housing complexes like Nydala and force them to watch bad TV shows. We're going to let our children be free, we won't try to control their lives."

"Yeah. Although ... although what if it's like some kind of law of nature? That children have to liberate themselves. That children have to do exactly the opposite of their parents. Imagine what our children will be like then—they have longhaired dads who smoke hash all the time and walk around barefoot and live in a commune and grow vegetables and listen to rock music and dance and believe in the great universal revolution. What will our kids do if they want to rebel?"

"Shave their heads."

"Walk around in army boots and uniforms."

"Listen to military music."

"Sing the national anthem."

"March in formation. Follow a leader."

"Drink booze."

"Enough! What a fucking nightmare. Even though it's never going to be like that, because the new man is going to build a new world, without borders and without class distinctions. Hallelujah."

"Hallelujah, brother. Let us load a bong."

"Hallelujah, praise the Lord. Deliver us from all our dark visions of doom. Teach us to live in the here and now."

"Forever and ever. Amen."

It's true. That's what we said. I'd forgotten that. Hmm. If that's the case, then the skinheads' kids and the children of the far-right Sweden Democrats will be happy, longhaired anarchists who burn the Swedish flag. No, of course it's not that simple.

But I remember that that's what we said. As a joke, as the worst and stupidest and most unlikely image of the future we could dream up.

21

"All right. I'm back now. Let's see if we can get to the bottom of all this."

It isn't until the nurse pulls up a chair and sits down facing me that I notice the name tag on her coat. Sister Anna. I see. She came into the room, checked your pulse and your breathing, and shook you gently, to which you reacted with a weak groan. Now she's sitting here with a black notebook open on her knee and a pen in her hand.

"I'd like to start by asking for your name and personal identification number."

"Göran Persson. 550119-4196."

I lean over toward her and whisper, "I'm not the same Göran Persson as the one who's prime minister of Sweden."

"I can see that," she says without batting an eye.

"Of course," I whisper, "because he is much heav—"

"And then this is your son lying here?" Sister Anna interrupts.

I nod.

"And his name is Jonatan Persson?"

I nod.

"Born?"

I nod and smile, but Sister Anna is very serious and very terse now. A professional woman, one hundred percent.

"He was born December 5, 1983," I say. "He's seventeen."

"So his civil registration number would be his birth date, 831205, plus …?" she prompts, waiting for me to supply the last four digits.

"I don't know. I don't remember."

Sister Anna looks up, contemplating me. She's completely expressionless, her face is completely unreadable and blank. I don't get it, didn't we tell each other our earliest childhood memories an hour ago, what's happened? Maybe she's just tired, I think, maybe it's been an exhausting night in the E.R.

"He's going to make it," she says. "We'll assume that this is a case of alcohol intoxication and nothing else. Drunk, in other words. All his readings should return to normal now, blood pressure and pulse are good. His degree of consciousness is increasing. No external injuries, his shirt is a little bloody as you see, but he doesn't have any wounds. Perhaps his condition is due to a combination of alcohol and pills. Does he have any substance-abuse problems?"

I shake my head.

"What do you know about his drug-use habits? Does he drink a lot? Often? Do you know anything about his friends? Do you know who he hangs out with?"

Soon I'm going to have to explain, I think. Then I sigh, shake my head and say, "Nothing. No, I don't know anything about that."

"Nothing?"

I shake my head and lower my eyes, down to her white clogs.

"I'm asking for his sake. So that we can help Jonatan as much as possible. I'm not trying to pry."

I fully understand that. Does she think I'm some stupid, sulky child?

"Did you know anything about his plans for this evening?"

I shake my head.

"Is he taking any medications? Obviously, we've already checked that he doesn't have diabetes. But does he have any other chronic conditions?"

I'm going to have to explain. "I don't know anything," I whisper. "I don't know him."

"What?"

I notice how her concern and surprise make her muscles tense, suddenly she's ready to make a run for it as she sits there just a meter in front of me.

"I don't know him," I repeat. "He's my son, but I don't know him."

When I look up I see a small wrinkle of displeasure in the middle of Sister Anna's forehead. But I also see that she's relaxed again, the slight fear has flown away, it's gone as if it had never landed on her in the first place. I can't help but smile, and my smile makes her eyes narrow and stern.

"I haven't seen him in eleven years," I explain with a sigh. "We separated when he was five, his mother and I."

Sister Anna studies me, waiting for me to continue.

"I ... I've had problems," I say.

Now she isn't afraid. Now she keeps sitting there. She explains, "He had your phone number on a slip of paper in his back pocket. That's why the police called you. No wallet, no ID. Maybe he was robbed. But as I said, no sign of violence."

I nod. Then I shake my head.

"I ... I wouldn't have recognized him if I saw him on the street," I say, and feel irritated when I hear myself choke up.

I turn away from her. I don't want her fat, white-lab-coat pity.

"I didn't know," she says.

I nod, shutting my eyes. I sigh. Run my right hand over my face, rub my eyes and my nose.

"Where does he live?" Sister Anna asks after a considerate moment of silence.

"He lives with his mother and her new family," I say without opening my eyes. "In Falsterbo. At least I think so. He's only seventeen. He's still in school."

"At any rate, could I ask you for his mother's name and address? And phone number. We'll have to contact her, of course. Maybe she can give us some of the information that … that … you don't …"

I nod, stretch, and look her straight in the eyes. You've become a stranger, Sister Anna, we've become strangers to each other.

"Karin Hoff," I say. "That's his mom's name. I loved her. We met when we were seventeen. We lived together for seventeen years. Isn't that weird?"

I snort and continue staring at Sister Anna, but now I can't shake her. She's just sitting there, solid and professional, waiting, her pen ready. So I pull up my shoulders and give her a crooked clown smile. Then I give her the address.

"But I don't know if she changed her last name."

Sister Anna nods. "We'll find her." She shuts her notebook and gets up from the chair. "An assistant nurse will come and look in on Jonatan at regular intervals. He may throw up, of course. If he does, you should help him. You can always call for us. We're waiting for a few test results, but as I said …"

She leaves the room and closes the door behind her without finishing her thought.

You're lying where you're lying. You're breathing.

I don't have much time. We don't have that much time together. I have to tell you what I want to tell you before Karin comes. Then I have to go. I have to be gone by then.

Why did you have my phone number?

And what did you do? Why are you lying here?

And whose blood is it?

22

I have to tell the story. That's why you had my phone number, so that I would come here to you and tell you the story. Do you hear me? I know you can hear me. I'll tell you more.

Of course she called.

"There's a young lady asking for you," my mother said, and in her pleased tone I could clearly hear the hope that a nice little girlfriend would make me forget those hippie pals of mine that I spent all my time with.

I grabbed the phone and shooed away my mother.

"Hi. It's me. Karin. Do you remember me? You stopped by here the other night …"

When I heard her voice in my ear, I lost the ability to speak. I'd waited a whole day, hadn't done anything other than wait. I'd thought out a hundred beautiful things to say, I'd thought out words and ideas I wanted to tell her, but in a fraction of a second my head was as hollow as a Ping-Pong ball.

"Uh …," I said.

Everything that had happened on Saturday seemed so unreal, like a dream, like a fairy tale, like a slender wisp of smoke vanishing into the sky, like nothingness. Was she actually real?

"Hello? Are you there?"

"Hmm," I said, realizing that I was nodding as if she were standing there in front of me, able to see me.

Then I laughed and snapped out of my paralysis. "Oh, yeah, I think I remember you." I laughed again. "Karin you said your name was? You're the rich chick who was going to break up with her sorry old boyfriend, right?"

What? What did I say? Why did I say that? That wasn't one of the nice things I'd thought out. Now she'll be mad or annoyed. Now she's going to hang up. Now I'll never ...

"Boy, are you cocky," she laughed in my ear.

"Sorry," I said. "That's not what I wanted to say, I was just so ... happy and ... confused ... when I heard your voice."

"What *did* you want to say, then?" she asked.

Now I didn't hesitate. "That I wanted to see you. That I've been thinking about you. That I ... that I've missed you."

The receiver was quiet. Then she said. "You sure know what a girl likes to hear, don't you?"

I could hear from her voice that everything was good. Everything was very good.

We talked for three hours. Talked and laughed. My right ear was throbbing. It turned bright red. I saw it in the hallway mirror after I hung up the phone. I was as happy as the lyrics to a pop song and did a little dance into the kitchen, where my mother was waiting with dinner and a knowing mom-smile on her lips.

We were going to get together the next day, Karin and me. We were going to play hooky together and take the ferry over to Copenhagen. I was happy and in love. I was so happy and in love that it wasn't until I was lying in my bed late that night that it occurred to me she hadn't said anything about her boyfriend. Was he still in the picture? Was he history? An ex?

Just the idea that he had existed made me ice-cold. Had he also lain there with her on that mattress? Had she done the things with him she'd done with me? I'm going to castrate that bastard, I thought. Love, peace, and understanding sailed away like three helium-filled balloons.

PN

His name was Claes. He was a communist, of course. Marxist-Leninist-Maoist. Tall, skinny, and pimply, and wore shirts without collars. He was a few years older than Karin. They'd met at a meeting of their National Liberation Front group. He was one of those people who wished his father had been an honorable welder instead of a school principal, and that his mother had been an overworked cleaning lady instead of a senior psychologist. He did not disappear from Karin's life as quickly as I would have liked.

"He was so heartbroken," Karin said. "He feels betrayed. I'm afraid he'll do something stupid. I can't just erase him from my life."

Yes, you could, I thought. I want him to disappear. Go up in smoke. Emigrate to China. Die a painful death. Whatever. But of course I couldn't say that. And I also couldn't say that I didn't want her to get together with him anymore. You can't own someone else, you don't have the sole rights to another human being. That rule still applied. Karin was a communist, too. She'd taken the basic course and was chock-full of quotes from Marx, Engels, Lenin, Stalin, and Mao. She could talk about imperialism and materialism and idealism and dialectics and revisionism and the United Front and the dictatorship of the proletariat and lots of other stuff. And she loved to talk about all that. But I was a bad listener. Head over heels in love, love sealed off my ears, and I would watch her lips and her sparkling eyes and the soft skin of her throat while her words floated away like shimmering soap bubbles.

"You have to look at what the main antithesis is, there are loads of small battles to be fought, the battle for equality between the

17

sexes and the battle for the environment, but none of these battles must be fought in such a way that they impede the most important battle of all, the battle for a socialist Sweden."

"Hmm," I said, happiness thrilling through my veins because I caught a glimpse of the tip of her cute little tongue.

"Are you listening? Do you agree with me? Do you have an opinion?"

I turned off my sexual thoughts and tried to turn my rational brain back on.

"How?" I asked, after considering for a moment.

"How what?"

"How do you fight the battle?" I asked.

If someone else had said all the things she said, I would have responded with scorn and contempt. Obviously, I didn't do that when it came to Karin, but I wasn't afraid to debate things. I was already confident in our love. I was an idealist.

"You arm yourself with arguments. You learn from history. You expose the lies," she answered quickly, without hesitation.

"In other words, you talk," I scoffed. "You fight the battle by talking."

"Well, what do you think? Should we kill the capitalists and blow up shopping malls and take hostages like the Baader-Meinhof Gang in West Germany? That's not a revolution, that's just romanticizing violence, those are just ego-tripping terrorists without any ties to the working classes and the masses."

"No," I said. "I want people to fight the battle by how they live. Their way of being. Every laugh is a bomb against the capitalist pigs. Every happy person is a rebel. You fight the battle by not being part of it, by creating an alternative."

PN

"And smoking hash is a revolutionary act?" she asked sarcastically.

"Absolutely," I said.

"Individual happiness or romanticizing drugs has nothing to do with the struggle. Look at history. Look at how society ..."

"Kiss me."

"No. Listen to me ..."

"Kiss me. Come on. I'll debate Hegel with you for half an hour if you'll just kiss me now."

"All right already."

That's about how our conversations would go. Not quite so stilted maybe, but that's more or less how they would go. We'd already known each other for a few months of course, gotten to know each other, felt each other out, and gotten close to each other. We'd seen each other every single day of summer vacation. We were a couple, we were together. She still went to her meetings and I still sat up in Mattsson's apartment or in Kungsparken with my friends and smoked, but we spent most of our time together.

We were together. A smart, upper-class girl who was a communist and a middle-class boy who was a hippie. We didn't try to indoctrinate each other. Or did we? Well, maybe.

I quickly came to understand that I would not be able to fit Karin into my life with my buddies. In Mattsson's eyes she was disqualified for three reasons:

She was a girl. She was a communist. And she lived in Bellevue.

We lived in a guys' world. Guy talk and guy jokes. Girls crimped our style, got in our way, curtailed our freedom. And partnering off wasn't our dream—rather the opposite. From the

17

couples at school, we were able to observe that falling in love made you dumb and made you isolate yourself from the rest of the world, and every single one of us had witnessed how the nuclear family was a prison. And I've already explained what we thought about communists. And we were class-conscious enough that we knew what kind of upper-class riffraff lived in the mansions in Bellevue.

None of that mattered to me anymore. I had found love. It was like I'd been born again, like I was someone who'd seen the light. But I still didn't want to give up my old life.

Karen sighed and said, "They think I'm just some dumb upper-class chick," after we'd been to Mattsson's apartment together for the first time. "They were just trying to get rid of me the whole time. Didn't you notice that? But that Per-Inge seemed nice."

I nodded. Everything she said was true. But I wasn't ready to choose, not yet.

23

Do you understand what I'm saying? Can you picture any of this in your head?

There's so much I want to tell you. There's so much I want you to understand. And I only have a little bit of time. I have to choose from all the pictures that come up in my memory. I have to try to be clear. But I'm afraid I'm not doing very well. I feel like I've turned into some kind of dreary lecturer who wants to cram way too many facts into way too short a lesson. Forgive me. I'm doing my best.

I notice something else, too, as I listen to myself: I'm turning myself into a charming hero. As if I were telling some heroic fairy tale. Friendship and adventure and love. And drugs. An exciting drama, a comedic love story, starring Göran Persson. It even has a little bathroom humor.

That's not my goal, and only on a few occasions in my life have I felt like a protagonist, more often I've had to play sad, uninteresting bit parts. But now I'm telling the story of my first great love, and that's how it is when you fall in love—it makes you into a king. Another person makes you feel good. Makes you feel valuable. If it's ever happened to you, then you know what I mean.

I've realized that this is my only chance in life to tell you the story. Surely you hear my words, surely you understand what I'm saying? Yes, I know you're hearing me and understanding.

To summarize what I've said so far: I had a safe suburban childhood in the fifties and sixties. When I started at Pildamm High School, that's when I got to know Mattsson and Per-Inge and Jonny and started smoking hash and became part of the hippie world. Soon I had shoulder-length hair and the most tattered jeans in town. I took pictures. In May of my sophomore year I met Karin, as I explained. Her parents lived in one of the nicest stone mansions in Bellevue, although she had a little house in the corner of the large grounds. She started at Borgarskola after the summer; she was one year younger than me. During my two remaining years of high school I went to school only a third of the time, the other two thirds of the time I spent smoking hash with my friends or lying on a mattress with Karin. Then I was forced to choose. I chose Karin. And we started our life together.

I have to hurry along in the story now. I want to get to you. But first I have to tell you about our week of camping at Samsö in August 1973.

24

We saw the little flyer on the bulletin board at Huset, the music venue in Copenhagen. It was in Danish and it said, *Det Ny Samfund. Sommerlejr og festival.*

A big festival and a New Society. It promised freedom and joy and love and music and community. On the tiny island of Samsö between Själland and Jylland. Yes, that seemed like something for us. The camp was going to run all summer, Mattsson and Per-Inge and Jonny packed up their backpacks and headed off just after Midsummer, and I promised I'd be right behind them.

It took me a while before I was able to convince Karin, but at the beginning of August we took the train from Copenhagen's Central Station to Kalundborg, and from there a little ferry over to Samsö. I'd received a muddled postcard from my friends with directions for how to get there; we set out briskly on foot from the ferry terminal, it was a hot day in the middle of the summer, and we were sweating under our packs. But we didn't have to walk very far before we rounded a bend in the road and spotted a camp-ground out in a meadow. Hundreds of little tents, a couple of big circus tents and military tents, buses and cars outside, lots of old painted buses inside the camp area, too, thin trails of smoke rising up into the blue sky from small campfires, you could hear music, guitars, and little jingle bells and bigger bells, a jarring voice from a bad loudspeaker, the smell of wood smoke and organic soup and incense spread over the meadows and fields, yes, the smell of hash smoke, too, of course. We stopped. I pulled out my camera and took a few pictures. I later made a successful enlargement of one of the pictures, grainy and with nice gray tones. I framed it, and it was part of our lives. It hung in the kitchen when you were little.

It was a picture that was part of our lives until it got smashed and torn to pieces.

So, we went over to the camp and walked in through a big portal. It said "Welcome to the New Society" on the sign.

I told Karin, "Welcome to the New Society."

She didn't respond, just peered around wide-eyed.

And, boy, was there a lot to see. The first people we met were a group of well-dressed Japanese tourists who were sweating in the sun; one of the men was wearing a suit and staring at two top-less young women who were dancing in front of them, while the Japanese women looked away and hurried along the path toward the bus that was waiting for them outside. Then we came to an open area with a huge bulletin board that was covered with slips of paper and little flyers in Danish. I thought that maybe Mattsson and the guys might have left us a message, so I pulled Karin over to it to look. No, nothing for us, but there was a lot of other interesting stuff:

Have to take a shit outdoors? Follow these steps: Grab a shovel—dig a hole—take a shit—refill the hole—mark the site with your shovel.

Hash cake 1.5 grams 8 kroner. Primo acid. See Preben on Nepal Street.

Welcome to Camp Samsø! Please read this message before you enter the camp. We are human beings, not animals. We have chosen to build a new community, one that may have different values than the community you live in. We hope that you will respect our right to make this choice! Sit down among us. Talk to us, dance with us, rejoice with us.

The love tent is open by the supermarket.

After an acid trip try a healthy and nutritious strawberry compote! Available at the grocery store!

"I don't get it," Karin said, wanting to keep moving.

"You don't understand the Danish?" I asked, confused. "I thought everyone from Malmö could understand Danish."

"Not me. Come on."

I remember the flyers on the bulletin board because I took pictures there, too. Actually, that was one of the pictures in my *Love, Peace and Understanding* exhibit at the Hasselblad Center in Göteborg in 1978.

We continued on into the camp. People and tents everywhere, I thought it was like climbing into a dream world, everywhere I looked there was something going on: a group of naked children was building a tall tower out of boards and sackcloth over there, two fat farmers in overalls were standing over there arguing loudly with a naked guy with long hair whose whole body was painted, a woman wearing only underwear was dancing over there, she was dancing, with her eyes closed, to music from two guys who were playing an Indian drum and a flute, a group was sitting over there outside a tent passing around a bong, some chickens were running across the road over there chased by a mangy dog, Mother Earth & Sons were standing over there by their bus serving biodynamic food, pearl necklaces and earthenware bowls were for sale over there, a group of monks dressed in orange robes was walking over there, red and red-and-black and black banners were flying over there, there was a stage over there, there was a little post office over there, there were showers where men and women and children were showering all willy-nilly, food was being served over there, and there, outside a worn camping tent, Per-Inge was lying on his back completely naked, staring straight up at the sky with a serene smile on his lips.

"I see you've converted to Taoism," I said, pointing at the yin and yang symbol that was painted on his chest.

"Only half," he said calmly, not seeming a bit surprised to see us. "On my back I'm an anarchist."

Per-Inge rolled over onto his stomach to show off the black and red star that covered his back. Then he jumped up and hugged us.

"Guran, you bastard! And Karin, you little cutie-pie! Guess what I found!"

"What?"

"My third eye. Everyone has a third eye that we've forgotten to use."

"Oh," I said.

"And no, I don't mean the one we have in our butts," Per-Inge continued, "I mean the one in our foreheads. You just have to find it. And then open it."

"Where's everybody else?" I asked.

"Mattsson's probably over in the love tent screwing, and Jonny's probably taking acid with some Scottish guys he met. Guran, fuck, man, how cool that you're here, we'll have to arrange a little welcome bong and then ..."

"What's ... what's it like here?" Karin asked. "What do you guys do here?"

Per-Inge stared at her as if he didn't understand the question. Then he thought about it and gave her a broad smile. "This is the New Society," he said, his smile becoming more and more radiant. "Two thousand people live here. But there's no police, because we don't need police, because everyone is nice. Everyone shares everything. No capitalists. No crooks. We dance and listen to music and talk and are high as kites all the time. You can really live like this. This is the New Society. There are only two problems. One is that the Hare Krishna guys keep walking around jingling and droning on and on with their goddamn boring songs all over the place, and the other is that this place is teeming with tons of tourists who are always gawking. Today, there was even a busload of fucking Japanese people. Can you believe it? People are coming all the way from fucking Japan to gawk at us. We're like world news. No shit. And they all had identical suits and cameras and they walked around taking pictures of girls' tits until people got sick of them and chased them away. No shit ..."

He burst out laughing.

"We saw them," I said, nodding.

Karin and I set up our little cotton Tarfala tent nearby, and after a few days we'd started to get used to the New Society and, well, everything Per-Inge said was true. You could really live like this. People really do want to live together in peace. People really do want to laugh and dance and make love and be free. Deep down inside, people are good. You *can* build a new world.

Even when someone went into our tent and stole Karin's purse and her money I didn't start having doubts. Clearly, there were idiots here, too. After all, we all came from the cold world out there. Clearly, you couldn't create the New Human in just a few weeks. But Karin was mad.

"You said I could leave my stuff in the tent."

"I know, but ..."

"I want to go home," she whined.

"But ... school doesn't start until the twentieth ..."

"I have to go home. I told my mom we were on a package vacation to Costa del Sol. I have to be home tomorrow."

And so it was. Against my will, I packed up my backpack and then we set off, leaving the New Society and heading back to the old one.

Sitting on the train on the way to Copenhagen I thought again: Well, now I know that it can be done. It's possible to build a new world. Now I've seen that it's possible.

I was happy. There was hope, in spite of everything.

Karin was quiet the whole way, staring at the flat Danish landscape outside the train window.

Many years later, when our life together fell apart, she said that that week on Samsø was the worst week of her life. She'd been scared to death the whole time, she said. All she'd seen was filth and shit and drugs the whole time, she said. She'd seen only unhappy, lonely, confused people there, she said. The New Society, she scoffed, that was just a bunch of bored big-city kids at scout camp.

I don't know. For a long time I thought there was something there. An energy, a desire. I carried the memories and pictures from that summer week with me for a long time as a sort of dream, a vision. Now they've faded, and my dreams for the future have gotten smaller and more private. In the end, just a comfortable little piece of happiness for myself, that's what I want. The New Society feels way too distant.

Maybe Karin was right. Maybe that was just an adventure game for affluent children and children from social-welfare states. I don't know. I know less and less.

25

Drugs. Maybe I should say a little more about drugs.

You wound up here in the hospital because of drugs. I missed watching you grow up because of drugs. Or, more specifically, one drug. The same one in both cases: the Mighty Alcohol. Drug of Death.

When I was seventeen I lived in a drug culture. But all the same, the drugs weren't the most important thing. Do you understand? I lived in a community, and drugs were a part of that community. Community first, then drugs. I've smoked hash and marijuana hundreds of times, eaten it and drunk it in tea, I've sniffed cocaine, smoked opium, I've chowed down on uppers, I've been on LSD trips and I've eaten mushrooms.

I'm not telling you this to brag, to make myself seem cool. All right, I admit that there was a time when I thought I'd had experiences most other people hadn't, but I realized a long time ago that my drug use for some of my teenage years isn't anything to be proud of. Not at all. But I'm not ashamed, either. No. I've done or given up doing a lot of things in my life I'm ashamed of, way too many things; many memories make me blush and shudder with shame, but never the fact that I used illegal drugs for those years.

Wasn't it dangerous? Potentially lethal? I know the most dangerous combination, the one most people die from. Sure, we saw other people around us waste away and die. The junkies. I was no junky. And sure, LSD is a powerful drug, and the truth is, we never knew what we were stuffing into ourselves. And sure, for years and years I had flashbacks. I could be sitting in a room and suddenly notice that the walls and the ceiling were starting to bubble, and shapes and colors would dissolve and mix together. Sure it's dangerous, lethal. I never wanted to fly, never felt dread, never had any serious psychoses.

Were we criminals? Just little things, just what I've already told you. I never dealt drugs to finance my habit. Smuggled stuff back into Sweden from Copenhagen, of course, sure, and was very close to getting caught a few times. But on the whole, my drug use didn't bother anyone, didn't wreck anything. Never any violence, never any threats, never any noisy gangs roving through the city, never any vandalism. Or ..., do broken-off Mercedes hood ornaments count as destruction? If so, I confess. We collected those in a plastic bag at Mattsson's apartment.

"When the bag's full, there'll be a bonus prize," Mattsson laughed. *"Eine Reise nach Hamburg. Jawohl."*

Wasn't it addictive? Absolutely. Even smoking hash is addictive, no matter what they say. But when the hippies stopped, it was possible to quit, even though it took quite a few years before the cravings went away completely. But smoking tobacco is a harder habit to break, at least it was for me.

We were living in a drug culture. Yes, we thought using certain drugs would change not only us but also the society. "Legalize marijuana" was just as common a slogan as "U.S.A. out of Vietnam." Smoking hash makes you nice, peaceful and happy—nice, peaceful and happy people were going to build a new world. In some way we thought it was a historical wave of progress and we were the vanguard. "Before there was slavery and poverty and the oppression of women, now we have democracy and prosperity and equality, and now psychedelic drugs are here to lead humanity to the next stage." That's more or less it. What we didn't know was that American fighter pilots were smoking their own joints before releasing napalm bombs over Vietnamese women and children. What we didn't know was that lawyers and judges and soldiers and politicians in the United States were smoking marijuana as a nice little party drug. Without becoming particularly nice or peaceful. We were wrong. Society won't be changed by having more people smoke hash, at least not changed for the better. But it's not the most dangerous or the worst drug.

I've met a lot of junkies, real junkies, the kind that let the drugs take over. I've sat there with junkies in various treatment programs, we sat in a circle and examined our lives inside and out. We admitted to each other that we became powerless in our addiction. But the junkies are a different sort. I don't recognize myself in their stories.

They're always about children who were abused, always the same awful tales, the old saying is always true that abused people become abusers. I was never like that.

If I could choose, I would wish that you not use any drugs at all. First of all. Second of all, that you protect your freedom and your independence, that you don't become a slave. Third of all, that community comes before drugs.

Why am I lecturing you? Why am I playing the role of assiduous schoolmaster? Because I want to tell you about the most dangerous combination. The lethal combination.

I have way too much experience with the most lethal combination. You'll get to hear the sad, shameful, humiliating part of my story soon.

Loneliness and alcohol. That's the combination I'm talking about.

Yup, that's the most dangerous combination of them all.

And I sigh, and an icy chill grips my heart as I see you lying here. Why were you alone? Where are your friends? Why didn't anyone take care of you?

26

I finished high school in 1974 but didn't officially graduate. What did I need a diploma for? It was a relic of the old class society when only upper-class kids got to finish school. Still, there were only five people in my class who didn't actually graduate, and consequently didn't get to participate in all the traditional Swedish graduation celebrations—wearing the student cap, going to the ball, and riding around in a decorated hay wagon or cruising in a shiny old American muscle car. Of course, I was one of those five who said thanks, but no thanks.

"But think of your grandmother," my mom begged. "Surely for her sake you could ... Just a small party for the family. And you can borrow Krister's student cap."

"No way," I said. "And besides, he's got such a fat head. How could I wear his cap?"

"But, Göran, please ..."

"Not on your life," I said, and had my own little graduation celebration with my friends in Mattsson's apartment instead.

Normally, I would have put up with just about anything for my grandmother's sake. I loved my grandmother. Grandma Signe. I'm sure you don't remember her. She died before your first birthday. When you were just a few weeks old, we visited her at the nursing home and she held you in her firm, experienced mom grip even though she was ninety years old. She'd had eight children of her own, three died when they were little and two later on in an accident. She'd been hard up and dirt poor her whole life and married to a man who drank and beat her. Now, she was wrinkly and gray-haired and stocky and almost blind, and she would shuffle around in the hallways there, walking with two canes, wearing a light-blue housecoat and bedroom slippers with her stockings sagging. But she was completely with it mentally. She was still interested in everything going on in the world, and everything going on with her children and grandchildren.

And she still knew how to hold a baby. So, obviously her old body remembered that position. I took a picture of you two. You must have seen it, right? You're resting there so safely in her stick-thin arms.

Ten years earlier, when I finished high school, Grandma was ten years younger but already old, of course.

"And what are you going to do now, Göran?" she asked. "Now that you're done with school."

"I'm going to travel a little," I said. "See the world."

"That sounds wise," Grandma said, nodding. "Travel while you're young and strong. You learn a lot from traveling. But what about little Karin? What does she have to say about your heading off to see the world?"

"I am coming back," I said.

"And then you'll continue on in school, right?" Grandma said. "I hear that you've been getting good grades."

"Yeah. But I don't know what I'll do then. I haven't decided ..."

"No, it can't be easy being young today," Grandma said with a sigh, "when there are so things to choose from ..." Yes, I had gotten good grades, strangely enough, since, as I mentioned before, I was absent for most of my senior year, dedicating myself to the pursuit of love and illegal drugs. My final GPA was 3.3, with a focus on social studies. If I'd gone to class I might well have gotten a 3.9. Then I could have been a lawyer or something. Then everything would have been different.

If.

What a word.

The other day on the radio I heard that there are these historians who research what the world would have looked like *if* something else had happened. If the Third Reich hadn't been destroyed, if Caesar hadn't been murdered, if the Cuban missile crisis had led to a war between the United States and the Soviet Union. What an extraordinarily pointless thing to do. Those researchers might as well be playing Tetris.

There is no If.

There's cause and effect, events influence each other, it's all weaving a web, puzzle pieces are forming a pattern. I'm not saying that there's a purpose, but actually that thought is the one that sometimes gives me the most solace.

The fact that I'm sitting here with you now telling this story indicates that, doesn't it? It can't just be a coincidence, can it?

17

And what about you? School? Grades? Which classes did you like best? Was school easy for you, or did you have to work hard? Do you care? Are you struggling? Do you have plans, plans for the future, career plans?

No, I don't have any good fatherly advice to give you. No sage advice. It would be silly if I even tried, since I was such a complete failure at being both a father and a grown-up.

I've already given you my best advice: Don't combine alcohol and loneliness.

27

Oh, by the way, another thing happened that spring before school ended. I reported for duty, because military service was compulsory in Sweden back then, too.

My experiences in the Swedish Armed Forces were limited to a single day in Kristianstad.

The idea that we would do our military service was as inconceivable as thinking that we would get crew cuts. Pretty much zero, in other words. There were lots of myths and stories going around about how other friends had managed to get exemptions or been granted conscientious-objector status, so we were curious and a bit anxious as we climbed onto one of the chartered buses in Södervärn early one chilly morning, the buses that were going to take us and a hundred other guys to the regiment in Kristianstad where we would muster. A hundred guys that the Swedish Armed Forces were going to turn into men.

Per-Inge and Jonny and I all reported for duty at the same time; Mattsson was already done: "I had to go in and see this officer who said I should hand him this fucking Tommy Gun that was standing in a corner, and I said I refused, and then he said again that I should give him the Tommy Gun, and I said again that I refused, and then I got to go home. Now it'll be jail, first one month, then two months, then three months, then four months, and I'll be fucked in the ass every day by a ton of criminals who hate longhaired conscientious objectors."

That's what he'd said, and now it was our turn.

When we got there we had to fall in, we each got a wooden tag with numbers on it to hang on a chain around our necks and then we had roll call. I felt like a cow being pushed into line with a hundred other eighteen-year-olds. Then we had to undress for a medical exam and some tests.

"Man, look at all these hot asses," Per-Inge said, plunging his hand down into his underwear.

Two soldiers who weren't any older than we were rushed over and led him away, and then he was gone. Jonny disappeared right after that, he was sound asleep sitting upright on a bench, completely exhausted because he'd been up for two days straight smoking hash. So I was the only one left.

I had no plan. I'd just thought it would all turn out OK. So I just stayed in line, with my tag around my neck, got examined and tested, and then we came to a big lecture hall, and there we were supposed to answer questions in a booklet. I remember two of the questions:

1. If a train takes a curve too fast, will it tip over toward the inside of the curve or the outside?

17

2. Assume that the wind is blowing in the direction shown by the arrow in the drawing. Draw a flag on the flagpole and smoke from the chimney.

I realized that the time had come for me to pack it in. I stood up and went over to a soldier who was one of the exam proctors and said that I didn't want to be there anymore, and then I had to go see an officer in an office.

But I was never ordered to pick up any weapon, no, he just talked to me nicely and looked at me with a concerned look in his eyes and wondered what was up and what I wanted, and I stammered and started blushing and was on the verge of letting myself be talked into going through with the mustering, but finally I braced myself and said, "I can't be away from my mother for that long. I already miss my mom. I can't do my military service, there's just no way."

The officer cocked his head to the side and studied me, then he just shrugged his shoulders and waved me on my way.

So I got my exemption.

We spent the rest of the day shoplifting books and clothes from the Domus store in Kristianstad, then we took the bus back to Malmö.

You haven't mustered yet, have you? I mean, you're only seventeen. What's it like these days? Now only people who want to do their military service have to do it? Or what's it like?

I think there ought to be another kind of national service besides the military one. I think all eighteen-year-olds, boys and girls, should serve for six months, learning useful stuff like how to tell poisonous mushrooms from edible ones and how to change a baby's diaper and take care of old people and stuff like that. And put out fires and administer first aid. That's how I think it should be.

28

Yes, I wanted to see the world. I had tons of plans when school ended.

Take the Trans-Siberian railway. Participate in international work brigades. Hitchhike across America, from the East Coast to California in Kerouac's footsteps. Travel through Europe and visit various communes and alternative societies. The world was my oyster. I planned and read. There were names in map books that made me shiver with excitement and anticipation: Marrakech. Tangier. Kirkenes. San Francisco. Big Sur. Isle of Skye. Reykjavik. Havana. Katmandu. Sarek. Verona. Samarkand. Connemara. Amsterdam.

The world was waiting out there, and my friends were all starting to say their good-byes.

Per-Inge had already gone to India, Jonny was going to move in with an old man who lived by Vombsjö, an old recluse who sat there all alone in his little cottage and meditated and studied Zen Buddhist texts, and Mattsson was hanging out waiting for his trial. They caught him when he was standing there in the toy department at NK handing out toys to the kids and, fool that he was, he had four grams of hash and two Purple Haze trips in a matchbox in his jeans pocket, and, fool that he was, he started fighting with the store security guards, and, unlucky as he was, two patrol cops showed up before he managed to get away.

That was the situation. The old world was falling apart, the new one was waiting.

And Karin listened patiently to all my dreams and plans. She still had a year of high school left, then our life together would begin. For a couple of weeks that summer we went to Emmaus Björkå up there in Småland and worked sorting clothes to send to Third World countries, then she wanted to go home for her National Liberation Front group. She helped organize the meetings and demonstrations and sold the Vietnam Bulletin outside the government-run liquor store every day during her summer vacation. Guess who was a member of the same group? Exactly: Claes. Claes the ugly, Claes the dumb. But he was history now, he belonged to the past, the future belonged to us, Karin and me.

Nowadays it seems like everyone travels after high school. Everyone goes to Australia and Thailand, everyone works as an au pair in London, everyone studies Spanish or works at some bar in Spain. Or is that not how it is? That's not how it was in my day. Most people started working or moved to Lund and went to college. In my day, there were only a few who went abroad.

I was going to be one of them, I'd decided. But in the end all my planned adventures turned into one month of traveling by Interrail. I had planned to be gone the whole fall, but it didn't turn out that way. There were three reasons why it didn't turn out that way:

One. I was traveling alone, and that was lonely. All the exciting people I thought I'd meet were obviously off traveling somewhere else. In four weeks, I talked to only three people, not counting railroad personnel and the people who worked in the youth hostels.

Two. My money ran out and I couldn't find any nice little side jobs. I worked at the port in Newcastle for two days, but the other longshoremen teased me and made fun of me in a Scottish accent that I couldn't understand, and besides my back hurt.

Three. In Glasgow I got robbed by a heroine addict who shoved me up against a wall late one night, put a knife to my throat, hissed something unintelligible and stole my wallet and my passport.

I gave up and went home. The triumphant return I'd planned to my hometown fizzled out into nothing at all. On a rainy September afternoon I was standing outside the school waiting for Karin. When she saw me she hurried over to me and hugged me tight.

"I thought you were going to be gone for such a long ..."

"I missed you," I lied, stroking her soft hair.

Have you seen the world?

I don't think lugging a backpack to Australia necessarily helps you know more about the world. On the other hand. On the other hand, you get perspective on your own life by seeing people who are living different lives.

Do you feel like I sound like a father all the time? Do you feel like I actually sound like a gloomy professor? Sorry about that.

29

"You're still telling your story?"

Sister Anna is back. I turn toward the door slowly and look at her. Which Sister Anna is it this time? Is it Sister Anna the gentle, with the inquisitive, twinkling eyes, the Sister Anna who steps out of her uniform and becomes a person, a fellow human being?

Or Sister Anna the strict, cold, impersonal career woman? Sister Anna, you are a mystery dressed in white.

"I couldn't get hold of Jonatan's mother, your ex-wife. She wasn't home. But I talked to the baby-sitter, who put the daughter on the phone, who promised she'd tell her. So, she'll come here."

Sister Anna, you're not being clear. She this, she that. Who's coming here, Karin or the baby-sitter or the daughter? Who is the daughter, is that Karin's daughter or the daughter of the man she married, and how old is this daughter, five or fifteen or twenty? Sister Anna, this won't do! But good that Karin wasn't home. That ought to give me a little more time before she gets here.

Oh well, if she's fifteen or twenty she wouldn't need a baby-sitter now, would she?

"Everything OK otherwise?"

Yes, Sister Anna, everything is OK. I'm nineteen years old now. I just came home from my somewhat disappointing trip-to-go-see-the-world. I can't move back in again with my mom and dad, that goes without saying, so I find an apartment in the picturesque Gamla Väster part of town, west of Lilla Torg square, and start working as an orderly at Eastern Hospital. West and east. Karin moves in with me, not officially but for all practical purposes.

"I'll leave you two alone. We're still waiting for some test results that I hope will be in soon."

Sure, Sister Anna, bye-bye. You're not the one I want to tell the story to. It's for him, the guy whose pulse and breathing you just checked.

Yes, it's your story I want to give you. Now we're living together, the woman who will become your mother and I. My parents have visited hers in their fancy mansion. Ooooooh, that was so painful, my bumbling Social Democrat dad and my distrustful Social Democrat mom paying a visit to the wealthy. My dad, wearing his threadbare Sunday suit, sat there staring at the floor the whole time and my mom was snooty and disagreeable, and the worst thing, the most painful thing of all, was that I was ashamed of them. Karin's parents were just trying to be nice. They weren't acting superior or condescending at all. And in the meeting of the well-bred stone-house upper class and the frugal row-house–dwelling middle class, Karin's parents triumphed 7–0. I thought my own parents were just drab and dull.

I was ashamed. I would never be like them, never.

Well, now I'm nineteen and I have my own apartment, a one-bedroom with a darkroom, and Karin is a senior and is still a committed communist and I'm working with the fools and the lunatics and the confused at Eastern Hospital. They have all sorts there, schizophrenics, manic depressives, psychotics, neurotics, senile people. They amble around there, all over the place in corridors and wards and out in the park, they're subjected to electrical shocks and lobotomies and medication and isolation and straitjackets and therapy, and I carry around my heavy bunch of keys and collect horrifying pictures that come out later on in my nightmares.

During that first month I wake up sweaty and confused every night and Karin has to comfort me and calm me down with her cool hand and her soft body. Every morning I think, *this will not do.* Then I think, *I need the money. I'll get used to it.*

Yes, I needed the money. I had food and rent to pay for now. Well, I got used to it. But I didn't know then how used to it I got.

I thought I would just work there for six months while I waited for Karin to finish high school, while I waited for my real life to begin.

30

The very worst picture from that first phase at Eastern Hospital doesn't have anything to do with the patients. I can see their eyes, their eyes staring or empty. I can hear their voices, their monotonous, meaningless ramblings and desperate howls and joyless laughter. I can feel their fingers and hands grabbing hold of my upper arms and holding onto me. I remember their fits of rage and resignation and deep sorrow, and how many of them lived in completely different worlds, worlds only they could see, where they were subjected to forces and powers that we others couldn't even imagine.

But there aren't any patients in the worst, most dreadful pictures in my head, just three cackling orderlies. And then the seagulls, of course.

Seagulls represent freedom, no doubt about it. Gliding on their glossy white wings between the blue sea and the blue sky.

Following the ferries and fishing boats, screaming and fighting for food, sitting proudly and warily on the wharves and bollards and piers.

Seagulls represent summer and vacation. Seagulls represent happy childhood memories. Seagulls represent freedom. That's how I think it is for most people, and that's how it was for me, too. But now I have a hard time looking at seagulls and shorebirds without thinking about what happened one morning in October

1974 at Malmö Eastern Hospital. Still.

It was up in the utility room on the second floor. We used to drink coffee there and take a smoking break when all our morning duties were done, but when I went up there that day three of my colleagues were leaning out the open window laughing and shrieking:

"Check out that one over there!"

"Bam! Crash landing!"

"Look! Look! At those two over there, look!"

I pushed my way through to see what was going on. Ah, they were feeding the seagulls, flinging out bits of French bread, but then what was so entertaining about that?

"Hey, Göran! Check this out! Want to see something neat? Look!"

I leaned out. The gulls and shorebirds were flapping around out there fighting for the pieces of bread the guys were throwing out. Seven or eight seagulls were lying on the ground under the window, not moving. Some of them were bloody, and then I noticed that several of the seagulls in the air were acting weird, like they were dizzy or drunk. They were flying around in con-fused circles, they were flying all topsy-turvy, they were crashing into each other, they were crashing into the trees, some of them had bloody beaks, some were plummeting like shot-down fighter jets onto the grass below.

"Cool, huh?"

I turned and looked at Håkan, a big guy with short-cropped hair who'd been working at the hospital for many years.

"I don't get it," I said. "What's going on?"

"We're feeding the seagulls," Håkan gloated. "Thorazine. And needles."

It took me a few seconds to understand. They had prepared the pieces of bread they were throwing with medication or needles, and the seagulls were doing nosedives to get the bread and then they swallowed it and would get drugged or get a needle in their throats.

"Fucking A," I said, turning away.

"But Göran, shit, man, they're like fucking rats, man. No one wants them here in the park. They chase the house sparrows. They're already totally weird. Shit, man, these seagulls are mental cases, for fuck's sake. We're doing them a good turn."

I gulped and walked away.

"Go cut your hair, faggot, junkie bastard, communist fuck!" Håkan shouted after me.

I just walked away. I didn't try to stop them. I didn't even tell them to cut it out. That's how chicken I was.

But the picture of those flapping, bleeding, crashing seagulls still haunts me. And the picture of those three cackling orderlies all dressed in white in the window. And the picture of me walking away with my head bent down.

I worked there as an orderly all spring and Karin graduated, yes, indeed, in full old-fashioned style with a student cap and singing and a ball and limousine and a big party with family and friends in their fancy home, and I got drunk and yelled, "This is capitalism!" from the top of the stairs, and then stumbled and tumbled all the way down, and all the nicely dressed party guests had to take little hops to the side so as not to be mowed down like bowling pins, and when I finally managed to come to a stop, I was lying at Herman Hoff's feet. Herman Hoff, the factory owner. Karin's dad. Your future grandfather. My father-in-law, one might well say, although no one ever did say that.

"Whoops-a-daisy!" he said. "You all right?"

And he helped me up, and I mumbled something and fled out into the yard, and Karin followed me and we giggled like crazy and then made our escape from her graduation party. I gave her a ride on my bike back to the apartment, and we devoted the rest of the night to love.

She wore her cap the whole time. When I see happy, young female students before school gets out at the beginning of the summer I sometimes think of that. But those are just my memories bubbling to the surface. I'm not some dirty old man, no, no. I'm not like that, no, no.

When I was eating breakfast a few weeks ago I saw Herman Hoff's obituary in the newspaper. There was a picture, too, and a little paragraph. *Factory owner Herman Hoff, 78, passed away after a brief illness. He is survived by his wife Anna-Clara and his daughter Karin and her family. Herman Hoff was born* ... etc.

I was startled to see the picture. It must have been at least twenty years old, because he looked exactly the way I remember him. Clear blue eyes, gray hair brushed back, neatly tailored suit, an old-school gentleman capitalist. The truth is, I was a little sad to see that he was dead. The truth is, I liked him. He was always up for a good discussion about anything. Sure, he had opinions about my hair and my clothes, but he accepted them as a fairly unimportant detail, a generational difference.

"You'll grow up, too, someday, Göran," he would say, laughing, and then clap me on the shoulder. "By the way, I was chatting

17

with my barber this morning, and he promised he'd give you a free haircut. 'It would be a pleasure,' he said. I might even be able to get him to pay you to let him cut your hair. What do you say, Göran? Should I make you an appointment?"

That's the kind of stuff he'd say. But I liked him. He was funny and honest, stood by his ultraconservative opinions, but he was still a good listener. And he liked me. He was interested in my pictures, and he loved you.

Were you close to your grandfather? Did you go to his funeral? Yeah, I'm sure you must've. How's your grandma doing, then? Is she living in that big house all alone?

My parents were never as interested, not in me and not in you. They weren't interested in being grandparents. They just wanted to be left in peace with their little garden plot and with their car trips and while they watched TV.

31

Here we are now. This is where we've come to. You don't need to worry. I'm not going to try to tell you everything. I won't spill my whole life out over you as you lie there completely defenseless. I won't drown you in a sea of little amusing or not so amusing episodes. No, I'll choose what's important, what led to everything turning out the way it did.

The Greatest Hits of My Life.

That's a tough one. Who among us can simply choose what was important in his or her life, what governed the paths he or she's chosen?

Still, I have to keep trying. My childhood, parents, youth,

friends, the spirit of the times, falling in love, ideas. Yes, I've told you about all that. Now I've come to our life together. And maybe grown-up life.

Is a twenty-year-old a grown-up? My dad was, and his generation. When I turned twenty in 1975 I didn't feel grown up, and nowadays it seems like nobody does. Youth lasts even longer now, doesn't it? People kind of grow out of childhood faster and become adults slower. Or? I mean, who wants to be a grown-up?

And, I mean, I did start out by saying that often I don't feel grown up even now.

But what does it mean to be a grown-up? Taking responsibility for your life, taking care of your own food and clothes and a roof over your head. Making your own choices. But it's something else, too. Maybe it involves settling down, waking up from the dream that everything could have been so much better. Maybe it also involves having to stop running back to Mommy and Daddy. "Mommy, comfort me, I'm sad and lonely. Mommy, hold me." "Daddy, look what a good job I'm doing, look at my nice car/ my big house/my pretty wife/my little baby/my important job. Daddy, praise me." Yes, some people contend that we're never really grown-ups until our mothers and fathers are dead. As long as we're still sons or daughters we're always looking to our parents. Maybe that's true, I don't know. You haven't had any father to run to, at least not the one sitting here, the one who was your father in the beginning.

But we haven't gotten there yet. No, I was going to talk about our life together.

About living together, as a family.

Why is this so hard?

17

And can I even explain it so that you can understand? Can any seventeen-year-old understand what it's like to live with another person? Can anyone at all understand or explain the world that two people build together out of love and hate and compromises and consideration and contempt and security and freedom and truth and lies and deceit and trust and suspicion and hope and despair?

Karin moved into my apartment after she graduated. She changed her address, and suddenly the future was here, the future we'd just been toying with in our mutual dreams. Now we had to make all our wild and beautiful plans real.

The nuclear family was an obsolete phenomenon. Locking ourselves away in couples or in little mommy-daddy-baby families had been ruled out. No, we were going to live together, together with others. There were extended families and communes all over the place. Up in Norrland, in northern Sweden, there were whole villages populated with longhaired big-city kids who were living on soy beans and gruel, who were farming and raising animals and building the beautiful free new world. And that summer, too, we worked up in Bjökå, where the Emmaus Association bought the entire old glassworks village and was toiling away with its solidarity work, collecting clothes and sorting them and sending them to liberation movements in southern Africa. We could move there.

But one day Karin said, "Now I know what I want. I want to start law school in the fall. I got accepted at Lund University. I think I'll do more good as a lawyer than by sorting clothes or pulling weeds."

Do more good for whom? I wondered.

I didn't even know she'd applied to the university.

"For the oppressed. For the people. For the revolutionary struggle," Karin answered, her voice unwavering. "There's going to be a need for lawyers. There's going to be a need for people who know the law, who know the law just as well or better than all those reactionary old fogies who …"

And so on.

That wasn't my choosing a path in life. Karin chose her path, and I followed her. I loved her. I wanted to be with her. That's why. And the world would wait for us. Even if she was going to study for four and a half years in Lund, the world and the communes would still be there when she was done, she could do her district court service anywhere. That's what she said, and I believed her. But I refused to keep living together in my little apartment, and soon we found two couples who were part of Karin's National Liberation Front group who were happy to share a nice, new five-bedroom place in Lund with us. So we moved to the Fäladen neighborhood in Lund and lived in a commune.

It was Gunilla, who was studying historical economics, and Sven-Erik, who was studying math, and Maria, who was studying philosophy, and Mats, who was going to be a kindergarten teacher, and Karin, who was in law school, and me—I was working as a mental health orderly at Saint Lars. Five communist academics and one longhaired laborer.

It wasn't how I thought it would be. I'll say that from the beginning.

There were interminable discussions about cleaning days and dishwashing days and clothes-washing days and responsibilities, and what music we would play and which TV shows we would watch, and about hash smoking and eating meat, and guests and parties and money. There was noise and harsh words and tears. There was icy-cold silence. There was disdain and antagonism, and yet ...

It wasn't like that the whole time. We had pleasant spells, too, great conversations over tea in the evenings, chaotic breakfasts with everyone running around and crashing into each other, delightful dinner parties with tasty casseroles and red wine and hundreds of flickering candles. There was always someone to talk to, and you could be excused if you didn't want to join in.

Actually, we had a really nice time; that's what I think now, at any rate. Actually, we'd started to get a rhythm worked out in our communal living arrangement until Hugo came, and then everything was ruined in two short months.

Things were happening out there in the world, yes, things were happening in the world that affected our little life. America pulled out of Vietnam. The world's strongest military power was actually conquered by a tiny group of people fighting in Indochina. That meant, for example, that Karin now sold the newspaper *Fib/Kulturfront* instead of the Vietnam Bulletin outside the government-run liquor store and at Lilla Torg square, and the fact that Salvador Allende's government in Chile collapsed in a military coup supported by the U.S. and led by General Pinochet in September 1973, which resulted in tons of Chileans moving to Sweden, including a twenty-year-old student named Hugo who came to Lund to study sociology. He put up a 3x5 card at the student union in Lundagård that he was looking for a place to live, and Gunilla saw his card and thought we could surely find room for one more person. It would be an act of solidarity, after all, to let Hugo live with us, and of course no one could object to that, so he moved in. That was in December. And by February the commune had already fallen apart with tears and harsh words and shattered porcelain and yogurt in people's hair.

Hugo. How should I describe him? Stubble and dark brown eyes and attractive laugh lines and a smile that made you feel special, that made you feel as if you were his best and smartest friend. That was what Hugo was like. He was easy to love. And he wanted people to love him. This ended up capsizing our little commune.

One bleak, wet winter night I came home from work, and just stepping into the hallway, I could tell that something serious had happened. It wasn't unusual, as I've mentioned, to hear heated discussions or quarrels, but now I heard Sven-Erik bellowing from the kitchen, "You, you … goddamn … fucking … you goddamn cunt …!"

I'd never heard Sven-Erik raise his voice or use any swear-words before. He was smart, he was a Trotskyist, he wore glasses with big black frames, he could be mean or sarcastic when we were discussing politics, but otherwise he was always good-natured and considerate. When I heard his voice I knew this wasn't just some normal argument about the cooking or cleaning.

"Fuck you, you fucking traitor, you fucking … liar, you fucking … you fucking … you fucking slut …!"

Everyone except Hugo was gathered in the kitchen. Sven-Erik was standing by the sink. His face was chalk-white with anger.

17

When his vacant eyes discovered me, he fell quiet, his mouth gaping like a fish on the pier, before he hid his face behind his hands. The others were sitting silently around the table, and I asked what had happened. Before anyone could answer, Sven-Erik screamed, "Ask Gunilla what happened! Ju-ju-ju-just ask her!"

I turned toward Gunilla, but she just quietly shook her head.

"Well, answer him then, you fu-fu-fucking coward!" Sven-Erik screamed.

Gunilla didn't say anything.

"Sven-Erik, why don't we talk about this together …" Karin started, but Sven-Erik cut her off. "She fu-fu-fu-fu-fu-fucked Hugo," he sobbed, turning away.

"What?!"

That was Maria, who couldn't help herself. She was staring at Gunilla with her black eyes, and right away we all understood that Maria, too, had let herself be seduced by that handsome Latin American smile. Her boyfriend Mats also understood it. Without a word he got up from the table, picked up the salad bowl in both hands, threw it against the wall, and then disappeared out in the hallway. Everything was quiet for a few seconds. No one moved. No one said anything. But the sound of the front door slamming shut broke the spell.

Gunilla started crying. Maria stood up, looked around, took a carton of yogurt off the table, and dumped it out over Gunilla's hair. With great seriousness, as if she were doing an important job or creating a modern art installation, she let the yogurt flow over Gunilla, who didn't seem to understand what was happening; at any rate, she didn't react. When the carton was empty, Maria inspected her work, and then disappeared into her room in a few quick steps without saying a word. Gunilla just sat there, her face buried in her hands, her tears and the yogurt mixing on the table in front of her. And Sven-Erik seemed to have been inspired by Mats. He took the whole dish drainer and threw it onto the floor, screamed some more ugly words at Gunilla, and then left the apartment.

When Gunilla stood up and snuffled her way into the bathroom, I sank down into a chair across from Karin. The kitchen was a disaster area full of cucumbers and tomatoes and shards of porcelain and utensils and yogurt and broken glass, and we looked at each other and in the end we just couldn't help but laugh, and our laughter cleaned all the hatred and jealousy and sadness out of the air. We laughed and laughed and laughed, until an icy thought brought me to a freezing halt.

"What is it?" Karin wondered aloud.

"Not you too, right?" I asked, feeling how I was starting to shake with fear in anticipation of her answer.

But Karin shook her head and laughed.

"Although he is cute," she said, laughing.

I was serious now.

"But you're cuter." Karin laughed.

I believed her. I trusted her.

Our commune ended there, obviously. The next week Karin and I moved to an attic apartment on Tomegapsgatan. The other four all moved out. Mats and Maria evidently managed to salvage their relationship after her little Chilean fling. We stayed in touch with Gunilla, but Sven-Erik went off to Göteborg, if I remember right. We sometimes saw Hugo in Lund. He would always stop to chat.

He was friendly and cheerful, as if nothing had happened, and we would march in the same demonstrations and shout together: *"El pueblo unido jamai sera vencido!"* *"Salvador Allende, presente! Che Guevara, presente!"*

And those seven months we spent in Fäladen are actually my only experience with communal living, if you don't count the institutions and treatment centers I visited much later, although three couples sharing an apartment isn't the same thing as living in a commune. No, I think a commune is something else, something more lasting. And so I can hold onto that dream along with all my other unrealized dreams.

"The dream is over," John Lennon sang.

None of my dreams are shattered. I've never really woken up to that realization. No, they're hibernating, my dreams. My dreams as a seventeen-year-old, my dreams of another world and another way of living together.

My dreams are hibernating, waiting to become reality.

32

When Karin told me she was pregnant, I was twenty-one. I wasn't a grown-up. I thought my life hadn't started yet. I'd just been putting stuff off. I was working as an orderly waiting for my real life to begin.

I could've become a young father. My life could have taken a whole different direction. But that was never really an option. I didn't even have time to think the thought before Karin said, "I'm thinking of getting an abortion. Of course."

I accepted that it was her decision to make, and as soon as

she said that I immediately stopped thinking of her pregnancy as anything other than a temporary little sickness that would soon be cured.

It wasn't until after you were born that I thought of what had grown in her as a potential human being. A sibling. Before that, it was just an abortion. A problem that was taken care of. A thin thread that was severed.

I don't mean that we did anything wrong. I don't mean that we weren't in agreement, your mother and I. I just mean: after the instant when I saw you come out into the world it didn't feel as simple anymore, as obvious. The other thing, I mean. The abortion.

Nowadays, every child is alive because his or her parents chose not to have an abortion. Well, not all of course, but still ... "Thank you very much," every child ought to say. "Thank you very much for allowing me to be born, Mom and Dad."

But it's the woman's decision, I still think that. We had never exactly discussed contraception. Karin took her birth-control pills and I hadn't offered any other solutions.

"Using a condom is like taking a bath in rag socks," Mattsson used to joke.

Guy talk. But it sure was nice and convenient not to have to worry about it. And even when it didn't work, I didn't need to worry about it.

Now I understand that the abortion wasn't as easy for Karin as she wanted me to think. I remember that she was changed when she came home from the hospital. I saw it but didn't know what I should do. It was as if she were still mourning something. She wouldn't look me in the eyes anymore. She was kind of hunkered down and stooped over, and it took many months before she straightened up and found her old sense of pride again.

I also understand that that created a crack in our love, a thin, little, almost imperceptible crack, but suddenly it was there and later, along with a lot of other stuff, it contributed to everything falling apart.

That crack formed in both her love and mine. But it was so faint and delicate that neither of us saw it, and neither of us could hear that the tone had changed.

33

We lived in that apartment in Lund for ... let me think now ... almost four years. They were good years, as I remember them. If we'd stayed together, Karin and I, we could have sat there in our rocking chairs when we were old with lap blankets on and talked about those years, and we could've pulled out pictures from our memories and said, yes, things were so good back then and those were exciting years and so much happened then. Yes, that's what we could've said.

Yes, a lot happened and we met lots of people, and I'm sure that's why couplehood didn't feel as claustrophobic as I had feared.

But I started getting together with my old friends less and less. Mattsson still lived in his apartment in Malmö. He had enrolled at the University of Lund and then used all his student-loan money on a bunch of hash. He talked as much as before. He had as many crazy plans as before, but I thought I detected a tired fog in his eyes. That stickiness, that glueyness that affects everyone who keeps smoking hash. Jonny had left his guru in Vombsjö and found a new one: L. Ron Hubbard. Yes, Jonny became a Scientologist. He took expensive classes. He worked for the Church of Scientology. He would walk around downtown handing out offers for person- ality tests and trying to convert people, and he had a new goal in life: to become a Clear. I stayed in touch with Per-Inge. He would send these remarkable letters with vividly colored stamps from India or Nepal or Tibet. He would stop by and say hello when he was home in Sweden, and he was very proud that he'd gotten two poems published in the journal *Lyrikvännen*.

I cut my hair. At one time long hair had stood for freedom, for freedom and rebellion. Short hair meant narrow-minded, meant scaredy-cat, meant nine-to-five drone. Crosby, Stills, Nash & Young sang "Almost Cut My Hair." Boy, that was a typical David Crosby song, a nightmare of a song with nasty distorted guitars. But then suddenly I discovered that all that didn't apply anymore, and suddenly long hair was just a lot of work, because it would get greasy and you had to wash it every day and comb it and take care of it. So one day on the way home from work I went to a barber and said, "I'd like a Kennedy cut."

The barber just stared at me.

"Just kidding," I said. "But cut it short. Leave about an inch. Give me a normal-guy haircut."

"I'd be delighted to," the barber said, smiling and licking his lips.

Karin didn't recognize me. It's true. It took her three seconds before she realized it was me.

"It's going to take me a few months to get used to this," she said, kissing the back of my neck. "But you're cute. You look like this guy I had a crush on when I was eight."

But soon we got used to it. And, oh man, was it nice! Short hair was freedom.

Maybe, I've thought, I grew up a bit then.

Some things we did together, some things we did on our own. Karin was still active in politics, of course. She was a member of the Communist Party of Sweden, SKP, which formed after the Communist League Marxist-Leninists, KFML, split up and the hard-core communists in Göteborg created the more orthodox and more revolutionary KFML(r). Later, that turned into KPML(r).

The struggle against the imperialists—the Soviet Union and the United States—was the most important item on the agenda. And in Sweden we also felt American imperialism in the form of cultural imperialism, what people called cocacolonization— bad, commercial Hollywood movies; bad American commercial music; bad, dumbed-down American TV shows; bad American fast food; and ads, of course. There weren't any ads on Swedish TV or radio then; that was just totally inconceivable.

America was the country we hated most of all. In America, black people were oppressed; in America, only rich people had access to health care; in America, little babies were eaten by rats, and old people were dumped at train stations and bus stops because no one wanted to take care of them. And people in America were shallow and stupid and fake and ostentatious and dollar-obsessed. And afraid of getting old, and afraid of dying. America was a nightmare vision of the kind of society we didn't want to have. And of course America was the biggest threat to world peace, and everywhere in the world where the people tried to take power,

America would pop up and support some dictator or military regime that would reestablish the old oppression.

That's how it was then. That's what we thought. But there were people who loved America, too, of course. The Swedish *raggare*, for example, who like to drive around in big American muscle cars.

At any rate, Karin's political convictions led to my learning to dance the *polska*. It's true. I learned the *slängpolska* and the *bakmes* and lots of other traditional Swedish folk dances, because our wonderful old Swedish cultural heritage was what we possessed to counter all of the seductive, glitzy schlock that was coming out of the Great Imperialist State in the West, so we started folk dancing. It was fun. There was like a weird little underground movement of young folk musicians and dancers, and it was important to us that it was folk dancing, not *gammaldans;* that was a cheesy pastime for old people and not the exhibition folk dances that national romanticists were performing. No, it had to be folk dancing, and the older the music, the more the bourdon strings buzzed, the better. But, boy, was it fun. During all those years in Lund we went dancing every week, and we went to Korrö and Ransäter and Dalarna to gatherings and get-togethers. Now, it's been ages since I last danced, but I can still hear the difference between a *polska* from Skåne and one from Dalarna and one from Norrbotten. How many people can say that these days? And how many people even know what a *polska* is?

And isn't it odd that it could be a kind of political statement, dancing old dances? Or baking your own bread or picking blueberries? We did that, too, you know. And there was a big glass jug of blueberry wine simmering and bubbling in a corner of the bedroom. Our wine was never that good, if I'm going to be honest, but it was sweet and strong.

Well, so the dancing was something we did together. But there was other music, too, and we were both active in Musikforum and Kontaktnätet, helping out with concert arrangements and with all the bands that were touring in Sweden then: Samla Mammas Manna and Risken Finns and Träd Gräs & Stenar and Arbete & Fritid and Turid and Kebnekaise and Nynningen and Røde Mor from Copenhagen and Norrbotten's Järn from Luleå and Vømmøl Spelmanslag from Norway and lots of others. Those groups and artists played all different kinds of music. There was political activism and free jazz and ballads and folk music and pop and rock, and people were open to all kinds.

Lots of people came to the concerts, and for two summers we organized a music festival outside Häckeberga. That was great, a couple of summer days of music and happy people and food and people camping out in tents. Yes, for me that was like a little reminder of the new world I had glimpsed in Denmark a few years earlier.

Those were good years in Lund. We were doing well together. We did stuff. We met lots of people. That's how I remember it.

We were doing well together, Karin and I, and yet, when I thought about the future, about my future, it wasn't a given that she would be part of it.

Or, rather, I'd started keeping a tally. I'd started thinking, *I've given up this and this and this and that important thing for your sake. So now you owe me. So, later I can cash this in.*

Do you get what I mean? Ugh! That sounds totally crazy,

doesn't it? It sounds sick. But it's something I've thought about a lot when I think about Karin and me. That whole thing about a tally sheet. I'll try to explain it better later.

I haven't said anything yet about the most important thing that happened during those years in Lund. My life took a new direction there.

More and more often my camera had just been lying there at home, but when the Academic Society in Lund organized a photography competition called *Lundabilder* I picked it up again. I took a series of pictures outside Saint Lars's Hospital, photographed the patients and staff and buildings. Then I made prints out of them at a friend's place, and entered them.

Then I forgot about the whole thing. Yup, it's true. And then I got a phone call one evening that my pictures were going to be in an exhibit at the Art Gallery, and that what's more I'd won first prize. Seven hundred dollars.

"Seven hundred!"

That was almost a whole semester's worth of funding for Karin. I scurried down to the government-run liquor store and bought two bottles of bubbly that we shared, and I was so radiantly happy and my whole body felt like now, now something was happening. Now my life was taking a turn, now the world was opening up, now the future was beginning, now ...

Yes, well, you could certainly say that that was true. My life did change, it had a new direction, maybe new goals as well. I'm not talking about the money, you know. I'm talking about the fact that I suddenly felt like I understood what I was: a photographer. That's what I was. That was my gift. The gift I'd been given.

And there was nothing I would've rather had, nothing I would've rather been.

The exhibition in Lund quickly led to a professional career. Things started to click, and everything started working together. *Vi* magazine published some of the pictures. I got an offer to do a photo essay on any topic for the magazine, and pulled out my old Samsö pictures and compiled them into a sequence that I called "Paradise Lost?" and that I was later invited to exhibit at the Hasselblad Center in Göteborg.

The truth was that the hippie era and hippie dream already felt distant and a little exotic. In London, the first punk groups had already started pissing in public and sticking safety pins through their cheeks.

At any rate, in 1978 I quit my job at Saint Lars's Hospital. I got a part-time job for the labor-movement newspaper *Arbetet* and the regional paper *Skånska Dagbladet* and sold pictures to magazines, but not much money came in. My income was irregular and uncertain, but with Karin's school funding we were able to manage.

I was doing great. It wasn't my little brush with fame or notoriety that tickled me most. I mean, sure, it was nice to see my pictures in different places and read good reviews, but mostly I was happy to have found my niche. I was happy. I was a photographer. In the phone book it said: *Göran Persson, photographer.* Suddenly, I got to meet artists and authors and craftspeople and cultural people, and I felt at home with them—much more at home than I'd ever felt among my coworkers at the hospital or among academics in Lund. It felt almost like my earlier friendships, like we were all coming from the same place.

And I wanted to hone my skills. I read, I discussed things with other photographers, I bought a new camera, I took a class on darkroom techniques. I tried to cultivate my gift in various ways.

And just as I had done occasionally in high school, I saw the world in pictures again. Shadows, light, and nuances, suddenly every instant was a potential photograph, every person, every tree, every building was a potential motif. My eyes became sensitive.

Yes, the years in Lund were filled with dancing and concerts and bread baking and politics and Karin's studies and my nascent career as a photographer. Those were good years, and I'm sure Karin would never say otherwise, in spite of everything.

On New Year's Day 1980 we left Lund. Karin was going to do her district court service in Malmö. Papa Herman helped us find an apartment in Sofielund and helped us out with a little deposit also, and so we filled our boxes with books and odds and ends, and with the help of some buddies we moved back to Malmö. It wasn't a hard decision. After all, Malmö is a real city, a vibrant city. Lund is really mostly a student ghetto, with way too many tech geeks running around in pink tracksuits playing with water pistols.

34

Am I wearing you out? Well, I guess you're just lying there on your mattress. Your only job right now is breathing and gathering your strength and listening. Letting what I'm saying sink in. And then trying … to learn something. To understand. To see more clearly, more plainly. Not about me, that's not what I'm going for, not most of all. No, that you should understand yourself better, that's what I want. In telling you about my life, I want to give you your own.

And soon you'll make your appearance in my story. Now it's just … let me see … one, two, three, yes, less than four years until you're born.

When we came to Sofielund, the neighborhood was a bizarre mix of newly renovated and freshly fixed-up apartment buildings and old ramshackle working-class tenements, full of young people and civil servants and welfare recipients and criminals. It was like that all the way out to Möllevången. We had a nice apartment on the fourth floor of a building near Lantmannagatan, a two-bedroom place where I was able to set up a decent darkroom in a closet. The biggest problem was that the walls were so thin. There was an immigrant family above us and it sounded like they rearranged their furniture every night, and they always had their TV on at maximum volume. To our left there was an older man who drank and had parties and screamed and shouted and hollered, and a couple about our age lived to the right of us, and every night they had such loud sex the bed would creak, and she would moan and squeal. Every time I met that cute woman in the stairwell I was embarrassed and turned away, even though she was always friendly and said hi to me. Their bedroom and our bedroom shared a wall, and Karin and I would look at each other and smile and feel like grown-ups.

"They've been at it for a while."

"Hmm."

"You want a man with that kind of stamina."

"Go get yourself one, then."

"Nah, I don't want to. But maybe you should practice that a little …"

"Should we get started and practice it now?"

"No, I have to go to sleep. Seriously. I have to get up early tomorrow. Good night."

"Good night."

Karin was a lawyer now and was working for the county administrative court, and I was a freelance photographer. We had an apartment, we had a coffeemaker, we had a sofa and a bed we bought at IKEA and furniture we bought at Myrorna, we had bookshelves full of books, we had a stereo system and three crates full of records, we had china and silverware and pots and pans and a terra-cotta teapot. We were like a little family. Still, I was keeping that tally sheet. And we never really talked about our plans for the future or compared them.

Of course we were active in the Anti-Nuclear–Power Campaign. Of course we participated in all the marches against the Barsebäck Nuclear Power Plant just south of Malmö. And when the referendum came, we were reminded of the kinds of nasty dirty tricks the Social Democrats would resort to to stay in power. What we had known as seventeen-year-olds was still true: Sweden's Social Democrats and big business got along quite well together. But it was painful, and it is painful that people already seem to have forgotten what happened when the Swedish people went to vote on whether or not the country should use nuclear power.

What happened after that? It was like time started moving faster. The days started melting together. I don't know.

In 1981 it had been nine years since I'd met Karin at a crosswalk here in Malmö. 1981 was also the year I made my big breakthrough as a photographer, and it involved Karin.

It was a Sunday morning in April. We'd stayed in bed until eleven and were enjoying our day off. And then I got up to put the coffee on, and when I came back Karin was sitting naked on the edge of the bed. A bright light from the foggy world outside the window had transformed her hair into a halo and given her skin a soft sheen. Her face was that of a thoughtful little girl, a little schoolgirl who suddenly got caught up in some thought and forgot everything else.

"Don't move," I said. "Don't think about anything else. I want to take a picture of you."

"I'm naked," Karin said, but she didn't move from the spot. "You know that I don't want my picture taken without my clothes on."

"I can take a picture of your face," I said as I got out the camera and switched lenses. "Your face is always naked, isn't it?"

I took a few quick pictures, worried that the moment would be gone.

"I can take a picture of your shoulder, can't I?" I said, turning the camera to the right. "Your shoulder and your arm?"

I turned the camera farther to the side, and took a few more pictures.

"There, good. Thank you."

"If my breast shows up in any magazine, I'll sue you," Karin said.

"Yes, my love," I said. "Come on. Let's eat breakfast now."

A few days later as I stood in the darkroom with the film, I discovered a picture where you could just glimpse Karin's naked shoulder, arm, and hip on the left edge of the frame while the rest of the picture showed an empty room with a luminous fog outside a grimy windowpane. I made a 10x16 copy and studied it carefully. Fantastic! Although Karin only showed in a few millimeters of the photo, her presence filled the entire picture. I started shaking as I stood there leaning over my photo, and I knew right away that I had discovered a way of capturing a portrait that I had to explore. The next week I took twelve rolls of people in different environments. I let them pose as if for a portrait, but always turned the camera slightly away, so that you could only just glimpse or sense a person in the finished photo.

When I was invited to participate a short time later in the joint exhibition Young Photo at the Modern Museum in Stockholm, I chose a series of pictures of rooms and environments where at the very edge of the frame you could just see a finger, a bit of a shoe, an ear, a few strands of hair or an elbow. Naturally, I called my pictures "Portraits," and I received a degree of notoriety that I could never have imagined. The big papers did stories, I was interviewed in *Rapport* and *Kulturnytt,* and my pictures were published in several other countries.

Turning the camera away from the subject, looking sideways, taking a step to the side, that was my whole idea. That took me far. And I hadn't seen Ola Billgren's paintings, I promise. It was only many years later that I discovered that for a while he and I had been working with exactly the same idea.

The success of the Stockholm exhibit resulted in work and money. I sold several pictures to the magazine *ETC,* which had just been launched. I was invited to exhibitions all over Europe. And I got a great half-time newspaper job at *Sydsvenska Dagbladet* that gave me a lot of freedom. I also met with a certain amount of fame, a modicum of celebrity status. People saw and heard my name. Yes, there was a short period in history when the name Göran Persson was known as the name of a successful photographer. I find it highly unlikely that a single person in this country would think of me now when he or she hears the name Göran Persson. But if someone did, it would probably be my mother.

I don't know if I got a bit of a swelled head, but maybe I started having a kind of pride or self-confidence that I hadn't had before. And maybe that was one of the reasons that I tried to leave Karin.

I mean, I had thought, *Never.* I had thought, *Always.*

Always us, until one of us dies. Let all the others break up and get divorced and have their relationships fail, but never us. We're forever. You and me forever, baby. That's what I thought.

My starting to think differently had to do with several things, and maybe my success as a photographer was one of them. I don't know. But running into Jonny at Pildamm Park one nice, clear fall day was definitely one of the reasons.

"I've found my way home now," he said.

"Are you a Clear now?" I asked.

But he explained that the Church of Scientology was a profit-hungry, authoritarian organization, and that luckily he'd figured that out, so he was able to get out in time, with his mind and his independence and a little bit of money intact.

"I didn't know that what I was looking for was so nearby," he said. "I didn't need to search in Tibet or India or Japan or among Indian tribes or from some greedy old science fiction writer or in the distant past. What I was looking for is right here, right now. I was blind, but now I see."

And then he said the name of what he'd found, what he'd been searching for the whole time.

"Jesus. Jesus Christ. He loves me and I love him. He loves me even if I'm not strong. I don't need to do any exercises. I don't need to collect points. He loves and forgives. He bears my sins. I don't need to qualify for his love. I've been blind, but now I see."

He talked for a really long time about his new life, and his eyes were bright and clear when he told me that the church had room for everyone. But it was what he told me about our old friends that I carried with me from our meeting.

"Mattsson, yeah, he moved up to some village in Västerbotten. I went up there to see him last summer. It was nice, pretty, just five or six houses, but they've fixed everything up nice, not nice enough that I'd want to live there, but they're farming and keeping chickens and pigs that run around free all over the place, and they have their own school, there's tons of kids there, too. They've built their own little world. He met a girl there who already had four children, so suddenly he's the father of four. Mattsson, can you imagine?"

"How about Per-Inge?" I asked.

"Haven't you heard?" Jonny asked, looking at me in surprise.

I shook my head.

"What?"

"He's dead."

"What?"

Jonny looked at me seriously before he elaborated.

"Did you meet Jennifer? No? Well, he'd gotten together with

a girl he met somewhere on one of his trips, and they'd moved in together and eventually bought a little house out in Videdal, a yellow house with a yard and apple trees and everything. And he seemed so happy and content puttering around there, you know how Per-Inge could be, like a little elf. And anyway, one day when Jennifer came home from the day-care center where she works, Per-Inge had hanged himself. He was hanging there in the kitchen, dead. Can you believe it? Per-Inge. I had seen him just a few weeks before that. He was completely normal. We wrestled on his lawn, and he told me about his vegetable garden and currant bushes and his compost and how he wanted ..."

"What?"

"How he wanted to have kids, how he wanted to be a father. And then he goes and hangs himself."

I didn't believe it was true. I didn't want to believe what Jonny said. Not Per-Inge. No, not him. He was the last person you'd think wouldn't want to live anymore, he was so full of life.

Running into Jonny that day and hearing what he told me changed my life. First, of course I was thinking about Per-Inge, and I felt guilty that I wasn't there. Maybe I could've helped him and prevented what happened. Maybe I could have said the right words. I kept coming back to what he was thinking, what could have driven him into such a bleak state of hopelessness. Then I started thinking about Mattsson. Then I started thinking about myself.

How was *my* life? What plans and dreams did I still have? Which ones had I given up on? Had I allowed myself to be lured and seduced by a little fame, and forgotten what was actually real?

Was there a risk that I, too, would start to speculate that death was the final way out of a prison I'd constructed around myself?

I sat home at the kitchen table one day and thought, *I'm twenty-seven years old.*

I remember that so well. It was as if I hadn't realized until that day that I was actually a grown-up. Or should be. I was twenty-seven years old. I couldn't keep putting off my life. And when Karin came home from work I said, "I have to move out. I have to live on my own for a bit."

She sank down across from me at the table and looked at me in silence for a long time.

"What do you mean, *have to?*" she asked finally. "Why do you *have to* do that?"

Because otherwise I might kill myself, I thought, but I never said that. I understood that that would sound pathetic.

"I have to ... I have to feel like I'm choosing my life, that I'm not just letting stuff happen. I don't want to wake up one day and discover that ..."

"Am I stopping you?" Karin asked. "Am I stopping you from doing something you think is important? Am I holding you back?"

Yes, I thought.

"No," I said.

Silence filled the kitchen like a cold, clammy fog. And Karin's voice was flat when she said, "OK. But if you move out, I never want to see you again. None of this 'we're taking a little break to see what it feels like' nonsense. And then stay friends. If you still want to move out tomorrow, then you can, and you'll be free and won't have to be tied down to me anymore. That would be best, although you might want to think it over carefully first. Think about whether I'm really what's stopping you from whatever you want to do. Because I ..."

She hesitated and swallowed, and a little sadness made her voice unsteady when she continued, "... was thinking we would live together because ... I want to ... because I love you."

That's what she said.

That's exactly what she said.

And I knew that I had to stay.

I knew that that's what I really wanted. I knew she was right. I knew I was an open book to her, that she knew me better than I knew myself.

Do you understand? When I said I wanted to leave her, she asked me to stay. That's true. She didn't let me leave.

_____

35

Karin. A twenty-six-year-old woman now.

How had she changed? Was she living a life she felt she'd chosen herself? Yes, I was always convinced that was the case.

She was the most beautiful, proudest, strongest woman I knew. And she was a grown woman, the angry girl in a faded jacket and worn jeans was gone. True, Karin often walked around in jeans still, but they were a more expensive kind now, and not all cut up and frayed. She would often wear airy cotton dresses in pastel colors. Her hair was long and straight. She wasn't frumpy in the least, but she was a grown woman, yes, absolutely.

She hung out with lawyers and law students but hadn't given up her ideas or ideals. She was active in an amnesty group, and a member of the Left Party. Yes, it's true. Ten years earlier she thought the Left Party Communists were revisionists, cowardly reformists and class traitors, but since most of the people she worked with were deeply right-wing you might well say that she held her own. She even got a little involved in local politics. She was a deputy member of the cultural committee, and attended group meetings every other week.

Karin still had faith. She was an unwavering socialist. Yes, for a long time she had continued to call herself a communist, even when it was all but forbidden. Sometimes I've envied her that, her ability to believe in something. I myself am cursed with never being able to fully let go of my skepticism. I've never been able to fully accept Marx or Jesus or Buddha or any of the other idols. There's always a tiny bit of doubt left, always a few objections up my sleeve. Always lukewarm. Rarely hot or ice-cold.

But maybe that's an asset, after all. At least I don't have to be embarrassed or apologize for stupid things I thought or said. So, A.A.'s wording of "God-as-we-understand-Him" suits me perfectly. I'm happy to confess my belief and my reliance in that sort of deity. God could be any positive force. For some people God means the sense of community they find in the A.A. group. And for some people GOD is an acronym for Group Of Drunks. That works fine. That little bit of faith is enough for me.

Sometimes I would lie awake at night and watch her sleep. Then she was a little girl again, sleeping so soundly with her mouth half open, mumbling something unintelligible, turning a little and moving in her sleep. I thought about our shared history, about everything we'd done together, about how we'd watched each other grow, and my heart would fill with warmth. I will never hurt her, no never. I will protect her from all harm. I will always be there for her.

I never loved Karin more than when I watched her sleep.

And often I would remember that Joni Mitchell line: "All I really, really want our love to do is to bring out the best in me and in you, too." I'd quoted that to her one of the first times we met during that first blissful period when we spent all our time getting to know each other and exploring each other, and took delight in everything we discovered about each other.

But days and weeks and months went by before we really found our way back to each other again after I'd said I wanted to move out. We never talked about it, but we were both more attentive to the other. We chose all the words we said to each other carefully. We searched for hidden meanings. We studied each other carefully for signs. A little fear and a little caution had come over us, but slowly it ebbed and we dared to trust each other again. Maybe you could say we'd learned something. I don't know. Maybe you could say that in spite of everything it brought us closer together. I don't know.

There was a blizzard over New Year's in 1982. We were supposed to go to a party in Bjärred but didn't dare venture out. We stayed home, just the two of us, sitting at our kitchen table. We drank two bottles of sparkling wine, and got a little tipsy.

"I love you," Karin said, her eyes fixed intently on mine.

"Good," I said.

She smiled and waited, and I let her wait a long time before I continued, "I love that you're so smart when I'm so dumb."

"More," Karin said.

"And that you're so beautiful," I said.

"More," Karin said, smiling.

"And that you say that you love me."

"More," Karin urged.

"And ... and ... and ..."

"And you're happy because I want to have a little baby with you," Karin said.

And that, one might say, is when you were born. At a kitchen table in Sofielund on New Year's Eve 1982. You were born from our wanting you, first Karin and then me. I wasn't hard to convince. I thought that ... that now was the time in my life. That was part of it. And maybe, I thought, a baby would help me settle down, finally feel at home. A baby would silence that voice in my head that was always repeating that life should be lived some other way, that I had given up something important that I believed in. Maybe I would be a grown-up.

Besides, I knew that if Karin had made up her mind, I had no choice. Besides, it turned out that Karin had stopped taking her birth-control pills two months earlier.

Then there was a while where we were waiting for her to miss her period.

"Damn it! Not this month, either. What if it doesn't work, what if we can't, what if there's something wrong with me?"

"Or me," I said.

But we were never seriously concerned.

I was going to have an exhibit in Oslo in March, and Karin came with me for the opening and a little weekend getaway, and we took the ferry from Copenhagen and we sat in the bar and drank drinks and a bad cover band named the Pink Panthers played and we danced and we were happy and we stumbled back to our cabin and created you.

You began in a cabin on the ferry to Oslo, created by a happy man and a happy woman who loved each other. You were wanted and eagerly awaited. It's pretty hard to think of a better beginning.

In the morning we ate the buffet breakfast as the ferry cruised up the narrow Oslo fjord.

I guarantee that no stomach in the history of the world was better documented than Karin's during the nine months that followed. After we found out, I took at least one picture every day.

"Maybe you shouldn't do that. Take pictures," Karin said, crinkling up her face. "What if something happens? What if it doesn't go well? What if …?"

"Everything will be fine. Nothing will happen," I said. Already I'd grown.

Karin was more beautiful than ever that summer and fall. She carried you with such a majestic pride. Her eyes sparkled. Yes, there was a radiance to her whole body. When she walked through town, everyone turned to look at her, and everyone who encountered her smiled and felt lighthearted. She was like a flesh-and-blood advertisement for Life & Love & Hope sent out by God. It's true. I saw it. But I wasn't able to capture it on film.

We joined a parents' group at the prenatal clinic, we practiced psychoprophylaxis, we practiced various breathing techniques, we read everything there was to read about pregnancies and childbirth and caring for infants, we followed your development in

Lennart Nilsson's photography book and watched you grow from a tadpole to a fish to a mammal to a little almost-person.

"But we're not buying anything. No baby carriage, no cradle, no clothes, no cute little toys. It's bad luck. We're not buying anything until he's born. Until we've seen that he's ... the way he's supposed to be."

"Or she," I said.

But Karin was convinced that you were a boy. She knew it from the beginning.

We sang to you. Do you remember that? We sang to our little unborn baby. We sang lullabies when you were swimming around in Karin's tummy, and we played classical music every night. We'd read that that was good. We played baroque music so the apartment boomed, and got a little revenge on our neighbors. Have you ever felt like Bach and Handel and Vivaldi seemed sort of strangely familiar to you?

You were scheduled to be born on December 13.

"Typical. That's a national holiday! We'll come in there in the morning, and they'll be celebrating Santa Lucia at the hospital and all the midwives will be bridesmaids and all the doctors will be carrying stars around on sticks and no one will have any time for us. They'll just be singing and eating gingerbread and saffron buns," Karin said, trying to giggle away her anxiety.

But you didn't want to wait. You were in a hurry to get out into the world. Early in the morning on December 5, Karin woke up because the bed was all wet, and she woke me. "It's time. Are you coming?"

She was totally calm. I was totally confused.

And scared. Yes, I was petrified. That something would

happen, that something would go wrong. I was scared for her. I prayed to a God I never believed in: "Dear God, let everything be all right."

Everything was all right. We took a taxi to the hospital. We got to the delivery room at six thirty. The contractions had started. I was breathing along with Karin, and holding her hand. The midwife was big and fat and firm, and her name was Alva, and you were born without difficulty at 7:59 a.m. on December 5, 1984, at Malmö General Hospital. I was the second person to see you after Alva. You were wrinkly and red, and I counted quickly: One, two, three, four ... Yes, ten fingers and ten toes. And Alva glanced at you and said that you were a handsome little guy, and then she set you on Karin's breast. Or was her name actually Alma? At any rate, it was a good, solid midwife's name.

I didn't have a camera with me. Karin had said absolutely not, and it never even occurred to me to stand there taking pictures. I was needed. Yes, I had to help out. We were going to give birth to a baby together.

Of course, I carried the picture of you as an absolute newborn in my head. I think it was from a little later, of course. I think the umbilical cord had been cut. You're lying on Karin's shoulder now. She's looking at you, her eyes exhausted. You smell like life. I'm sitting on the edge of the bed. I'm leaning over and I'm happy.

That picture, that moment. Yes, if I had to pick just one, that's the one I'd pick.

No one who has seen a baby being born can ever forget it. Everyone who's seen a baby being born knows that there is hope, despite everything there is hope. Everyone who's seen a baby being born looks at other people with fresh eyes. We were all so pathetically helpless. And we've all taken love for granted. Therefore, there is hope.'

You smelled so good.

You weighed seven pounds three ounces and were twenty inches long. On the dot. A perfect little person. I could hold you in my hand. You were almost bald.

And now you're lying here.

And now I'm sitting here. Here's where we ended up.

36

Do you remember? Do you remember what it was like to be born?

Per-Inge claimed that he relived his own birth during an LSD trip.

It was tight, he said. It hurt like hell, he said. It was like being several meters underwater and struggling to get up to the surface. You know what direction to go, you're struggling toward the light up there, but it feels as if your head's going to explode. That's exactly what it was like, he said. "I struggled my way toward the light. I was doing so well living there in my mother's soft, dark belly, I was doing acrobatics and somersaults in there, but now I knew that a new era was going to start, there were changes underway, big changes. Yes, indeed. And a force drew me toward the light, and I was compelled to fight my way onward, even though I felt like I was coming apart. And then I was there, and the glaring light stung my eyes like a thousand searing knives, and someone gave me a hand and helped pull me out the last bit, and then I was out in the world and it was cold and I was freezing and I couldn't breathe, I was dying, but then my lungs filled with air, and I found my mother's nipple and sucked the first bit of milk into me, and then I turned and there was my father and he smelled like tobacco, and already I longed to go back in where I'd come from."

That's what Per-Inge said.

"And since then I've longed to go back," he said. "I was never supposed to leave my mother, I should have stayed in there."

And Mattsson grinned and said that the other night when we came home it had looked as if Per-Inge was working on crawling into Tessa through that hole she had between her legs. "Ha ha," Mattsson chuckled. "So that's what you're always doing with all those girls, you're trying to get in."

"Yeah. I'm on my way home." Per-Inge laughed. "I don't belong out here in the cold. I long to go back to the womb."

That's what he said, Per-Inge, who's dead now, who didn't want to live anymore.

37

So. Now you're in the world. You exist and you smell good and you have ten fingers and ten toes. So we buy all the accoutrements, everything a little newborn might need.

A crib and a baby carriage and a bassinet and a changing table and a baby carrier. And cloth diapers, of course. For the next few years our home is constantly filled with cloth diapers drying, constantly filled with the sweet smell of baby poop.

But not a ton of stuff. No, you're not going to be buried under a ton of unnecessary stuff: a soft Waldorf doll and wooden toys for your hands, a beautiful mobile for your eyes, that's enough. And music and nursery rhymes and lullabies for your ears, never has any child been sung to as much as you were. Do you remember? Do you remember how I sat by your crib every night and thumped you gently on the bottom and sang, "Diddle, diddle dumpling, your plump little rumpling ..."

Do you remember?

Karin sang all the time, too. And told you nursery rhymes and goofed around.

"This little piggy went to market, this little piggy stayed home, this little piggy ..."

Fuck.

Fuck, fuck, fuck.

Why are you lying here reeking of alcohol?

Fuck.

You were supposed to be the world's strongest, freest, happiest person. Fuck. What could we have done that we didn't do? We sang and read and ... and took you out for plenty of fresh air and went to concerts and plays, and protected you from TV and loud noises and getting the sun in your eyes, and took care of you and tried to give you the best start a little human baby could have. Why are you lying here? Well?

There are kids who grow up in poverty and wretchedness and without love. There are kids who grow up with parents who are addicts. There are kids who are abused by their parents. There are kids who don't have any parents. You had us and we wanted to give you everything. We showered you with love and kindness.

17

You were a prince who ruled and controlled our lives.

Why are you lying here stinking? Do you have any reason whatsoever not to be doing well? Well?

"I don't think chewing him out is going to help ..."

What? A girl, a young woman has entered the room without my noticing. I don't know how long she's been standing there by the door, listening. Could that be the half-sister? Or a girlfriend?

"Who are you?"

"I'm Josefin," she says, kneeling down next to the mattress.

"I'm—" I start, but she interrupts me.

"I know who you are."

"Look, Josefin," I try to explain, "I'm telling him—"

But she interrupts me again. "I heard what you're telling him."

Then she says that she needs to talk to Jonatan for a minute, and asks me to leave the room. I don't know why I listen to her.

the young woman

He didn't notice me arrive. I didn't mean to sneak in, I mean, I wasn't trying to eavesdrop, but I didn't want to interrupt, he was talking about when you were little, he was talking about what good parents they were, and then he started chewing you out because you're lying here, and then I couldn't help but say that surely there was no point in that, and then he just stared at me as if I were a ghost.

He's so much like you. Or the other way around: you're so much like him. I mean, I've seen the picture you have over your bed, but you can't tell in it how much you guys look alike. It's the eyes. Looking away. And the mouth. And the hands. And ... everything, I can see you in almost everything about him.

Hanna's baby-sitter told me you were here. She said the hospital had called, and I biked over here right away, but then I had to argue with this grumpy nurse for like fifteen minutes before she would let me in.

I'm sorry. You.

I know it's my fault.

Although it's a little bit your fault too because I was so darned disappointed in you, not for what you said but because you were carrying around so much inside yourself. For so long. That you'd been considering that without my even realizing it, and that you didn't talk to me. Fuck, I totally thought I knew you, I thought we could never hide anything from each other, I thought no one had ever been so close to me before. I've told you everything, I've told you things I never thought I would tell anyone, I've been an open book to you the whole time, from the first time we met, and then ... and then you've been hiding such a huge piece of yourself from me.

Understand that I was disappointed. Understand that I was hurt. Understand that I was pissed off.

Sure, you'd been drinking, you were a little drunk. But not so much, not then, you meant what you said. I know, I said things I shouldn't have said, too. I'm sorry, I wish I could take my words back, chew them to bits, swallow them, I wish they'd never left my lips. But it's because I was disappointed. Understand that.

I've always thought you're not like the others. Like the other guys, the boys and the men. I've thought that since the first time we talked, and I love you for being who you are. I felt like suddenly your shell cracked and someone I hadn't expected at all emerged. An alien that I didn't want to meet.

Am I stopping you? Am I stopping you from doing something you think is important? Am I holding you back in some way? That's what I was wondering.

All right, I was a little drunk, too. But not so much. You know that.

2

It feels like we've known each other our whole lives.

If you hadn't come flying into the girls' locker room that day, if we hadn't met that night at the concert, if we hadn't wound up in that storeroom, maybe I would never have gotten to know you. We could have gone to the same school for four years, walked past each other in the hallways, sat in the cafeteria or up in the library at the same time, maybe even been in the same classes without ever starting to talk to each other, without getting to know each other. It could've been that way. There are so many people who just pass you by.

Now of everyone you're the person who's closest to me. The one who lives in my heart. Yes.

You weren't like other guys. You're not like other guys. In junior high, I mean, the guys were like a different species, lazing around like big dumb, puppies or something. Big, scruffy, overgrown puppies who drooled and bounced and came running and knocked things over when they turned around or when they wagged their tails in their childish glee. Not that all the girls were contemplating life or the world or the future, not that all the girls were writing poetry or painting or playing the flute, but, still, the girls were more like ... like humans. The guys were just a problem. Big, lazy puppies with bad manners. Barely housebroken. Mostly interested in the most basic stuff: in getting drunk and sports and girls' bodies. In getting into fights and competing for power in the classroom and in the schoolyard. Driven by their most primitive urges.

And there really isn't much difference now in high school. Most of the guys are still at that level. There's a bunch of guys from the suburbs here whose families come from various macho cultures. They're grown-up in another way, a scary old-fashioned way. They greet each other every day with a handshake, and they dream of manliness and money and power, and about beautiful and obedient women to show off to their buddies. All right, I'm being a little unfair now. A little racist. But mostly that's how it is. And then there are the usual soccer nuts and party boys and the minor thugs and the major thugs. But you're not like the others. You follow your own path.

That's what it is. You want to follow your own path.

Never be someone who follows someone else.

You guard your independence so much. You're so afraid of being tricked into something you didn't choose yourself. You'd rather be on your own than go with the flow.

I noticed that right away. That you weren't like the others, that you were different. I mean, everyone knows the different kinds of people there are. The stuck-up hip-hop crowd with their contemptuous sneers. The bleached-blond soccer guys bellowing out their songs at drinking parties. The trendy boys with their sad eyes, I feel most at home with them, but often they're so full of their own greatness or their plans or their suffering.

You came along and didn't fit into any of those pigeonholes. I was hesitant, maybe I was a little afraid, maybe you unmasked me in some way. You seemed so confident and so mature. So free and independent.

No, not really confident. Expectant, cautious. But not cowardly.

I'll be honest: I wasn't that interested in boys. I even thought I would do just fine without guys. If you get what I mean. But that was before I met you.

3

From a purely technical point of view I could charge you with assault and battery. It was your hand that held on, it was your arm that made me fall, although you'd have just as much right to charge me and say that it was self-defense. And you and I both know that that would be the most truthful picture.

We were like two squabbling three-year-olds in a sandbox.

I just mean, if I didn't love you as much as I do, if I wanted to hurt you, then I could charge you.

But you can trust me, I would never lie to hurt you. And you know that I trust you, like I've never trusted anyone. I even passed you the knife, you remember that? Do you get how much I trust you?

Then of course I got scared.

Scared that you would run into trouble. You'd had so much more to drink than usual. And I got scared that you would hurt yourself. And that you would drink more. I did start to understand why you drank, you were carrying around that pain that you wanted to numb, a pain I never even suspected.

I got so scared.

Mostly scared that you would harm yourself. I've never thought that before, but tonight that thought swept through me like an arctic blast. A deathly chill that made me shiver.

I've been looking for you all night.

Now I'm here with you, you're breathing, you're alive.

Now I'm warm again.

·

I've done so much thinking during these hours, I've thought about you and about us. This is what I thought: It's your weakness I love.

Don't get me wrong, it's not that I want to be the strong one, the one in charge, the dominant one. No, that's not it. This is what I mean: all the guys I've met seem like they're afraid of weakness, of their own weakness. They hide it in different ways, they hide it behind muscles or attitude or style. You're braver than any guy I know, you're brave enough to show your weakness, your insecurity, your fear.

Everyone despises weakness. We've talked about that. But I love your weakness.

I love that I found you. That we found each other.

You're the guy all girls dream of. No, I guess not all. Not the worst of the bimbos, obviously, and not the worst of the jock girls either, but the others. The ones who have brains and pride, the ones who don't allow themselves to be fooled. The ones who aren't desperate. Ah, that I was the one who found you.

I should tell you the story. Yes, I'll tell you now, when you're lying here with your eyes closed. If we were sitting face to face I would never do it. I'm not as brave as you.

But sometimes you're a chicken when it comes to talking about feelings. Have you ever said once that you love me? I'm not one of those silly little girls who's gaga for romance, you know that, but if at any time you had ever said that you missed me or longed for me, then … fuck, now I'm nagging. Nagging and pestering and complaining. Why am I doing that? I just want to sit here and watch you breathe, and be happy that you are and long for your hands and all the things your hands can do.

Fuck, what did you do? Idiot.

When I see your slender wrists I just want to cry. When I see your hands. Your hands were made for stroking. Open, your hands should be open and soft. I know what your hands can do. Your hands were made to play guitar, I love watching your hands when you play. Have I told you that? You know what I love more? Well, watching you make sandwiches. You're so careful when you spread the margarine on, you work at it for so long to get it even and smooth, then the soy cheese, then two tomato slices. You work so meticulously, concentrating as if you were creating a work of art. And when I sit there across from you at the table and watch, I shiver with happiness. But you'll never get to know that, of course.

Your hands weren't made for holding on. Fuck. Why am I nagging? I didn't come here to nag, I didn't come here to tell you a bunch of stuff you already know, I came here to say I'm sorry.

Do you understand? I'm apologizing. Do you get it? I want to be with you. Still. Always. I know I pushed you into a corner, you turned into someone else, I made you into someone else, you were beside yourself, I know that, I saw how surprised you were, how disconsolate you were after you realized, when you snapped out of it, I …

"Ahem. Pardon me."

4

Sigh. Shit. Now he's back. The old man. Göran Persson, not the prime minister, no, the absentee father, the famous photographer, the alcoholic, the one who makes threats, the quitter. He's standing there in the doorway. He comes in and shuts the door behind him. Shit. He looks so lost, so confused. But clean-cut, no stubble, nice clothes, no alcohol smell.

"Hi," he says. "I'm Jon's father. I was just telling him about ... I was just telling him a bunch of stuff I should have told him a long time ago, but ... well."

He swallows, hesitating.

Wow, you guys are so alike. He could be you.

"I'd like to finish ... telling the story ... before ... before Karin, before Jon's mother gets here. I ... I may only have this one opportunity."

I wait. What should I say? He's asking me to leave. I don't want to leave. But he has your eyes. Oh dear. Now he's holding out his hand, he's going to introduce himself for real, now he tells me again that he's your dad and says his name is Göran. I knew that already.

"Josefin," I say, although I'd already told him my name.

"Are you ... are you his ... are you together?" he asks, seeming almost embarrassed.

I nod.

Then he says he came here because Jon had his phone number on a piece of paper in his pocket, and the police called, and ...

"Do you know what happened?" he asks suddenly. "Do you know why he's lying here?"

I nod.

"He drank too much. He was ... sad. Or ..."

Desperate is the word, but I can't say that, not without having to explain something I don't want to, and hardly could anyway. Not to him.

When he mumbles something about how drinking doesn't help, it pisses me off. Yeah, says you, I think. I mean, how much did you care? Where was he when you needed him? Yes, I know why you had that slip of paper in your pocket, but I'd never tell him, never.

You told me about the pain, about the emptiness, and about the unimaginably awful thing that happened when you were only five.

The weird thing is that the anger washes away in a few seconds, it disappears down the drain, *slurp,* what's left is a ... sadness, a small sorrow. The weird thing is that I feel a kind of ... solidarity, yes, actually, with him. He and I share something. He, the big quitter, and I.

And then there are his eyes. Your eyes. But yours are closed now.

"Couldn't you ... couldn't you keep telling him the story even with me here?" I ask.

He thinks about it. He's quiet for so long that I'm about to say that I can go out into the corridor and wait there, when he clears his throat and says, "When Jon was born I had the idea that I would tell him about myself. About who I was before I became his dad. You think about that kind of thing when you become a parent, you think about what shapes a child, you think about your own childhood and your own parents, at least I did, and I thought that I know nothing about my own mother and father, I don't know who my father was when he was seventeen or what the world he lived in was like, I don't know what my mother was like when she was a little girl, I don't even know, I thought, how my own mother and father met. Every person should know that, I thought. So I thought I would tell Jon, I even started writing down some of my childhood memories and things like that, but then ... well ... then other things happened ... and ... you probably know about some of them."

He stops talking and gets lost in his own thoughts. I wait, watching him. His hands are also yours. Or the other way around. And that little wrinkle at the one side of the mouth.

"Now I had an opportunity to tell him," he says meekly. "Now, tonight."

But you should really tell the story when your son can hear you, I think, and as if he could hear what I was thinking he says, "I know Jon has heard me. And ... I was almost finished with my story. I've told him a bit about ... about my childhood, and about when I was seventeen, and about how I met Karin, and about our life together, now I've gotten to when Jon was born. There's just one more thing I was going to talk about. The hardest one."

"I'll step out for a bit," I say, standing up.

But he shakes his head.

"No," he says. "Stay. Maybe it's a good thing that you're here. Yeah. I think it's good."

He pulls out the chair from the little desk and puts it next to my stainless steel stool, then he sits down, leans forward and looks at you for a long time in silence before he says, "I'm sorry."

the father

1

She's cute. She has gray eyes and long hair and high cheekbones, she looks like one of the main characters in a very famous Swedish children's movie, she is so cute that I have a childish sense of pride: yes indeed, this is Josefin, my son's girlfriend, yes indeed. Absurd, I know. But still.

She has dried blood under her nose. She shouldn't have that, it doesn't suit her. She's earnest.

No, wait. Not cute. Beautiful. Yes, she is. Beautiful and earnest and wise. Strong. So much integrity that I almost feel embarrassed and start stuttering.

Here sits the proud papa.

Now I'm telling the story not just for you, I'm telling it for her, too, for Josefin. I thought maybe that would be good, maybe she can be my witness.

Forgive me, Jonatan. I didn't mean to accuse you of anything.

You're breathing. You're alive. That's what's important.

You can learn something. You can learn something from everything that doesn't kill you, isn't that the saying?

That would be the worst thing: if you died. When children

die before their parents, that's the worst thing. That should never happen. If there was a God he would never allow that. But now the world is full of parents who've lost their children. Children who've died from starvation, from diseases, from American bombs or Palestinian bombs, or Catholic or Protestant or Islamic bombs, from sharp knives that sliced apart their soft bodies, from lead bullets that tore up their insides, they've died in car accidents, they've drowned, they've been trapped in burning buildings, they've been poisoned with drugs. Or taken their own lives, in deep desperation.

The oceans of tears their parents cried were also deep. Think of the millions of parents in the world who've lost a child. Imagine being forced to go on living.

That would be the worst thing: if you died before me.

OK. I know. I haven't shown that that's how I feel. I haven't been present in your life. I sound like a hypocrite, I understand that.

But I've known the whole time that you were alive. And now I'm here, aren't I?

You're the best thing I've done.

In my life, you're the best thing I've done. Do you understand?

I have learned something since I was seventeen.

I'm the last person who has the right to accuse you of anything. But it's true that we tried to give you the very best during those first years, your mom and I. We were careful parents. We had read, we had thought.

Loudon Wainwright sang, "Be careful, there's a baby in the

house," and we tried to be careful in every regard. By the way, have you heard of Loudon Wainwright? Nah, I'm sure you probably haven't. Oh, here's tonight's music question: Who was he married to? Nah, obviously you wouldn't know that one. Kate McGarrigle. One of the Canadian McGarrigle sisters who made three great records. Nah, I'm sure you haven't heard of them either, of course. Early seventies. But they got divorced later, Loudon and Kate that is, they got divorced when their daughter Martha was just a little girl. Her older brother's name is Rufus, and he has his own singing career now. Yes, I did mention that, didn't I? That I carry around a surplus of worthless musical trivia in my head.

Naturally, we shared the year of parental leave that Swedish parents get. First Karin stayed home for six months, then I did. She kept breast-feeding you until you were a year old, and already had little razor-sharp teeth that chewed up her nipples. But breast milk prevents allergies, that's what we'd read.

And later we started giving you other foods, although of course we didn't buy jars of baby food from the greedy multinational corporations. We made our own food, we mashed fruit and beans and potatoes into various gray mixtures that we stuffed into you with a teaspoon.

You grew. You started walking. You wore a soft little helmet on your head so you wouldn't get hurt when you took a tumble. You started talking.

There was a period in my life when I was just a dad. Sure, I was working, too, I was taking pictures, but I was fulfilled by being a dad.

Everything takes so much time, it fills your life. I had no idea before.

17

Changing diapers. Potty training. Making the food, feeding. Putting on pants and shirts. Putting on the little snowsuit. Tying the shoes. Carrying you down the stairs. Getting the stroller. Going to the park. Feeding the ducks. Going shopping. Going home, going up the stairs. Taking off the little snowsuit and shoes. Making the food, feeding. Potty training. Changing diapers. Washing diapers. Playing. Napping. Making food. Reading a book. Taking off the clothes, changing diapers, putting on pajamas. Singing, sitting by the crib, thumping you on the bottom.

There goes one day.

And another and another.

But that's not what I want to tell you. Karin can tell you about your first years, maybe she already has. I hope so.

I turned thirty and had a big party at a park outside Veberöd. Family and friends and music. None of my old friends, just new ones and our mutual friends.

When Karin turned thirty the next year, we went to Greece. Do you remember that? I mean, we weren't the kind of people who went in for package tours, we'd never done that, but now we went with Vingresor and wound up at this nice little inn on Lesbos. Do you remember? The blue ocean. The colorful fish in the clear water. The hot sand. The sun. The warm evenings at the taverna. You were, let's see … you were only two. But surely you remember?

Do you remember the seagulls? When we took the ferry one day to another island, tons of bright white gulls followed the ferry, they flew with the sun on their wings and dove and fought for pieces of bread and other stuff the people were throwing, and we stood there at the railing, I held you in my arms and you fed the seagulls, they would come swooping and pluck the pieces of bread out of your little hand, and you were laughing so happily. Do you remember? The sky was so blue, and the ocean. Karin was afraid the gulls would bite you.

We were a little family. We went on vacation to Greece.

But …

Was that how it was supposed to be? Had I chosen my life, had I made my dreams come true? Was I steering, or was I sitting in the back seat, just along for the ride, and if so, was the car even going in the right direction?

I'd laughed at all that stuff they say about turning thirty. We'd laughed together, Karin and I. That kind of thing was beneath us. We weren't like the others, not fooled like they were. Still, there was something that was starting to gnaw at me. No, that's not true. The picture of a glass that's so full it's overflowing, or a drop that hollows out the stone is more accurate. I'd been collecting. I mentioned that before, I was collecting credits. I got one credit point for every idea, every dream, every plan, every piece of myself I felt I'd given up. That I could cash in later. But how? I had only a very fuzzy idea about that.

Can you understand this? Can a seventeen-year-old understand this? Can anyone at all understand how I was thinking? I can't understand it anymore myself …

There's one thing I'm totally sure of: so many unhealthy thoughts, so many peculiarities and horrors and so much hate flourishes in every couple relationship that you could make a dozen horror movies, every little family contains a dozen horror movies, yes, that I'm sure of.

At least, that's true if you shut yourself off behind your front

17

door, then the mildew grows and eventually everything takes on this musty smell. You don't notice it yourself, but everyone else does. And nobody says anything, the old withering tactfulness keeps everyone's mouth shut.

So maybe in the seventies we were right, after all: there are healthier ways to live together than in the sacrosanct family unit.

We moved from the apartment in Sofielund to a new development with a yard out by Riseberga. We didn't want to live downtown with a three-year-old with all that exhaust. So, you're almost four now, and have been going to day care for two years. You must remember being in the Bumblebee Group and Miss Annika and Ronja, that chubby girl who was so in love with you, who wanted to hug and kiss you all the time? Surely you remember that?

We bought a condo with a yard in Riseberga. We had money. Karin's income went up year by year, she was a lawyer now and was working on refugee issues in a small law firm, she was good, she worked hard, she was gone a lot, her career took off.

My career as a photographer went in the other direction, I wasn't into it anymore, I was satisfied with my half-time job at SDS, taking pictures of accidents and politicians and people celebrating their anniversaries and celebrities, yes, I even covered sporting events for a while. I'd sit freezing by the goal at Malmö FF's home games. I spent the rest of my time being a father.

I was the one who stayed home with you in the evenings while Karin worked. She was doing important things, she was earning money, not that I'm complaining, I'm just saying I was the one who stayed home. I was the one who watched you fall asleep.

2

We're products of the time we live in.

Yes, that's what I've said. And, yes, I believe that. We don't want to admit it, but we're products of our time. We're influenced.

We're products of our parents.

That's also true, and we don't want to admit that, either. That's what I think.

I remember all too well the day when I realized that.

It was a fall evening in 1989. The Soviet empire was crumbling, my life was about to do the same thing. I didn't know it that night as I sat dozing in front of the TV. There was some European Cup match flickering before me on the screen, you were asleep in your bed, I was sitting there and from outside in the fog I heard the ice-cream truck.

It was then, exactly then.

It was then that I thought: What am I doing?

I got up, suddenly I was wide awake, I went over to the window, glanced out across the parking lot, a thin rain formed a glowing ring around the streetlight, I saw the ice-cream truck's sign between the buildings.

My brain was as cold as a winter's night, and my thoughts sparklingly clear. Is this what I wanted? I wondered. Is this what I've chosen?

I wondered, How did I wind up here?

It felt like waking up from a dream. Like coming out of a fog. And that's when I realized: I'm living my father's life all over again. I'm sitting here in a row house dozing in front of the TV.

17

I have a wife and a Volvo. I'm planning vacation trips. I'm paying my insurance premiums. I've got a bit of a beer belly.

Was this what I wanted? No. This was a lifestyle I had once despised. And I was right. I was true then, and false now. I'd forgotten my most precious dreams. I'd just taken the easiest path.

I was thirty-four years old. It had been seven years since I'd said: We're going to change the world through the way we live, through our way of being. I was so much wiser then, so much more honest as a seventeen-year-old, seventeen years ago.

Do you understand? Of course you can't understand, no seventeen-year-old can understand a grown-up understanding of treachery, of course you can only scoff and think I was being stupid and pathetic. Naturally, you're right. But that night I thought I'd had a paralyzing insight, and when Karin came home I tried to talk to her and explain, and it turned into a long night and the distance between us grew with every rejoinder we exchanged, and the misunderstandings erected towering walls and dug deep moats between us. My life started to fall apart that night. That moment of clarity I thought I'd had just led to a dead end, with me bashing my bloody forehead against a brick wall.

3

Karin. I lost her that night.

Something I said and something she said cut the last threads between us. Then we lost ourselves in the cold and scorn and cheap, spiteful remarks. We opened up a secret closet within our relationship and out poured lots of things we'd tried to stash away and hide, sticky trash and malicious little monsters, and rats with sharp, nasty teeth.

Karin. I've never loved anyone the way I loved her.

I promise. You grew up in a home filled with love, don't believe anything else.

Karin, the rebel girl, the upper-class girl from Bellevue. She, too, was the child of her parents. Her father's girl, oh, that was so clear now. Actually, of course, it had been clear for a long time. I could see the kind of friends she found to hang out with. They were people like her. Sure, she was actively working with refugees and immigrants, but more and more she had grown back into her old class. That was, of course, one of the things I pointed out to her when we were arguing, and that was, of course, one of the things she refused to admit or acknowledge.

I lost Karin that night.

I woke up before her the next morning. In spite of everything we'd slept in the same bed. Now she was sleeping on the pillow next to me, and I looked at her and I was filled with such tenderness, I thought that everything would be good again. I thought that the two of us belonged together forever, but then she woke up and opened her eyes and turned away from me, and I understood that it was already too late.

What has she told you?

Maybe she told you something else. Maybe she told you a completely different story that involved other people as well. It isn't true. Everything was between her and me, just between the two of us.

I had hidden part of my life from her, but she had also hidden a large part of her life from me. We'd stashed away so much between the two of us.

That was why, that was what the mistake was.

Is she crying? The girl, the young woman. She's sitting there with her head bowed down now, but I thought I saw a gleam in those beautiful eyes.

"Are you crying?"

The young woman whose name is Josefin raises her face and looks at me, her eyes glistening. "Keep going with the story," she urges.

I hesitate, but she turns to look at you, and after a moment I do what she has asked.

The rest of the story is about my humiliation and my shame.

4

I don't remember anymore what I was thinking. Probably I was thinking that I could just run away from our little mommy-daddy-child game and start a life that in some way agreed with my old ideals and dreams, and you would be part of that life, too. A daddy-child game every other week.

That must have been what I was thinking. Something like that.

Nothing came of that thought. What came was a free fall down into the abyss.

I moved out after a week of harsh words, ice-cold truths and burning lies, of furious screaming and bitter silence. I left our condo, I left Karin, and I left you.

You weren't quite five yet when I left you. How could I have explained? How could you have understood?

I moved into a studio apartment on Ystadsgatan, by Möllevång Square. The only thing I brought with me from the house in Riseberga was a little clothing, some of my books and my Incredible Stringband record. I bought a bed, a table and a chair at Myrorna. Then my single life started.

I don't remember anymore what I was thinking. I only remember that already by the first weekend that you were supposed to stay with me that this wasn't going to work, that I was losing my footing and soon I would fall. Karin and I had decided to meet at Södervärn. When she left you, you started crying and wanted to run after her. I was kneeling down next to you and crying because you were crying. Karin came back and comforted you without even looking at me, and you calmed down and stopped sobbing when she walked away. When she walked over to the man who had come with her, I watched their backs disappear through the mist of my tears. At least she wasn't holding his hand. But hadn't I seen him before?

It was wrong from the beginning, and you were sad and scared the whole weekend. You'd become a stranger to me in fourteen days. We went to the movies, we went to the Technical Museum, we went to the bakery for a treat, we ate at a Chinese restaurant, and the whole time I felt foolish and ridiculous. No, this was never going to work. I understood that already from the beginning. Weekend dad? No, not me. It was all right for other men who had failed in their lives, but not me. Never. I knew it was wrong.

Either or.

I had no choice.

When I dropped you off with Karin on Sunday night, I got

drunk. Drunker than ever before in my life. I went from bar to bar until I couldn't walk anymore, I disappeared into the booze and noticed that there was a place where the liquor soothed, there was a place where the fear subsided.

But that wasn't why I started drinking. No, not to alleviate the fear.

I started drinking because I wanted to become an alcoholic.

I was counting on it. I wanted to sink so deeply into the mud that I'd reach the bottom. I wanted to lose myself, I wanted to be an irresponsible child again. I bet all my chips on a career as an alcoholic. And I succeeded. I dedicated nine years of my life to an extended suicide attempt. To obliterating myself, to numbing my brain and dulling all my senses. I even succeeded in eradicating the self-loathing.

And I was quick and efficient. Within a year of the separation I'd been transformed from the conscientious father of a small child to a homeless guy who slept in doorways and shelters or at the homes of other panhandlers. I carried everything I owned in a plastic grocery-store bag. I'd sold my camera and emptied my bank accounts, been evicted from my apartment. I drank cheap booze, I was filthy and smelled awful and I had succeeded in forgetting you. Yes, it's true. That was my real goal, to forget you.

Either or. Nothing in between.

One time I went out to the house in Riseberga to beg for money from Karin, but when I thought I saw you in the playground, my heart broke and I turned around. I …

"Jonatan said you came."

5

What? Little Josefin has a voice. She's looking at me now with a slightly accusatory, angry wrinkle in the middle of her forehead. She's cute. She's not a coward.

"What? What do you mean?"

"Jonatan says you used to come and sit by the sandbox so he didn't dare go outside. He says he remembers that. That he was ashamed of you and was afraid the other kids would realize that you were his dad. And that you used to call them late at night, night after night, and that he was terrified and started wetting the bed. And that Karin had to call the police when you would creep around outside the house at night. That you threatened her when she met a new man. Isn't that true?"

Sheesh, lady.

This eternal female silliness. True? As if there's a truth, one single one, as if in each situation there's a single truth. Yes or no. Why don't they understand that everything has a reason, that events are interrelated. Women! One-track minds, like an American president. "We're good. The others are bad. They're jealous of us and our liberty and our prosperity. That's the truth. That's why we bomb them. Those other people. People with slightly darker skin, people who smell different, people who believe in different gods." Pick a comfortable lie and call it the truth. As if there weren't far more complicated causes and interconnections.

"Is it true?"

Sheesh, lady. She's persistent. She makes me so tired.

I close my eyes, sigh, swallow, turn away. How can I make

her understand? But you understand, surely you understand, I've told you the story now, you can see how everything led to a black hole, to a bottomless sea to sink into, you have to understand, it doesn't matter what everyone else says, the only thing that means anything is that you understand, that you take in my truth, you who ...

"Oh, you two are so alike. He does that exact same thing, gets all quiet and turns away."

Do you hear that? Now she's making fun of us, she's mocking you and me. Honey, little Josefin, whom I don't know, if only she knew how similar she is to all the women I've known ... and one of them in particular.

"That's what Jonatan says. That that's the way it was. That you came. That you called. That you scared him."

"No!"

There is a limit, and now she's crossed it. Still, it isn't my intention to scare her, but her lies are crawling on my skin like ants, I can't sit still any longer, I have to get up, I don't mean for the chair to tip over as I stand either, I see her fear, she's cowering, crouching there, almost as if she thinks ...

"Don't be scared. I'm sorry," I say, stumbling back a few steps. "I didn't mean to scare you. I'm sorry."

I walk all the way over to the window without taking my eyes off her, I lean against the windowsill, behind my back a new day is starting to dawn, but the city is still asleep.

"You two are so much alike," she mumbles as she looks at you, lying there on the mattress between us.

Red ants, wasp stings, viper bites, stinging nettle, wrong,

wrong, wrong, this is all wrong, it wasn't supposed to be like this, I didn't get to finish my story, I've lost the only chance I'm ever going to have because of little Miss Angry, little Miss Hard-Core Feminist; dislike and disappointment and rage crawl into me, dig tunnels in me, undermine me, make me feel sick, ill, feeble, weak, make me lose my balance, I grab hold of the windowsill, then I sink down onto the floor and sit there under the window.

"How old are you?" I ask, without even trying to hide the hatred in my voice.

"Seventeen," she replies. "The same age as ... him."

Seventeen, and you think you know everything, think you have all the answers. Little Miss Know-It-All. Ha! That's so typical.

Naturally she gets scared again when I suddenly burst out laughing. She's even more afraid than before, sitting tensely on the little stool like a jack-in-the-box about to spring up while her eyes are fixed on me in suspicion.

I laugh like I haven't laughed in ages.

I laugh away my bitterness, it sails out the window and crashes to the ground to die.

I laugh at myself.

Suddenly, I saw myself from the outside, suddenly I heard myself. Suddenly, I remember the very first thing I said to you tonight.

Seventeen years old, I said. A person's never so smart as then, I said.

Now I'm laughing because I'm remembering. And because my memory is so short. And because I still occasionally have the ability to look at myself from the outside.

Then I stop laughing. Then I cry. Because I can't get close to you.

I don't know how long I sat there, I didn't hear her get up, I didn't hear her footsteps across the floor, but now I feel her hand on my cheek.

Her soft, comforting hand against my cheek.

The young woman. She's come to me to quiet my crying.

"Don't cry," she says.

the young woman

1

Yes, you two are so much alike it's scaring me. I mix you guys up and get all confused. He scared me, he got irritated with me and mad, then he felt ashamed when he saw I was afraid, then he started laughing, a kind of insane cackling, and then ... then he cried. He cried like a little kid, like a helpless little kid.

I go over there, drop down on my knees in front of him and put my hand on his cheek.

"Don't cry," I plead.

It takes a while before he calms down, but then he looks up at me. He looks at me with your eyes.

His eyes, your eyes, ask me to keep my hand there, his eyes, your eyes, say that he needs me. I'm a mother comforting an unhappy child.

Finally, I get up the courage to move my hand, and I sit down next to him on the floor with my back against the radiator. His pants legs have slid up and his hairy shins seem almost sickly white.

"You two are so much alike," I say.

He nods without turning to look at me.

"We've been together for two years," I say. "Jonatan and I. Almost two years. Two years this August."

His eyes are fixed on you.

"It all started with him seeing me naked," I say.

Yes, of course. Now he turns toward me. Surprised, naturally. I mean, that was my goal. I'm a little tickled by his curiosity, even I'm surprised when I notice that. I'm explaining something now that no one else knows, something that belongs to you and me, Jonatan. But he's not just any old person, right?

"We'd just started at Malmö Latin High School, both of us, it was the first time I had P.E. with my new classmates, or the second time anyway, we'd run three kilometers and I took a long shower afterward, it was nice, I just stood there and lost track of the time so I was the only one left in the locker room when I came out from the showers. I'd just dried off and set the towel down when the door flew open and a guy came in. It was Jonatan. Some of his new classmates thought it would be a funny joke to shove him into the girls' locker room, that's how mature high school guys are nowadays. And there I was, completely naked holding my underwear in my hand, and there he was, and when he regained his balance and discovered me, he stood there for three seconds, for three seconds he stared at me before looking away and mumbling, "Sorry." Then he stumbled on his way. The back of his neck was beet-red.

I was pissed, of course. Childish guys, if there's anything a sixteen-year-old girl is sick of it's childish guys. But I was pissed at Jonatan, too. For those three seconds. And then I was pissed at myself for feeling embarrassed whenever I would run into Jonatan in the hallway or in the cafeteria after that. I mean, I had nothing to be embarrassed about. So why was I blushing?

And I got it into my head that we were running into each other a little too often for it to be just coincidental, and we would end up sitting at the same table or being up in the library at the same time. So one day when school got out and I noticed Jonatan behind me as I crossed the schoolyard, I turned around.

"What are you doing?" I asked him.

"What do you mean?" he said, seeming like he had no idea what I was talking about.

"Are you following me or what?" I said. "Cut it out."

He just said, "I have no idea what you're talking about," and kept walking.

That was the first thing we said to each other. Not especially romantic, huh? Not the kind of love at first sight that people sing about. Not at all. Not on my part, at any rate.

And it might have ended there, that might have been the end of the story of Jonatan and Josefin. But that was hardly even the beginning. Because then there was that concert.

It was just a week later. I'm part of a musical society that arranges concerts, mostly small punk groups and hard rock and stuff like that, you know, and it's more or less the same people who usually come, but that night there was a really well-known ska group playing and the audience was unusually large. And it was crowded, because we have just a small space, it's in an old factory on Grängesbergsgatan that this educational association set up. So anyway, it was full of people and kind of rowdy, and people were dancing and some idiot poured a bottle of beer on me. My whole shirt was soaking wet and I was furious and sulking because I really wanted to see that group, and besides I didn't want to go home to my mom all covered in beer, and I was chewing that guy out, and then he was standing there, Jonatan.

He was just standing there next to me, and he shouted into my ear that I could borrow his shirt. And then he pulled a shirt out of his bag and waved it, and I was happy even though I was actually mad at him, and I pulled him into a room backstage, just a little storeroom, and it was then, exactly then when it happened, when we were standing there. Love at third sight. He handed me the shirt and asked if he should wait outside while I changed.

"Well, you've already seen everything, haven't you?" I said and pulled off my wet shirt.

The camisole I was wearing underneath was soaked too. I wasn't wearing a bra, I rarely do. But I was completely calm. Him, too. It felt so strangely natural and safe to stand there stripped to the waist in that storeroom with Jonatan, and I took my time putting on his shirt. It smelled good.

"I didn't mean to," Jonatan said. "That time in the locker room. They shoved me in."

"I know," I said.

We stood there feeling calm and safe. It was if we'd wound up on a deserted island, and we had no desire whatsoever to leave.

"Your shirt smells good," I said.

"Your shirt smells like beer," he said.

We laughed together. Then we started talking.

I noticed right away that he was different. He didn't fit any of my stereotypes. In my classification system for guys there was no cubbyhole for Jonatan. And that made me so happy. I didn't know people like him existed. What I mean is, I didn't know that Jonatan existed. Didn't know who he was.

It was so easy for us to talk to each other. After a few minutes, I said things to him that I've never told anyone. And he said things that were so familiar to me it was as if they were my own innermost thoughts. About life, about school, about the world. About music. About everything conceivable.

We talked about everything. We missed a whole concert, plus it was a band I'd really wanted to hear.

We were standing close to each other in the cramped storeroom, but we didn't touch each other. I didn't take my shirt off again, we didn't kiss or hug. Just this: When we were going to say good-bye, when the music had been over for a long time, and all the people had left the place and my friends in the music society had already started cleaning up and putting things away, Jonatan laid his hand on my shoulder and said, "I have to go now. Otherwise, I'll miss the last bus."

I couldn't respond. I was electrified. I'm sure it sounds totally ridiculous, but his hand on my shoulder lit me on fire. Inside. It's true. I'm about the least romantic person you'll ever find, and I can hear how silly that sounds, but when Jonatan put his hand on my shoulder I understood that there was such a thing as love. Or being in love, at any rate. I understood that the cheesiest pop songs might capture some element of truth.

Then … well, then there was us. I called him the next day. When I heard how happy he was to hear my voice, I caught fire again.

We were together. I don't want to lose him. Ever.

That's what I was thinking tonight when I was looking for him, I was so scared and worried and I was thinking: I was so lucky to find Jonatan. I won the best prize of all. I mean, not that he's some kind of saint or my hero or anything like that, no, I just mean that the two of us, we have something unique.

Ugh ... now I sound like the lyrics to some stupid song again. But it's true. I want to say it because it's true.

Why am I saying all this? I don't know.

The words are pouring out of me. And he's a good listener, he watches me attentively and nods.

"Tell me more," he begs. "Tell me more about Jonatan. I don't know him."

I hesitate, but just for a second. The anger I felt a while ago has subsided, it's gone as if it had never been there. Instead, remembering those first meetings with you gave me a tingly, happy sensation.

But what can I say, without letting you down? Would you want me to tell? Him? You were going to tell him, you were going to see him, I mean you'd found his phone number. But actually it's because you wanted to hear what he had to say, and now you have. Did you hear what he told you?

"It's better if you ask Jonatan to tell his own story," I say finally. "I think he wants to."

He nods. Deflates a little.

"Why is Jonatan here?" he asks after a long silence and nods toward you. "What happened?"

"He drank too much," I say. "He was ... sad. Disappointed in himself. I'll tell you later."

I don't say any more.

I don't want to share anymore. Not with him, not now.

We're sitting in silence again, next to each other on the floor.

What are we waiting for?

Everything stands still. A fan whirs, footsteps hurry past out in the corridor, then it's quiet again. There's a faint odor of liquor and drunkenness in here, that's you, you don't smell good. Outside the window it's getting light, and a gray light from out there mixes with the sharp fluorescent light in here.

We both jump when the door opens. A young girl dressed in white stands there in the doorway, she looks at us in surprise—we're sitting on the floor below the window—she mumbles something like "I was just ..." Then she goes over to you, squats down, takes ahold of your shoulders and shakes you a little, and seems satisfied when you moan. Without saying anything else, she gets up and leaves the room.

It's quiet. Then he whispers, "I'm sorry."

His voice is flat and dry. A twig among last year's leaves that snaps when you step on it, that's what his little apology sounds like.

The words hang in the room, float up toward the ceiling for a while before he continues, "I'm sorry that I scared you. I didn't mean to. I've been sitting here all night talking. I've been trying to tell the story of my life for Jon, and ... well ..."

His voice fades away, he loses his train of thought, he can't think how to put it into words.

"I'm sorry," I say, as a little echo. "I'm sorry I butted in. It's just because ... because I've heard Jonatan tell the story and I've been ... mad at you. Even though we've never met. Because I thought ..."

When I hesitate he quickly volunteers, "that I hurt Jon."

I nod and sigh, and know that I've said too much again. And all of a sudden I get scared again, I try to pull away from him, move cautiously to the side and hope he won't notice.

"Don't be afraid," he says.

I stop and sit there, rigid and tense. I hear his breathing.

Now he turns toward me.

"Nice, sweet Josefin. Nice, sweet Josefin whom I don't know, don't be afraid of me, you never need to be afraid of me again, I promise, we're sitting here because we love him, him, the one lying on the mattress there, we have that in common, we … Sweetie."

I force myself to look into his pleading puppy-dog eyes. I recognize that look. Still, I'm hesitant and doubtful.

Now I see his hand.

He's reached his arm out toward me, he's put his hand on the floor between us, he wants me to put my hand in his.

2

No.

Never in my life will I be able to understand where the fear came from.

The menacing sensation. The images in my head.

We're sitting there next to each other on the floor, he didn't say or do anything in particular, and yet, without my having a chance to defend myself or talk to myself sensibly, horrifying images race through my head. Horrifying scenes flash by like lightning in there, the images are suddenly there and I can't understand where they came from. In my head I see how he holds onto my hand, pulls me to him, puts his other hand around my neck, forces me closer, presses my head down toward his stomach, against his … No!

I close my eyes, want to jump up, want to run away, but I know that my legs won't support me.

And his hand lies there like a threat next to me, like a snake ready to strike if I move at all.

I've ended up in a nightmare. My worst nightmare has become real.

"Sweet Josefin, look at me."

No. Never. Your eyes are his eyes, and I can never feel safe in your eyes again if I see his eyes in yours.

I close my eyes with my face turned away from him. Images are burning in my brain, scenes involving him and me, scenes of violence and coercion and sex. I don't know where my images come from, I just know that I can't stop them, his hand hard around my neck, he presses my head down, pulls down his fly, and ...

His hand.

In reality, outside my head, he has lifted up his hand. In reality, here and now, he places his hand on my shoulder. Lightly and softly it rests there, but every second I'm waiting for his hand to close into a firm grip, hold on, hurt, force me.

I stop breathing.

Good God, let me wake up from this dream.

It's because I stroked his cheek, I think. That's why, he took that as an invitation. And because I told the story about my being naked, I created pictures in his imagination, I shouldn't have forgotten that a man is a man is a man, that a man's desire is a big, hairy beast that's always lurking around the corner, behind the friendly smile and the sympathetic words. Any man can turn into a rutting gorilla in a single second.

If I could I would have cried out, screamed out to the people in white I hear passing by outside the closed door, but my tongue is stuck to the roof of my mouth, it fills my mouth like a thick lump and makes me mute and helpless, I can't move, I can't call for help, I'm sitting shackled in front of a movie screen that's showing a snuff movie, that's showing close-ups of my face splattered with sperm, that's showing a heavy, hairy man's body against mine, I hear his moan and my stifled scream for help inside my head.

Save me!

Jonatan, you can save me. Yes, you're still here.

With my back I push myself away from the radiator and in spite of everything I manage to propel myself forward, I fall like a rag doll, roll, crawl, wriggle my way over to the mattress, yes, it's working, my feeble legs drag behind me like two logs but, yes, I make it to you, yes, I swivel up onto the mattress, put one arm around you as you lie there on your side, press myself in against your back, press my lips against the back of your neck.

Jonatan. You are the one I love.

Wake up now. This is enough now. We've learned something.

I want to go home now. With you. I want to take your clothes off and take a shower with you, scrub you like a little kid, shampoo your hair and lather you with soap, wash away all the bad stuff, I want to dry you off with the softest terry-cloth bath towel, I want to ruffle your hair, I want to brush your teeth for a long time, yes, I want you to smell good again, I want you to be you again.

Jonatan. Wake up now. I want to leave now, with you.

I want us to wake up and leave our bad dreams behind. Come on. Come on, let's go.

Everything will be all right.

We're going to liberate each other, you and me. Not confine each other.

You will be you and I will be me, and there will still be an us. There will always be an us. That's what I want.

Wake up now, Jonatan. I want to go home.

3

I didn't hear him stand up.

Now he's standing by the door looking at us.

And now I have the courage to look at him. He's someone else now.

All my fear is gone. Where did my awful images come from?

Seeing him standing there watching us, it's impossible for me to make sense of all the awful visions that paralyzed me just a few minutes ago.

He stands there hunched over, his back stooped, a sad, tired old man. His sadness hurts me, but I can't apologize again, that little phrase "I'm sorry" has already been overworked tonight. And what do I need to apologize for?

"You don't need to be afraid of me," he says, quietly shaking his head.

I'm embarrassed. What should I do? What should I say?

"He has one of your pictures over his bed," I say. "Jonatan."

He gets a few centimeters taller, straightens himself up a little, the sadness in his eyes is mixed with two teaspoonfuls of curiosity, a tablespoon of hope, and a pinch of pride.

"Do you mean," he says after a long and motionless silence,

"that he has a picture I took over his bed, or do you mean a picture of me?"

It feels as if he's laying his life in my hands with his question.

"He has tons of pictures that you took in his room," I say, "but over his bed he has a picture of you. It's old, of course, it's a picture of you and Jonatan when he's just one, but you look like yourself, I recognized you right away."

"Is it the one where we're both naked?"

There's a lightness to his voice now, a faint, flickering melancholy lightness. All my fear is gone.

"Yes, you guys are naked. Although he's sitting on your knee so there's nothing ... sleazy."

"I rarely take sleazy pictures," he says, taking on a smile that is both sad and beautiful. "I'm no Mapplethorpe."

"Who?" I ask.

"Robert Mapplethorpe. One of the best photographers in the world. But he took some pictures that could certainly be called ... sleazy. Lots of penises, actually, to tell—"

"Is he more famous than you?"

"Pshaw ... as a photographer I'm worth about as much as the toenail on Robert Mapplethorpe's little pinkie toe. But obviously I remember that picture you mentioned. It was taken using the self-timer in our apartment in Sofielund. I have it over my bed, too."

Please don't start crying now, I think.

But nope, not at all, now he's calm and collected, he's himself again, like he was when I got here. The desperate old man I saw there by the door a minute ago is gone.

"Ah, but you're far too polite," he says, still smiling, "when you say that I look like myself. It's been sixteen years since that

PN

picture was taken. Life has been pretty hard on me since then. Or
... why should I blame life? I've treated myself badly."

He's right, of course. It's true. The proud young father in that
picture is not the man standing before me now. Now his face is
plump, puffy and wrinkled, his eyelids droopy, his back stooped,
and an unappealing little paunch hangs down over his waistband.
Still, weirdly enough, it wasn't until I met him in person that I
saw how similar they are.

The look in the eyes, the voice, the gestures, the way he moves,
the way he ... is.

None of that shows in the picture.

"I've seen another picture of you," I continue. "When you are
just seventeen or eighteen, and you have shoulder-length hair. A
total hippie."

Now I'm bold enough for anything, now I'll say anything at
all.

And his smile remains. It's a wan smile, he's not beaming like a
radiant sun, no, it's a slightly hazy moon smile, but it's there.

"That's what I looked like when I met Karin." He nods.
"Jonatan's mom. You ... you must know her."

I nod. Don't ask me to tell you anything about Karin, I pray
to myself.

He reads my mind and calmly shakes his head.

Just like you do. Just like you surprise me sometimes by reading
my mind.

Then he stands there quietly and I lie here quietly, breathing
on the back of your neck, my dear.

All the nice things I'd like to say to you, everything I've never
said.

•

"Suddenly I feel so old," he says suddenly and grins, slightly embarrassed. "Old and like an outsider."

What should I say? I don't want to feel sorry for him anymore, I don't want him to want that.

"I don't want your pity," he says, proving again that he's a good mind reader.

"There's room for you over here, too," I say. "On the mattress, I mean."

I say it without thinking, the words fly out of my mouth like swallows, I mean for him to lie down on the other side of you, that we'll have you between us, protect you and warm you with our bodies. At first, he looks like a startled child, then he nods, comes over to the mattress and stretches out next to you. It's crowded but it works.

"Do you have room?"

He chuckles. "When I was a kid I was in the Boy Scouts. Sometimes when we went camping we played silly games. One game was called hot dog in a bun. It went like this: you and I are the bun and Jonatan is the hot dog. But ... but I don't remember what the point of the game was."

"Maybe it was just an excuse to get to lie close to each other," I say.

After a moment of silence he says, "You're as wise as a little owl, you are. I'm so glad Jonatan found you."

He's being honest, yes, I hear the delight in his voice, and I feel proud, as if I'd won first prize.

"Although he doesn't smell so good, your boyfriend," he says then, and laughs. "And my nose is three centimeters from his mouth."

"He usually smells better," I say, feeling warm and calm and effervescently happy.

Everything is going to be fine. I know that now.

4

After a while I ask him if he is done with his story, with everything he wanted to tell you, and he says that he told the most important things, he says the rest is emptiness and silliness, he says that he lost ten years of his life, he says that now he wants to find his way home to himself again, he says he's been sober for a year and ten months.

"Everything's going to be fine," I say.

"You were right," he says.

"What do you mean?"

"I did some stupid things then, after the separation. I wasn't myself then for a while, I got it into my head that the only way to survive was not to lose touch with my old life, or rather, to make sure that Karin didn't completely forget me, I didn't want to be erased, deleted like a typo, it was just a stupid game, but thanks to it I kept my head above water during the worst phase, I didn't want ... I never wanted to hurt her. And I was careful not to pull Jonatan into it. If she claims otherwise, then she's lying."

I lie there quietly, waiting.

"I let a feeling control my life," he continues. "Not hate, it wasn't revenge I wanted. It was desperation. And ... well, jealousy, of course. Never in my life have I been as dedicated to anything I believed in as I was to that sorrow and jealousy. I wasn't myself. I wasn't in control of my own actions. Or ... can you ever put the blame on anyone else?"

"So, what did you do?" I ask.

He doesn't answer.

So we lie there quietly, all scrunched onto the mattress, you and me and your dad.

Several times I'm on the verge of telling him things, I want to tell him something about you, about who you are, about what you're like, I want to help him get close to you, and I think about how I should describe you, give an accurate picture of you, I think about what it is about you that makes you the person I never want to lose. How can you describe a person? How can you give a picture of someone?

Maybe I could've told him about last Saturday. There was a demonstration against police brutality, and we were marching along Södergatan and shouting and singing, and a thousand cops were watching us and suddenly in the middle of the whole thing you stepped over to the side and got on the sidewalk and I followed you.

"What is it?" I said.

"This is ludicrous," you said.

"What is?" I said.

At first you didn't want to explain, but I pestered you and we walked over and sat down on a bench in Kungsparken and you said, "A bunch of young people whose parents are teachers or psychologists or lawyers or computer engineers are fighting with the cops because the cops won't let them dance in the streets. It's ludicrous. All of this talk about reclaiming the streets is just ridiculous. This doesn't have anything to do with fighting capitalism or commuting by car or commercialism or anything, this is just about a bunch of young people who don't have anything rational to do. Anything important to do. Who the fuck wants to dance in the street?"

"The last time we danced in the street you had a heck of a lot of fun, didn't you?" I reminded him.

"All right. Sure. But I wasn't waging some kind of fucking important battle. I would've had just as much fun dancing at a nightclub."

"But you never go to nightclubs, do you?"

"Nah, but I mean if I went. The world is on fire and hundreds of thousands of children are starving and dying of needless diseases every day, and then there's some teenagers in Sweden who think it's so fucking important whether they get to dance in the street or not. Don't you see what I mean? It's like people have this little lie and then they turn it into this giant truth so that they'll look good. It's like the Hultsfred Festival."

"Huh?"

"You know how it is. Fifty thousand young people and each one walks around in his or her everyday life thinking they're a little different and dressing a little different and listening to music that's a little different and thinking thoughts that are a little different, and then they get to Hultsfred and discover that there's forty-nine thousand nine hundred and ninety-nine other people who are exactly like them and who also think exactly like they do and who've been to the same concerts and the same demonstrations, and deep down inside, everyone came there to drink and party and lose their virginity and get away from their mom for a few days."

"I don't get what you're talking about," I said. "Didn't we have a good time at Hultsfred last year? Wasn't the music great?"

"Sure. It was fine. We had a good time. But don't you under-stand what I mean?"

"I'm trying," I said.

"It's always about people despising someone else," you said. "Feeling like they're better than someone else. More important. More honest. Or something. The anarchists are a little cooler than the anarcho-syndicalists, who are a little cooler than the socialists, who are a little cooler than the environmentalists. Hip-hoppers look down on hard rockers, who look down on punks, who look down on everybody. The whole thing is just ... silly. It's just a game. A bunch of kids who grew up with the comforts of the Scandinavian welfare state, playing. Don't you get it? Don't you get what I mean?"

That's how he is, the one I love. That should be a picture of him.

He wants to go his own way, always. He wants to know that he's doing what's right. He wants to keep an eye on stuff, he never wants to follow the herd, or do something just because other people are doing it. Or think something just because other people are thinking it. That's how he is.

And another thing is that he says things he doesn't mean, in other words sometimes he says the opposite of what he means just to test ... just to see what happens, just to avoid being pinned down in someone else's opinion. And to see what response he gets. If he discussed the whole protest thing with Karin and Claes he would probably say the exact opposite. Or like the part about going dancing. He hates to go dancing. I don't think he's been out dancing since he was in junior high.

I don't always understand him. I don't always agree with him.

If he says that somebody doesn't have any right to protest because his or her parents are academics or middle class, then he's wrong. If he says that the battle being waged is just made up, then he's wrong. Feminism, veganism, anarchism, antiglobalization and opposing the police state, all of that is deadly serious, all of that will lead to progress. My friend Sanna went to the World Social Forum in Porto Alegre. She met trade union representatives from Korea, poor women from Brazil, feminists from Palestine and Israel, environmental activists from the Philippines, anarchists from Germany, she met tons of people, she heard Noam Chomsky and Naomi Klein. There is a struggle, there is a resistance, there is a movement, it's not a game, it's for real. Another world is possible.

Sometimes he's wrong. But I love him for who he is.

Does that sound silly? I don't care.

And in which case: I could give a picture of you, I could tell your dad about our conversation last Saturday. But I don't. Instead I say, "I'll tell you what happened earlier tonight. I'll tell you why Jonatan ended up here."

I'm speaking into the back of your neck. He's lying on the other side of you, I sense how he's paying attention and waiting, but before I'm able to start, the door opens.

the mother

I've never been so scared in all my life. Well, one time. Two times.

We came home late, Claes and I, we'd been to a colleague's fiftieth birthday party, a big party down in Skanör. We had a good time. Some fiftieth birthday parties are just long-winded sit-down events with food and dreary conversation, but there was a blues band playing at this one, and there was dancing and, well, I drank a little too much. I did, I noticed myself that I was starting to get a little talkative and, well, overly affectionate, in the taxi on the way home I sat in the back seat and made out with Claes like we were two teenagers. Then we got home. Hanna had been home alone with a baby-sitter, a neighbor girl who was going to spend the night, too, I'd made a little food and some snacks for them and rented a movie. So, anyway, I was a little drunk and kind of in high spirits and even more affectionate when we got home and I thought the girls were sleeping, of course, so I pulled Claes into the kitchen with me. I wanted to do it on the kitchen table, no, I'm really not like that, usually I'm not like that, I stopped doing crazy, foolish things like that a long time ago, but it was the wine, you know, and up came my dress and down went my panties and Claes pulled down his pants and he was the one who discovered the note just as I flung myself onto the table on my back and put my legs up around his neck.

Strange, actually, that he noticed the note right then. Strange that he read it. Strange that he told me, that he didn't wait. I guess that probably says something about him.

The note the baby-sitter wrote. That the hospital had called, that Jonatan had been in an accident. She wrote *He's in the emurgency ward,* and even though I was more scared than I've ever been in my life, I noticed that she'd spelled it wrong. I guess that probably says something about me.

Claes stood there like a wilting tulip while I rushed in and woke the girls up, and they told me the same thing that the note said, and Hanna told me that Josefin called, too, and asked about Jonatan, and I called for a cab, now I was sober as a priest and scared like never before.

Jonatan, my darling baby. What's happened? What have you done?

Claes stayed home with the girls and I went to the emergency room at the hospital, and right when I was standing there stamping my feet waiting for the nurse who was admitting a guy who'd been beaten up and had blood all over his face, I realized that I didn't have any underwear on.

Anyway, then the nurse came and said that Jonatan was "suffering from alcohol intoxication." Then she said, "In other words, drunk," as if I were some silly goose or an irresponsible parent who needed to be reprimanded. Too much alcohol was an ordinary problem, my son just needed to rest and sober up, all his test results were stable. I was ashamed, felt like a schoolgirl. Taking up health-care resources with a drunk teenager, so unnecessary. A little of my fear is replaced by ... not anger maybe but irritation at any rate. Jonatan, did you have to put me through this?

But I'm certainly not going to be unfair to myself, naturally I was mostly relieved that it wasn't anything worse, during the cab ride in to the hospital I'd seen pictures in my head of traffic accidents, and Jonatan's body lying in the street, bloody and contorted, I'd seen visions of violence, skinheads with heavy boots kicking Jonatan's head, kicking the heck out of my son, yes ... I'd seen the most horrible pictures from the most horrible movies in my head and the pictures cut me like knives, and hurt as if the boots were kicking me. Of course I was relieved that he was lying here because he drank too much. Relieved, and slightly irritated.

And I answered a few questions the nurse had and then hurried to the room she indicated.

When I opened the door, I just stood there.

I was ready to rush in, I'd been seized by such a longing to see him, to hold his head in my hands, but I just stood there.

He was lying there on a mattress in the middle of the floor in the cold room. But he wasn't the only one lying there. There were three people crowded onto the narrow mattress. Josefin lifted her head from behind Jonatan and flashed me a weak, almost half-asleep smile, but there was also a man lying in front of Jonatan with his back to me.

I just stood there in the doorway and stared. Who was that? Why was a strange man lying there pressed up against my son?

I just stood there and felt the anger growing in me. I wanted to rush over to Jonatan, but there was a strange man in my way.

Lying there like a walrus, and he didn't even turn around. I mean, of course, finally, I went into the room, Josefin sat up and it wasn't until I'd walked over and squatted down next to her that I saw who the man was.

Not for a single second had I thought it was him.

He slowly raised his head from the mattress and blinked at me, it looked like he'd been asleep. He'd gotten fat, or round in the face anyway, and his hairline had receded a few centimeters. I admit it, for a brief moment I forgot Jonatan and just stared at him, a thousand different feelings and pictures and memories welled up in me and competed with each other, and just as a feeling of sorrow seemed to have won the gold medal, he grinned and murmured, "I see that you've stopped wearing underwear."

Then he rolled off the mattress, scrambled to his feet, hurried out of the room, and pulled the door shut behind him.

Göran, you bastard. I hate you. You're a pig.

2

Now I'm here. Now I'm sitting on a mattress with Josefin, my son's girlfriend. Jonatan is lying in front of us, he seems to be sleeping, peaceful, like a baby, he sniffles or snores every now and then. I kissed his cheek but quickly pulled back, he stank of alcohol and vomit.

I didn't believe it. That I would have to come pick up my son from the emergency room because he drank too much. I'm disappointed.

But naturally I'm relieved too, of course. It could have been so much worse, obviously.

I asked Josefin what had happened, she just said he was sad and got drunk. Her answer was hiding something from me, I saw in her eyes and heard in her voice. That irritates me, too.

Now we're sitting here. And I have to ask, "Why did he come here? I mean Göran, Jonatan's father."

"He was here when I got here," Josefin says. "He was sitting here telling the story …"

"Telling the story?"

"Yes, I think he'd been sitting here for a really long time. He told me he'd told Jonatan about his own childhood, and when he was young, and … and met you, and about when Jonatan was little, and … and why you guys separated. I just heard the end."

I can hear it right away in her voice. Clearly, as if she'd said it with words. She's chosen sides, she listened to Göran and believed all his lies, just as I once had. She was lying here on the mattress with him. Ha, if she only knew.

"I see. So he told the story?" I say, and even I can hear the icicles hanging off my words.

"Yes. He said that he'd always wanted to tell Jonatan the story, and that tonight he'd gotten the opportunity, and he believes Jonatan heard the whole thing," Josefin rattles off, as if she were teaching me a lesson.

Oh, you gullible little fool. I would never have thought that you could be so stupid and easily tricked.

"Why did he come here, then?" I ask. "How did Göran know Jonatan was here?"

"Because …"

Now she hesitates. I notice a cowardice in her that I've never seen before.

•

I have mixed feelings about Josefin, as they say. Sometimes it scares me that she always seems so strong and confident. So resolute. So secure, so impossible to upset. She never doubts, never wavers, is always so convinced of what the right path is. And Jonatan follows her so willingly and cheerfully. I suppose that's what troubles me most. Or irritates me, maybe. That he trots along behind Josefin like an obedient little dog. Since they met, all of her opinions have rubbed off on Jonatan, he's become her voice, her echo. And she's always so conscious of gender equality, always so meticulous about everything being one hundred percent fair in every situation.

I know I'm being unfair now. I know that Jonatan is smart, I know that he can think for himself. And of course I'm happy that he met Josefin, and that they're together, obviously I see how much fun they have together, I hear them laughing when they make their vegetarian food together in the kitchen, or sit on the sofa playing some game with Hanna in the evenings. They're good together, they're nice to each other, and considerate.

If only she weren't so strong. If only she could ever just let up on being so morally upstanding and capable. If only just once she could be an insecure little girl.

Maybe I'm just envious. I see how she stole my son. He never gives me even a glimmer of the handsome smiles and cheerful laughter he offers her. I'm excluded from their happy coexistence.

Persecuted mother-in-law syndrome. The gloomy old lady.

But I don't recognize my Jonatan. Or, I don't know my Jonatan anymore. He only shows me the exterior, as if I weren't worth confiding in anymore, getting close to. I don't know what he thinks or feels deep down inside. Before, I could always read him like an open book, he was never able to lie to me or hide anything. Now he's closed. It hurts me. But I'm being unfair if I say it has to do with Josefin, I know that.

He's seventeen.

He'll come back to me, I haven't lost him. A mom is always a mom. Everyone else can be replaced, everyone else can come and go, everyone else can leave and be left. But never Mom.

"Because ... Jonatan had his phone number in his pocket," Josefin stammers. "His dad's phone number. On a slip of paper. Someone had stolen Jonatan's wallet, so the police called that number."

"Why ...?" I start but stop right away.

She will not get to see my humiliation. I'll ask Jonatan later. Why he was walking around with Göran's phone number?

Shit. Everything is wrong.

An iceberg is growing in my stomach. Shit.

I hide my face in my hands and lean in over, Jonatan. Shit.

Göran, you pig. You won little Josefin over, and through her you'll win Jonatan back. You think. But never. Never, never, never. I won't be able to stop him from going to see you, I understand that he's going to want to do that at some point in his life, that he'll want to get to know his father, but I will never open the door to you. Never.

And all your lies will never become the truth.

I lift my face and look straight into Josefin's gray eyes.

"I'll tell the story," I say.

"What?" she asks, pretending she doesn't understand.

"I'll tell the story the way it actually happened," I say.

From her hesitant look I understand how Göran's clever lies have taken root in her. "Just you wait, just you wait, my dear, until you've heard the true version."

"I'll tell the story," I say again.

3

Göran and I met at a demonstration. 1972. It was a pro-bike demonstration—no cars downtown and pedal power, thank you very much—that kind of thing, you know. I went to every demonstration there was back then. Anyway, then there was a commotion with some of the drivers at a crosswalk, and I got hit in the head with a stick or something, so blood was gushing out, and I fell down and ... I was scared. That's when he appeared.

He's told me the story a thousand times, how he saw me fall and rushed over and pulled me out of the way and put me in a taxi so we could go to the hospital. I got four stitches, you can still see the scar. Look.

He had hair down over his shoulders and tattered jeans and a filthy T-shirt. Skinny as a rail. A little shy and awkward. He was cute, he sure was.

I was in ninth grade and already had a boyfriend. Claes. It's true, I was with Claes when I met Göran. I ... it's hard to explain. But when my parents came to the hospital, and when I saw the contemptuous looks my mom gave Göran, I made up my mind. Everything I did back then I did to rebel against my parents, I didn't realize it, of course, but I can see that now.

I was a wild teenager. I'd been with guys since I was thirteen.

I was in all the left-wing groups there were, actually that's how I met Claes, there were two kinds of teenagers back then, the peaceniks and the slackers, I was one of the peaceniks, obviously, but when I met Göran I realized that an even more powerful rebellion would be dating an actual hippie.

Wasn't I in love with him?

Sure, obviously. Still, it was a mistake from the beginning. Claes is the man in my life, we were meant for each other. Göran was a seventeen-year-long intermission from my life with Claes. A mistake that lasted seventeen years.

Actually, by the second summer I'd already come to see that it was a mistake. Göran dragged me to this hippie camp in Denmark, he had these burnout buddies of his who were going. I hated his friends from the beginning, they despised me because I hadn't read the same books as they had, and didn't listen to the same music, and because I didn't think the pinnacle of happiness was sitting around in a condemned apartment smoking hash all day long. Anyway, I went with Göran to that camp. It was a nightmare. It was a bunch of stoned, naked people, each of them believing they were Jesus or Che Guevara, running around in a filthy, muddy field, and the worst thing of all was that Göran was so happy there. He was seriously talking about how that was the beginning of the New Society. Heaven help me if that's the New Society! I felt ashamed of myself the whole week, I was playing a role there in order to survive, but I knew that I wasn't being myself, that I would never again run around half-naked and dance to a bunch of drums and some whiny flute.

Actually, I'd already understood it then, that Göran was a mistake. That he was building his entire life on a lie, and that he and I would never really be able to understand each other. Or ... I don't know if I understood that then. Maybe I was still a little blinded, blinded by love.

But I hated his buddies the whole time. Arrogant and condescending, always thought they knew everything better than everyone else. Especially this one guy name Lasse Mattsson. I ran into him a few years ago at a party, he went on to become some big shot at the Education Department, he was standing there in an expensive suit with a cocktail in his hand. Him! The guy who'd made fun of me and teased me because of my parents and their big house, now he was standing there at a party in upscale Höllviken, schmoozing, all polite and courteous. I didn't tell him who I was, and he obviously didn't recognize me.

Göran wasn't a real hippie, I suppose. He looked like one, but actually I think his so-called buddies looked down on him, too, he was kind of clinging to edges of that gang, walking around with a camera against his belly and trying to keep up, taking the same drugs as the others so he wouldn't be left out, I think that's how it was. But he always had this excessively romanticized picture of that time. He was so absurdly snooty about having been part of it, about having smoked hash and taken LSD a few times, as if that were some kind of accomplishment, as if he'd learned something important.

He was always good at fooling himself and fooling other people, Göran was.

17

4

Filthy. Everything Göran loved was so filthy. We worked sorting clothes up in Småland for two summers, slaved away like animals for solidarity. It was sweaty and there were tons of mosquitoes. And filthy, everything was filthy and everyone was filthy. It seemed like the people up there had never heard of soap or toothpaste.

And of course Göran thought it was so groovy to live with a bunch of people in a big, filthy commune, and toil away sorting filthy clothes to send to liberation movements in southern Africa.

He was finished with high school by then, and had rented an apartment in Väster. Oh yeah, you know first he was going to go out and travel all over the world, he wanted to see the world, that whole summer he talked about his big trip, and of course I thought it was sad that he was going away, but I still thought that it meant so much to him. I didn't want to hold him back, even though I could see that he was fooling himself with all that nonsense.

And sure enough, after just a month he came home with his tail between his legs, was standing there one day looking like a pathetic failure when I walked out of school.

Then, you could say that I moved into his place. And he started working as a nurse at Eastern Hospital, in the beginning he had nightmares every night about what he'd seen during the day, I had to be like a mother and comfort him.

And then I graduated from high school. I wanted to go to law school for political reasons, I wanted to change society from the inside. Politics meant so much to me even then. Politics was serious, it wasn't a game or some rebellion against parental authority. And it was purely a political tactic that some people would work to change the system from the outside and some from the inside. Göran never understood that. For him, my decision just meant that I was following in my parents' footsteps, that I was starting down a path that would lead to a well-paid, high-status job. Whenever we discussed politics it always ended with him saying: "Politics is the way you live." Yeah, right. I mean, he's demonstrated that with his own life. With his failure of a life. You sure didn't make any super revolution out of your life, did you, Göran?

5

"What is it?"

I'd stopped talking, I'd hidden my face in my hands again, and now I hear concern in Josefin's voice.

Yes, a little concern in spite of everything. I saw the suspicion in her eyes while I was telling the story, yes, even a glimpse of hatred, but all the same now she was a little concerned ... unless she's a really good actress, that is.

"It brings back so many memories," I say. "There's so much that I haven't ... haven't wanted to think about."

She nods.

Shit. Little Josefin. Of course you see through me with your childlike wisdom. You hear that I'm exaggerating too much when I talk about Göran. But I have to do that, not just for your sake but also for my own. I don't want to risk winding up wallowing in some foolish teenage nostalgia, of course I ought to be immune to all that since I have all the answers, I know the ending, I know how it all played out, still I feel like I mustn't take any chances.

"Did he talk about this time period?" I ask.

She shakes her head.

"I didn't hear it. I only heard the end. But probably he did, I mean, he said he did, that he'd told the story of ... well, of when you met, and so ..."

I don't know if she's lying. Maybe she's heard Göran's version after all. Little Josefin has shown sides of herself tonight that I've never seen before.

I look at Jonatan and think about what I've said about who Göran was when I met him, I think that Jonatan is the same age now that Göran was then, and suddenly it occurs to me, something that should've occurred to me right away, of course. It's strange how slow and sluggish the brain is sometimes.

"Does he take any drugs?"

Josefin pretends not to understand.

"Jonatan. Does he take any drugs? You have to answer honestly, I'm sure you understand that. Is there anything besides the alcohol that made him wind up here? Has he been combining it with anything?"

Josefin hesitates. Oh, you stupid little goose, don't you get it? His life is at stake, this isn't some nosy mom thing.

"He's lit up a few times," she says finally, her voice sounding uncertain.

"Lit up?"

"Yes, in other words ..."

"I understand," I interrupt. "Does he do it often? Did he do it tonight? Do you think he took anything else tonight?"

"No," Josefin says quickly and finally, letting that one single little no answer all three of my questions.

I have to believe her, I have no choice.

"He's … he's not like super into it or anything," Josefin mumbles. "But at Roskilde … well, everyone does it there."

I don't ask whether she does it, too. I don't care, and we have more important things to talk about. I have more important things to talk about. I continue on with the story.

6

I started law school in Lund in 1975, and we moved into a little commune in Fäladen together, there were six of us, it was Göran's idea that we should do it, he was so deathly afraid of family life, it was pretty much inconceivable for the two of us to live together just him and me. Of course, he would have preferred that we move out to some real hippie commune out in the woods somewhere and grow vegetables and run around naked and build our own little society, but it ended up being a modern apartment in Lund instead.

I let him decide way too many things back then, he had a way of convincing me. But our so-called commune was a fiasco from start to finish, there wasn't any sense of community spirit at all, just arguing and nagging and grumbling and irritation, every little thing led to these absurd arguments and behaviors. Besides, Göran was so turned on by one of the other girls there, a dumb cow named Gunilla, he was on her side in every single discussion, I felt so … so humiliated, it was like he wanted to test me in some way. Or punish me because we weren't growing beans in the countryside.

But then Hugo beat him to it. Hugo the Charmer from Chile,

Gunilla was the one who brought him into our apartment, and in only a few weeks he'd seduced both her and the other girl that lived there, Maria. They thought it was so exciting to know a real political refugee, I'm sure they thought sleeping with him was some kind of act of solidarity. And of course Gunilla had lost all interest in Göran from the first moment Hugo smiled his boyish smile and twinkled his brown eyes. And so our commune came crashing down with a big hullabaloo, and Göran and I moved into an apartment on Tomegapsgatan.

Then it was just him and me at any rate. Just him and me.

He was working at St. Lars then, did I mention that?

We'd been living in our apartment for only a few weeks when I discovered I was pregnant. I was twenty. I'd just started my law studies. The thought of my becoming a mother was completely impossible, I couldn't think it, I decided right away when I got the pregnancy test. And besides, I didn't know ...

I won't be unfair. It was my fault, I was the one who'd been careless. In two ways. It was totally my fault.

And Göran ... he was good then. Yes, I won't be unfair. He let me decide, he supported me, he comforted me when I was sad.

He just assumed that he ... that he would've been the father.

But ... well. The truth is that I didn't know.

He was good then, and I was embarrassed. He tied me to him, I ended up being indebted to him, that was why ... that was why we kept living together for so long. Yes. I've come to realize that since then. Even much later, once all the love was gone, I couldn't forget that I had betrayed him then, that I owed him.

Later, I found out that he had cheated on me and deceived me hundreds of times, he'd already begun back then, but of course there was no way I could have suspected that then.

I'm not trying to put the blame on anyone else. It was stupid of me.

I was ashamed and regretted what I'd done, and felt like an airhead. And it took a while before I could look Göran in the eyes. He never understood.

It turned out that my abortion tied us together. But I'm not going to be unfair. Those years in Lund were good years. In spite of everything that happened, in spite of everything I know now that I didn't know then, those were good years.

Göran started to grow up, he gave up some of his romanticized hippie ideas. He even cut his hair. That was a shock, boy, oh my God, I'd only ever seen him with long hair and then suddenly one day he came home looking like ... like a schoolboy. He'd taken a step toward becoming a grown-up and looked like a schoolboy. He worked and I studied, I was in Sweden's Communist Party and politically we hadn't grown any closer to each other, but we started doing things together during those years. We got into folk dancing. We joined a music society, and arranged concerts and festivals. We'd found issues that we could be actively involved in together.

And then there was that photo exhibit. I didn't even know Göran had entered his pictures, and then one night the phone rang and he found out that he was going to be included in an exhibit at the Art Gallery. And that he'd won seven hundred dollars. Seven hundred! You have no idea how much money that was back then. He was so happy, of course he was happy. I was, too.

Right then, right at that time, it felt like we could live a life together. That's how I felt, anyway. Later, I found out that Göran was carrying a lot of baggage around that I never got to see, but I'm certain that right then he was happy, I'm sure that he would also … well.

It wasn't just that exhibit and the money, it was that he suddenly figured out what he wanted to do. And he found a sense of pride. It said "Göran Persson, Photographer" in the middle of his forehead. Suddenly he knew what he wanted to do with his life, he had a plan that was real, unlike all the stoner dreams he'd been walking around with. He'd found his calling. And he loved getting to meet other photographers, we started hanging out with artists and authors, he was so happy to be part of the culture crowd.

I was happy for his sake.

It's true, I'm not going to be unfair. I was happy for our sake.

It wasn't my shame about that whole thing with Hugo that was keeping us together anymore.

7

Then we moved to Malmö, into a dark, dreary apartment in Sofielund. I was doing my district court service and Göran was a full-time photographer now. He had a little newspaper job at *Sydsvenskan*, too, or maybe he got that later … at any rate, we weren't students anymore, we'd left that world for good.

There was going to be a referendum that winter about nuclear power, and we both worked for the Swedish Anti-Nuclear Movement, we'd already started with that in Lund, of course.

We were for Option 3: an immediate freeze on new construction and phasing out the existing reactors by 1990. We went to meetings and demonstrations, and handed out flyers, and followed the debates. Now it was almost always Göran who was the most involved. And he was the most disappointed when we lost. Despite the Social Democrats' dirty tactics and fear mongering, almost half of Sweden voted for Option 3, but it didn't help. We lost. Göran took it really hard, for several months he was bitter and disappointed, he seriously believed that if nuclear power were phased out, the whole course of societal change would have been different.

"Now everything's going to go to hell," he said. "Now capitalism's going to take over. And we were so close," he sighed, demonstrating by holding up his thumb and index finger. As if he really believed we were only two centimeters away from the Revolution.

But in a way, though, he was right, later there was the whole debate about whether Sweden should join the EU and the referendum on that, which we also lost by just a few percentage points. But how different would Sweden have been if it stayed out of the EU and didn't have nuclear power?

Well, I don't want to discuss politics now. But Göran's reaction after the referendum`... it scared me. Something happened to him, he changed, I think it's somehow related to his wanting to leave me a few years later, to his wanting to break up without being able to explain why.

Although now I'm jumping ahead in my story, I'm skipping ahead.

What happened before was his big success. He took that picture of me in our bedroom. And then he was part of a big exhibit in Stockholm, it was at the Modern Museum, and then suddenly it just all took off, there was TV and radio and newspaper articles and interviews. Suddenly, he was a celebrity.

And yet, oddly enough, he didn't show the same joy he'd shown that time in Lund. He was proud, of course, he was obviously flattered at being invited to New York and Madrid and ... and tons of places. But still. Not that same joyful exuberance.

He wasn't the same. He had mood swings, he would sit and brood all night long, he took long walks by himself. And our life had also changed, a bit of the joy in our life together had vanished. I suppose that's why it meant so much to me when I saw Claes again.

Through the Swedish Anti-Nuclear Movement I got involved with the Left Party Communists, now they're the Left Party, and the very first time I went to a meeting I ran into Claes.

Claes, my old boyfriend that I broke up with when I met Göran. I hadn't seen him since we moved away from Malmö, we hadn't stayed in touch, but now he came back into my life. He made me happy. We had a shared history that I'd almost forgotten. And no doubt it was Göran's melancholy and erratic moods that made being with Claes feel so easy.

We started getting together. We didn't have a secret affair, no relationship, I mean, I wasn't unfaithful, Göran's lying if he says that. Not even a thought about sex, not by me, anyway. I promise. We ate lunch together, we went to the movies sometimes, we talked, he made me laugh, we enjoyed each other's company. Nothing else. But it's true, I didn't tell Göran about Claes, I admit that. And sometimes I was sitting at a restaurant with him when Göran thought I was at a group meeting.

White lies, a few. But not a problem, nothing that had to mean anything. No.

And when Göran said he wanted to move out one day, that he needed to live on his own for a while, I said no.

I said, "I want to live with you."

Yes, I said it.

It was so strange, one day he was just sitting there at the kitchen table and he said that. Everything was exactly the way it usually was, nothing in particular had happened, we'd been living together for ten years and then suddenly he says that he's been thinking, that he decided he needed to be by himself.

I was totally shocked. And I still can't believe that I asked him to stay. Everything would have been so much easier if our paths had split there. Everything would've been better and easier.

Everything besides one single thing, I know.

The reason we're sitting here, I know.

I had just started meeting Claes then, I knew that Göran and I should go our separate ways, and still I didn't hesitate for a second.

"I want you to stay," I said. "I want to spend my life with you," I said.

Yes, it's true. I said that.

It's so strange. And it's equally strange that he changed his mind. He took it back. He stayed. Even today, I can't understand why.

If I believed in God or fate everything would be so much easier, then there'd be some meaning to things like this, then you could say that the meaning is lying here on the floor in front of me. But I don't believe in God, I don't think there's any plan for our lives.

8

Now I sense Josefin looking at me, I can feel her staring at me. I'd almost forgotten her, I'm not telling the story for her anymore.

When I lift my face and look at her, she turns away, her eyes flit around and come to rest on Jonatan.

"Did Göran tell you this part?" I ask. "Did he tell this part of the story?"

She shakes her head.

"When I got here he was talking about when Jonatan was a baby," she says.

Of course. Didn't she say that before? I can't remember what happened ten minutes ago anymore, I've lost myself in much older memories.

No, I'm not telling the story for you anymore, little Josefin.

A seventeen-year-old can't understand adult life, I don't think so. I don't remember anymore what I thought when I was seventeen. Yes, I believed in the great Revolution and the new human. But did I ever think that there would be an everyday life, did I ever wonder what it would look like? I don't think so.

No, I don't think a seventeen-year-old can understand. Everyone has to make their own mistakes. Their own choices. Try to learn.

"Yes, now we get to Jonatan," I say, feeling how the smile I try to give her turns into a steeled grimace. "Jonatan comes into the picture now."

She tilts her head slightly and keeps looking at him, the one who's going to come into my story now, the one who's going to come into the world.

It would be easy to say that we tried to save our relationship by having a baby. Maybe that's true, but still that would be an over-simplification.

I was the one who decided, again, I was the one who said it. I wanted to first, and I put my desire into words.

And Göran said yes. Oddly enough.

One day it just came, the longing to be a mother. Without actually mulling the matter over I suddenly knew one day, my whole body knew. I knew the time had come. Maybe that comes preprogrammed in us women, I don't know, I mean I don't actually believe in biological explanations, but …

Well, suddenly it was there, a longing. And Göran just said: Sure.

I know where Jonatan came into existence. On a ferry between Copenhagen and Oslo. We worked it out. I've never told him that, I think I would be embarrassed, that he would have pictures in his head of his mother and father in a cabin on the Oslo ferry. His mother- and father-to-be.

Göran took thousands of pictures of my belly. I didn't like that. I thought: all these pictures that will have to be burned if some-thing goes wrong.

I was often scared. Sometimes I was convinced that I would have a miscarriage or give birth to a deformed baby, sometimes I was so convinced that I starting planning for a life after the catastrophe.

But everything went fine. Jonatan was born at Malmö General

Hospital on December 5, 1983. He weighed seven pounds three ounces and was twenty inches long. It went fast, now in hindsight it was an easy childbirth. When Hanna was born it was worse, much worse. And Jonatan was precisely the way he should be, such a perfect little baby, and yet ...

Yet I was hit by this sadness. I was completely unprepared. Everything had gone well, Göran was happy, Jonatan was lying there on my chest and I was hit by this sadness that I'd never felt before. I can't understand why. I should have been relieved and happy, too, but during those days when I was lying there in the hospital I was filled with a paralyzing black sadness.

I ... I can't explain it, I can't describe what I felt, now it seems almost unreal, but I know that I cried. The whole time. Except when Göran was there, I didn't want to show him anything. And he was so fulfilled by Jonatan that he didn't notice.

What did my sadness mean? I don't know. No feeling in my life has been as powerful and black as that.

I think ... I think I wanted to die.

How can a new mother want to die? Next to me in a little bed lay a newborn baby who needed me, and I didn't want to live.

I've never told anyone this.

I don't know why I'm saying it now.

9

No, why am I telling Josefin this?

She's sitting here and listening with her head cocked to the side, hiding from me, not giving any indication of what she's thinking.

I started telling the story because I wanted to win her over. Win Jonatan over through her.

But why am I being so honest?

Now I've wound up at a disadvantage, a little seventeen-year-old girl has gained the upper hand over me, by sitting here quietly and listening she's taken the upper hand. She tricked me, lulled me into a false sense of security, got me to turn myself inside out, I'm saying things that not even Claes ever got to know. Or Göran, of course.

"I don't want … I don't want you to tell Jonatan this stuff," I say, swallowing my humiliation.

I'm pleading with her. That little teenage girl there.

And she grows before my eyes, without hesitating she looks me in the eyes and keeps looking at me.

"I won't tell," she says. "I won't tell anything."

I look at her and hope that she can't see my suspicion, and the doubt in my eyes.

"The things you want Jonatan to know you can tell him yourself," she continues. "I think you should. Tell him, I mean. I think … no, I know that he would want you to."

Josefin. Now you're so wise and self-assured again. Maybe I should be humiliated when you give me good advice, but I know that this time you're right, and at the moment it feels like we're on the same side.

I'll keep going with the story, although I'm no longer sure whom I'm telling it for.

Yes, we were careful parents, I suppose that's what you heard Göran say. It's true. We'd read all the books, we wanted to give Jonatan all the best opportunities. We played music and sang to him. We painted his room in pastels. We bought an anthropo-sophic rag doll and wooden toys. I breast-fed him for a whole year, then we made our own baby food out of organic vegetables and beans. We used cloth diapers, there were cloth diapers hanging up everywhere drying, our apartment was transformed into a tall ship with zillions of teeny-weensy sails. It was Göran who said that. It's a good image. And we sailed along, two young parents who wanted all the best we could think of for our child.

Now it sounds like I'm bragging, doesn't it? As if I think we were better than other people. That's not what I mean. It's just that later everything got so sarcastic, with our squabbling and with Göran moving out, I don't mean that our carefulness was wasted, I just mean … ugh, I can't explain. Can you understand anyway?

Of course, we shared the parental leave. And maybe, specifi-cally for those early years, Göran was more of a father than I was a mother. Yes. I was in the middle of my career, I'd gotten a new job that I thought was exciting and important, but Göran … Göran seemed to give up his career. He said no to job offers and exhibits, he seemed like he'd stopped caring.

Maybe he really wanted to be a full-time father. Just a father, and nothing else. I don't know.

In 1988 we moved to a condo with a yard out in Riseberga. It had seemed so tough walking around with a little four-year-old in the middle of all the car exhaust in town. It was a nice condo, with a little yard and a garden plot where we could grow a few things.

Or so we thought. But nothing besides weeds ever grew in that little garden.

I don't know what I should say about the short time we lived out there. Jonatan grew, he had a baby-sitter, in town he'd been going to day care and we thought that was best, of course, but out there the waiting lists for day care were so long. We kept a journal of his development, wrote down funny things he did and things he said. Göran and I also grew, but in different directions. I had my job and politics, got together with colleagues, and stayed in touch with Claes the whole time. But it was still just friendship, nothing else, at any rate not from my side. But Göran's career went backward, and he started getting used to his loneliness. His old friends had been gone for a long time, and his new artist and journalist friends disappeared since he wasn't showing any interest in participating in that world anymore. It quickly became apparent that he had never gotten very close to any of them.

We'd joked about midlife crises, talked about stupid myths and self-fulfilling prophecies.

If you're not doing well you have only yourself to blame. I guess that's more or less what we thought. Burnout hadn't been invented yet.

Now it seems like I'm being evasive, as if I'm trying to procrastinate telling the hardest part of the story by talking about something else.

No. I'm just trying to give you some background, trying to find an explanation for what led up to that night in October 1989. I can't. I suppose everything I've said about Göran and me leads up to it in some way. There aren't any simple explanations.

17

10

I came home late that night. First I'd been to a meeting, and then I'd had a glass of wine with Claes. Immediately when I stepped into the apartment, I understood that something was wrong. Jonatan was lying in his bed whimpering, he wasn't screaming but making little squeaking noises as if he'd been crying for so long that he was too tired to keep going, as if he'd given up. Of course I was terrified, and rushed in and picked him up, yes, the pillowcase was drenched and his cheeks were wet with tears. The whole condo was freezing, the balcony door in the living room was wide open and the curtains were fluttering, it was a cold, gray October evening. It was drizzling and almost stormy outside, and the parquet flooring was wet quite far into the room.

It wasn't until I'd pulled the balcony door shut again that I discovered the TV. It was lying on the floor, tipped over with the screen smashed, thousands of small shards gleamed in the faint light from the hallway.

Jonatan clung to me so hard, pushed his little body against mine as if he were terrified I would leave him, and I felt his damp cheek against mine.

At first I thought there'd been a break-in, and that something had happened to Göran. I was just about to call the police when I heard music coming from the bathroom.

The bathroom door was locked, I hesitated there on the out-side, it could be a stranger in there, it could be anyone. But then I recognized the music, it was Joni Mitchell singing, and then I knew it was Göran.

I was furious. Madder than ever before. What was he doing? I knocked on the door and shouted his name. I kept doing that for several minutes, but nothing happened and he didn't respond. Then I got really scared.

What if he killed himself, what if he's lying there in the bathtub with his wrists slashed, what if he's lying there in a pool of his own blood?

And I started crying and pleading and begging on the outside of the door, still nothing happened, I just heard the music and maybe, maybe I heard a faint splash.

"Göran! Are you there? Are you alive? Answer me! Open the door!"

Jonatan had just started crying again, I carried him into our bedroom, tried to comfort him, then tucked him into our bed and left him there while I ran and got a screwdriver.

I knew what I had to do, I'd seen Göran open the bathroom door from the outside just a week earlier when Jonatan had locked himself in. It was easy.

I've never been so scared as when I pushed down on that door handle and opened the door. No, I had once. And again today when I found Hanna's note on the kitchen table. Deathly afraid three times in my life. This was the first.

Göran was lying in the bathtub in there. He was taking a bubble bath. The tape player was sitting on the edge of the tub and Joni Mitchell was singing in her squeaky voice.

At first I was just relieved. He was alive.

But of course I understood that something was wrong, that something had gone horribly wrong, and Göran just stared at me vacantly, his head sticking up from the bubbles, he looked like a dumb walrus, he didn't say anything, just stared as if he'd never seen me before.

I just stood there in the doorway and waited and seriously believed he'd lost his mind.

"No," he said finally. "I'm not sure I am."

"You are what?" I said.

"That I'm alive," he said. "I think I'm the living dead. I think I've turned into a zombie."

Then I was pissed. He was lying there feeling sorry for himself while Jonatan had had to lie there screaming frantically alone in his bed. I don't know for how long, but I'd seen how resigned Jonatan was, I'd seen he was shivering and trembling when I'd picked him up. I yelled at Göran, I screamed at him, I tried to get him to say something, but he just turned away and stared at the tiles. I wanted to go over there and push his head down under the water to get him to react, but of course I didn't do that.

In the end, I decided to take Jonatan and go home to my parents' house, but while I was getting him dressed and comforting him, Göran had gotten up out of the tub, and when I walked by lugging Jonatan, Göran was standing there outside the bathroom wrapped in a towel.

He was himself again, immensely sad, but himself. The vacant stare was gone as if I'd only been dreaming a few minutes earlier.

"Don't go," he pleaded. "Please stay. We have to talk. You don't need to be afraid."

Even today I can't believe I stayed. Anyone would certainly have run away from there, just fled, but I stayed. I tucked Jonatan in and sang to him, and then Göran and I sat at the kitchen table all night long and talked, and what he said then made me more scared and more surprised than the smashed television.

11

You can think you know a person. If you've lived together for seventeen years, if you have a child together, if you've grown together since you were teenagers. You share a history.

After that night I don't know anymore how close to another person we can ever come. Maybe they're right, the people who say that the world is a stage and we're playing our roles, even for those we're closest to, we're acting. Only when we're alone do we take off the masks. I don't know.

Obviously, some of the things Göran said I'd heard before. All the stuff about how he wanted to make his dreams come true, that he wanted to feel like he was choosing, that he wanted to be true to himself. I'd heard all of that before. What frightened me was his desperation. The life we shared had become a prison to him, none of what we'd done together seemed to be worth anything.

As if I'd been controlling his life, the whole time. As if I were his jailer. Just that and nothing else.

We'd slept in the same bed, sat at the same breakfast table, gone on trips, played with Jonatan, planned our future, and the whole time he'd been living in another world from mine. Another world that was more important than the one we shared.

He said, "I've come to a dead end with high brick walls everywhere."

He said, "Something has to happen. Otherwise, I'll kill myself."

Can you believe it? He threatened to kill himself. And wanted to make me responsible for it! Release me, otherwise I'll commit suicide, that's what he said.

Can you understand how it feels to hear that?

17

He was such a coward, he'd become so confused that he was trying to commit extortion.

Still we had a conversation, I cried, I was heartbroken as I listened to him, but we had a conversation, and maybe we would have been able to talk through it all, maybe I could have reasoned with him, led him out of his dead end if it weren't for what he said next.

He started talking about freedom.

I said something about security.

He talked about freedom.

I said something about being faithful.

He talked about freedom.

I said something about honesty.

That was when he started taunting me, and he shouted that if honesty was so important to me then he'd give me a real dose of honesty, and then he told me about the women. About the women he'd been with since we met.

As early as back at that camp in Denmark he'd fucked some drugged-out Danish hippie princess while I was sleeping in the tent. When he was out on his failed trip around the world as a nineteen-year-old he'd been with a girl in Scotland. Gunilla in Lund, of course, twice. A colleague at St. Lars, in a storeroom. A very famous ceramist from Helsingborg. An artist from Luleå. A Japanese photographer. When I was pregnant with Jonatan, he had an affair with a very young Japanese photographer. Then I don't remember anymore, then I covered my ears.

But he forced me to listen. He told me about his trysts, he described in detail who was on the top and who was on the bottom, who he'd taken from behind, who he'd gone down on, who'd gone down on him. He forced me to listen. And when he was finished he shouted, "Now you've got your honesty! Was it great? Do you feel good now?"

That's what a pig he is.

That's how much he wanted to hurt me, how much he hated me.

Can you believe that? After half a lifetime together.

That's when I took down the framed picture from the hippie camp in Denmark that was hanging on the wall in the kitchen, in every kitchen we'd had, and smashed it against the corner of the table. "Take that for your juvenile dreams of another life!" Then I took Jonatan and fled to my parents' house, and then our life together was over. Period.

I stop talking, I notice that I'd raised the volume of my voice, that I'd gotten carried away with my story. Josefin is sitting quietly, I hear her breathing.

"Well, you've heard Göran's version," I say, trying to find my way back to my own voice.

She nods.

"He didn't say anything about the women," she whispers.

"I'm sure he didn't," I say.

"But he said ... that you stayed," Josefin whispers.

"Stayed?"

"He said that a week went by. He said that he watched you sleeping, and ... and thought everything would be OK, I remember that because ... because I thought about it."

She's embarrassed. No wonder. She's wound up right into the middle of two people's most private, most intimate moments, it's

17

like she had to empty out our laundry basket and study our dirty underwear.

"Stayed? How could I stay after what he said? I never slept in the same bed as Göran again. But it is true that I spoke to him again, of course. But it was over then. Our life together ended that night."

Yes, it's true that we kept talking. I don't know for sure whether Göran actually thought we could keep living together, he tried to take it back, he tried to explain, it was as if he didn't understand that he'd crossed a limit. A limit to how much you can hurt another person.

Even his affairs with women, he tried to explain them away and minimize them.

He said, "Have we promised to be faithful to each other sexually?" He said, "None of that actually meant anything." He said, "It didn't mean any more than if I'd danced with those girls, or had coffee and talked." He said, "What's the big deal about sex?" He said, "It never affected our life, it was never about feelings, it was just a game."

Like a game? Like drinking coffee? Yes, that's what he said.

I said, "Why didn't you tell me about your encounters, then?"

He said, "I didn't want to hurt you."

He said, "You're the only one I loved."

He said that.

It seemed like he didn't want to understand that everything was over, that everything was too late. Even though he was the one who felt trapped in our life, it seemed like he wanted to keep going.

I suppose for Jonatan. No matter how abominably he acted toward me, no matter how much he deceived me and lied to me, I still can't deny that he loved Jonatan, that he was a good father.

But how could I risk living with him after what'd happened, how could I risk letting Jonatan live with him? Not a chance in the world.

12

We weren't married, so we didn't need to get a divorce.

Göran found an apartment by Möllevången, and I stayed out in Riseberga. Of course Jonatan was going to live with me, but we would share custody. Of course.

Once Göran realized that the whole thing was over, everything got much easier. We only talked about practical matters, our relationship turned into a sort of by-the-book negotiation, a sort of business transaction. Everything went very fast. He didn't want to take anything with him when he moved out, just some clothes and some old records. He didn't even take his files of negatives. And when he moved out, Jonatan and I moved back in again, we'd spent that week at my parents' place. And just a month later Claes moved in with us, and then he had to deal with his divorce, and that was a complicated, heart-rending story involving a hysterical wife and two crying children.

No. In all the discussions with Göran I didn't mention Claes a single time. Not even when he humiliated me with that description of how he'd screwed around. I didn't say anything about Hugo, either, of course. I … I don't know why not. Because I was afraid of Göran, because I was a coward, because I was still ashamed and knew that I was only faking when I demanded honesty, or ... or because I didn't want to hurt him anymore. He hurt himself so much. I don't know. But I'm glad I didn't say anything.

He met Jonatan just one time after that. It was so sad, it was like the worst kind of Hollywood tearjerker. Jonatan didn't want to go, he cried and protested, I had to comfort him and cajole him, we met Göran at Södervärn and I practically had to force Jonatan to stay when I walked away, I had to bribe him with everything I could think of. I knew right away that that part of our business arrangement wasn't going to work out, and Göran understood it, too, he wasn't too dumb or too blind yet.

Children need a father. I believe that. Especially boys. But maybe not necessarily the biological father, and since Claes moved in with us so quickly, that solved that problem. But for Göran, of course, it was a catastrophe.

Claes has been a good father. Jonatan liked him from the beginning, there were never any problems. I've never lied to Jonatan, never bad-mouthed Göran, not even during the period later when he made our lives into a kind of hell. Maybe you don't believe me, but it's true. I've thought the whole time that Jonatan would want to get to know Göran, sooner or later, and I've seen the pictures in his room now, I get that he's started wondering about his father. His first father. So if that's the case I think I did a great job, despite everything Göran did.

After that weekend with Jonatan I lost touch with Göran.

I was ensconced in a new life. We'd weathered a storm, a nightmare was over. I wanted to think about the future, not about what had been. I suppose that's natural, I'm sure everyone would've reacted that way.

Jonatan didn't ask for Göran a single time. That's true. Maybe I should've been happy about that, that he'd also put the past behind him, but it frightened me a little.

Are people so replaceable? I mean, you can't help but wonder. Although surely it was some sort of defense mechanism for Jonatan, a psychologist would certainly be able to explain it.

A few times I actually tried to get in touch with Göran, but his phone was disconnected after a few months, and he wasn't home when I knocked on his door. I even called his parents, but his mother told me off. Then I thought, *I'll let him live his own life now.* I mean, that was what he wanted. Why should I care? I'm doing well, I'm living with a man I love, Jonatan has a father. Why should I care about that man who hurt me more than anyone else in this world?

I had just made up my mind that Göran was out of my life for good when he popped up again.

It was a lovely fall evening, Jonatan was out playing in the sandbox, it was a good neighborhood in that sense, there were always kids out there, we never worried about letting him go out to play.

But this one evening he came back up with tears and snot on his face, he was more sulky than sad, it took a little time to get him to tell us what had happened, but in the end he said that there was an old man down in the playground who had scared him. Or maybe didn't actually scare him, he was sort of more confused. And I walked out onto the balcony, and there was a man sitting on the bench down there next to the seesaw. He noticed me right away, we stared at each other for a long time before I recognized him. It was Göran. He looked like a homeless person, like the old guys you see shuffling around in Möllevång Square, unshaven and disheveled, wearing an old quilted jacket and a pair of frayed, stained jeans, bedroom slippers and no socks.

My first thought was that he was wearing a costume, that he was playing a role. It's true.

"What do you want?" I yelled.

He didn't answer, just stared at me.

"You scared Jonatan!" I yelled.

He stared at me, then he stood up and walked away without a word.

That night I asked Jonatan. No, the man hadn't done anything, he'd just talked so strangely.

I don't know if Jonatan recognized his dad. He never mentioned it, but for some reason I had the idea that he had. And that that was what had scared him.

13

Then Göran's game of terror began. For a good six months he transformed our lives into a horror movie, a thriller.

Already that same night the phone rang, I'd fallen asleep but Claes was up working on something, and when he answered at first there was just silence. Then a man had asked him who he was and if he lived there, and if I lived there. Then the man had asked how often we fucked. And then he hung up. It was only then that Claes understood that it was Göran who'd called.

The next night he called again. Claes answered this time, too, he tried to talk to Göran but just got a lot of sex talk in response.

The next night, I answered. He was quiet when he heard my voice. I was mad, I asked what he wanted. "You've got your freedom now," I said. "Is this how you want to use it?" I threatened to call the police if he didn't cut it out. He was quiet the whole time. When I hung up, I thought I heard him crying.

I thought it was over, then. The phone was quiet the next night, and the next, I thought he was dejected, sad, lonely, I thought my voice and my words made him come to his senses. I thought it was over.

The next day Claes got a letter at work, in the envelope he found a pornographic picture with a photograph of my face pasted onto it.

That same night the phone rang again. It was quiet on the line when I answered. He didn't say anything, just hung up again.

After having been woken up yet again, we contacted the police. I mean, we knew who it was, we didn't want him to go to jail, we just wanted him to stop. We were still more angry than scared, and I still had a certain amount of understanding for Göran. His sadness and loneliness must be immense, I thought.

I'm not trying to make myself sound better than I am. I'm no saint, I mean, I've told you about my deception and my lies. It's true that I hated him when we separated, but it's also true that he was a part of my life. And that he's my son's father.

It was Claes who convinced me to contact the police. For Göran's sake, too, he said. So that he can get help, he said. Yes, I thought.

I probably imagined that by calling the police, the problem would be solved. Not at all, to the contrary. The police couldn't find him. He'd disappeared, as if he'd been swallowed up. There was no address, no government agency had any contact with him, no one knew where he lived or what he was doing. Göran had succeeded in making himself invisible to the world. I don't know how much in the way of resources the police put into the case, and despite the fact that both Claes and I were both quite well connected we weren't able to influence the matter, the police probably just did a very cursory investigation. I mean, in spite of everything, the whole thing didn't involve any kind of felony.

Maybe we should have waited before contacting the police, because when Göran threatened to seriously take over our lives we got no help, the police just said they'd already looked for him without any luck.

Yes. Of course we didn't know then that we'd only seen the beginning.

There weren't any more nighttime phone calls. The next thing that happened was that Claes received another letter at work.

No picture this time, but it was still about sex.

More than a week went by before Claes let me read the letter, he'd crumpled it up in a rage. At first he was going to burn it, then he thought he'd turn it over to the police, then he pushed it into the very back of a desk drawer, and then suddenly one night when we were talking about Göran he went and got it and let me read it. And what I read, once I'd smoothed out the crumpled ball of paper, was a manual. Instructions, written out very formally.

Instructions about how I liked things.

Sexually, I mean. A detailed description of what gives me the most pleasure, but also of what I don't like.

Can you imagine? Can you imagine a person who would do that?

Claes thought it was disgusting, of course, he had actually never planned to show me the letter, but the strangest thing of all was that I ... that I ...

Yes. It reminded me. I mean, Claes and I are good together, both during the day and at night, if you get what I mean, we're good together in every way, but when I read Göran's letter it reminded me that he knew me better. Everything it said there was correct. He knew what I wanted. I mean, it's not that weird, we shared a bed for so many years, Claes and I had lived together for just a year, it takes time to get to know another person, also in that way. But it reminded me. And of course that was exactly what he wanted.

Shit. Why am I telling you this?

Josefin isn't even blushing. But surely she must think I'm gross.

"I don't know why I'm telling you this," I say, and a great weariness washes over me.

Josefin looks at me with her earnest eyes.

"I've told you things that I've never told anyone," I say. "I'm turning myself inside out. I don't understand why."

"It's good," Josefin says. "It's good that you're telling this story."

Despite her youthful wisdom, I'm not sure she understands. I mean, I'm telling her things about myself that normally no person would reveal to anyone else. I'm letting her see into my most secret spaces. I'm putting my life in her hands. Strangely enough, I haven't hesitated, everything has just flowed out of me, my thoughts and my memories have become words without any protective filter getting in the way. Maybe she's right, maybe that's good.

"Göran ...," she begins.

"Yes?"

"He didn't say anything about all this. He didn't say anything about any phone calls or letters. He just said ... that he did stupid things. That he wasn't himself. That it was a way for him to survive. And then he said ..."

"Yes?"

"That he wanted to be sure that you didn't forget him."

I can't help but laugh.

No, heaven knows, he was making sure that I didn't forget him.

But quickly I get serious.

"You haven't heard the worst of it yet," I say.

14

It was a week before Christmas. Nothing else had happened after that letter, we started hoping Göran had given up, that he was gone for good. And we'd started looking forward to celebrating our first Christmas together, Claes had still been fully preoccupied with his divorce the year before, and the entire Christmas holiday had been a chaotic mess of crying children and feeling guilty. But now we felt like we no longer needed to think about everything in the past, we could leave it all behind us, and we devoted ourselves to building up our own family life, creating our own traditions. We'd baked gingerbread and watched the Advent calendar on TV together every night, we lit candles and hung decorations and hid packages in the closets. We were a completely normal little family about to celebrate Christmas.

It was just as we sat down at the kitchen table and lit the fourth Advent candle that we heard the sound of bells from down in the courtyard, and Claes peeked out and said, "Look, here comes Santa Claus already."

And we peered out through the window and saw tons of children flocking around someone dressed as Santa Claus down there by the playground.

"It looks like he's passing out Christmas presents," I said. "Don't you want to run down there too, Jonatan?"

And of course he rushed off, eager as a little mouse.

Obviously, we thought it was something the tenants' association had arranged, I mean, there was a group that arranged a midsummer party and summer dances and community workdays and such. And we stood there at the window, Claes and I, and smiled as we watched how Jonatan hesitated before he got up the courage to approach Santa, we saw how Santa picked a package out of his sack and gave it to Jonatan. Then I saw how the Santa looked up at our window. He was wearing one of those dreadful stiff plastic masks, and when I saw him turn toward us, an icy wind rushed through me. Claes never noticed it, and Jonatan came bounding back up with his Christmas present right away, he sat down at the table and ripped the paper off. What could I do? I couldn't yank the year's first Christmas present away from him. I studied him closely as he opened the package, I saw that he was disappointed. Good, I thought. Better disappointed than scared.

It was a framed photograph. A picture of the three of us, taken when we were buying our Christmas tree the day before.

"How nice," I said quickly. "A picture of us buying our Christmas tree. How nice, look, Claes is just about to pay for it. What a nice Christmas present you got from Santa."

Jonatan smiled a hesitant smile, and Claes just stared at me.

That was the first picture.

After that we got one a week. Pictures of ourselves. Everyday pictures. It might be a picture of Claes getting off the bus. A picture of me when I was eating my lunch. A picture of me on the balcony. A picture of all three of us feeding the ducks in Pildamm Park. One picture every week. A little reminder of something we'd done during the last week. They came in the mail, or they were also stuffed directly into the mail slot, or they also came to me or Claes at work. One time a delivery service even brought me a photo while I was in a meeting with an asylum seeker.

He took over our lives.

We couldn't go anywhere, couldn't do anything without looking nervously over our shoulders. He was out there somewhere. And he had a good telephoto lens.

He took over our lives. I couldn't forget even for just a minute that Göran was out there somewhere. I mean, you said as much yourself a little bit ago, didn't you? That that was what he wanted. Not to be forgotten. Well, he succeeded. And he was ruining us. We tried to keep Jonatan out of it the whole time, but obviously he noticed when we would get irritable or frightened, when we started staying indoors and didn't want to go do things with him.

And the police, yes, well, I've already told you about that. They couldn't do anything.

Can you imagine how that feels? That there's someone out

there watching you all the time? No, I don't think anyone can imagine that.

To get away from it all, we went to the Canary Islands on vacation, it was a package vacation and there were a few tickets left and we went with just a few days' notice. And even though we were so far from home it still took until the last few days we were down there before we were able to enjoy the sun and the ocean. But Jonatan had fun, he talked about it for a long time afterward, about the long beaches down there, and he learned to swim then, although he was only five years old. Or six. Yes, I guess he was six. Then, when we came home we were happy and tan, it felt as if a nightmare were over.

On Monday, one of the secretaries came into my office.

"A man came by and wanted me to give you this," she said, holding out an envelope.

At first I was just going to tear it up and throw it away. Or stuff it into the paper shredder. I was convinced that there were pictures of our vacation in it, a picture of us on the beach, a grainy, slightly blurry picture, the kind the paparazzi take of Princess Madeleine when she's sunbathing topless with her new boyfriend. In the end, I tore the envelope open. No, there wasn't any picture inside, he hadn't followed us to the Canary Islands. Of course not. There was just a brief message from Göran. He'd written *Welcome Home* on a piece of paper from a notepad. It meant: I'll keep taking pictures. I'll keep following you.

He'd gotten into our lives. He was taking over our lives. Can you understand?

All the happiness drained out of me. I walked around frozen.

What should we do? We started tailing each other to see if we could detect Göran, we contacted private detectives, we tried pulling all the strings we could.

Nothing helped. The pictures kept coming.

I could have killed Göran then. It's true. Or ... no. But that's how it felt. I would've done anything if I could only just be free.

The spring came. A tired, pale, joyless spring.

One sunny April day I went out for lunch, I no longer had the strength to worry about whether I was in his sights or not, I didn't have the strength to run away anymore. I was sitting on a bench in Slottsparken, I was watching some schoolchildren playing, it was a whole group of toddlers from some day-care center, one-year-olds and two-year-olds out toddling around and chasing the ducks and enjoying the green grass and the blue sky. I couldn't enjoy anything anymore, that's how it felt. All of my joy was gone.

That's when I discovered him. I saw him when the sun reflected off a lens up on a hill, leaning against a tree, he was standing there with his camera raised. I stood up quickly. Then I stayed standing. At first I'd intended to rush up to him, then I thought I'd turn around and run away, but I just stood there and stared straight into his camera lens.

Naked and defenseless I stood there, like a little mouse hypnotized by the snake's eyes.

With my arms hanging at my sides I stood there, and then my tears began to flow. Two rivers of sorrow ran down my cheeks.

I couldn't do anything but stand there and cry. I didn't notice that the children around me had stopped playing, I didn't hear that one of the day-care workers was concerned and asked me something, I don't know how long I stood there, but through my tears I eventually saw him lower his camera and turn around and disappear.

Then it was over.

Then no more pictures ever came.

15

It's going to be a beautiful day. Outside the window the early morning sun is glittering over the city, the sky is light blue like the jerseys worn by Malmö's soccer team, Heavenly Blue, and you can just hear a faint roar from the first early traffic down there.

Now I feel how tired I am, I'd like to stretch out next to Jonatan there on the mattress. He's still sleeping and breathing peacefully. I laugh out loud, and Josefin looks at me, startled.

"I was thinking about Jonatan," I explain, swallowing a yawn. "He has no idea what he started tonight, he's just lying there sleeping so soundly."

Josefin nods and gives me a brief smile.

"Some things happened before he wound up here, too," she says.

"Tell me," I ask. "Do you know what happened?"

Josefin nods again.

"I was there," she says. "I know what happened at home in my apartment. But then he left, then I don't know."

"In any case I want you to tell the story of what happened," I say. "Now that I've given you my entire life."

"Not truly," Josefin responds, shaking her head.

At first, I don't get what she means, but then I understand that she doesn't think I've told my story all the way to the end.

"OK," I say, shrugging my shoulders.

Actually, I think before I keep going with the story, my story is kind of more about Göran than about myself. I've hardly said anything about my own dreams, my plans and my thoughts. I've turned him into the main character in a story about my life. But I suppose that's because of the way it started, I mean I started telling the story to give her a picture of him. And really *he's* the main character, the one lying here on the floor. Really.

Göran vanished from my world when he vanished behind those trees that day in April. After a few weeks without any photographs, I realized it was over. For some reason, my tears in his viewfinder had made him stop what he was doing. Had he only just then understood how much he was hurting me? I don't know, and now I just wanted to forget him.

So we were going to try to build a family life from the ruins and debris, Claes and I and Jonatan. We realized that we couldn't keep living in Riseberga, but when Claes heard through some of his contacts about a house in Falsterbo that was going to be available, we had our first big argument. No way, I said. Only conservative wackos live in Falsterbo, I said. I don't want Jonatan growing up with that group, I said. It's so nice there, Claes said. The sand dunes. The light over the peninsula. The moors. Living by the ocean surrounded by nature, and still close to the city. We couldn't have it any better. Jonatan couldn't have it any better.

I let myself be convinced, and now I'm glad I did. Claes was right, the ocean and the light and the beaches helped the wounds heal. Sure, the area was populated by conservatives, but some of them have become our friends, some of them turned out to be good neighbors and helpful and nice in every way. But there's a

whole bunch of narrow-minded idiots down there, too, and quite
a few racists, as I'm sure you know.

Suddenly something occurs to me, something I obviously should
have thought of right away:

"Didn't you say earlier that Jonatan's wallet had been stolen?
And didn't he have his keys with him, too?"

Josefin nods.

"I have to cancel his debit card then," I say, and start rooting
around in my purse for my cell phone, "and then I have to ask
Claes to try and find a locksmith who can make it out to the
house today, he probably had his address in his wallet, we have to
replace the locks, otherwise I won't be able to sleep tonight ..."

Josefin puts her hand on my arm and stops me.

"Wait," she urges. "There's no danger. Jonatan only had like
fifty bucks in his account. And the card companies reimburse that
kind of thing. And you'll have time to call the locksmith later.
Finish telling the story first. Please?"

I sigh, hesitating.

"Please. Tell me about Jonatan," Josefin beseeches. "How did
he handle all of this?"

I nod and set my purse down again. Yes. I want to finish the
story, too.

16

"Jonatan started wetting the bed again when he was six. Every
morning, his sheets were wet. Ultimately, I had to borrow a mattress from the children's clinic, one of those mattresses that has an

alarm that sounds when it gets wet. I was so afraid that he would still be wetting the bed when he started school, what if his classmates thought he smelled like pee? Or if they went somewhere for school, a sleepover somewhere.

I was often afraid when Jonatan was a child. Afraid that he would be left out, that he wouldn't have any friends, that he would be different, that he wouldn't be invited to parties. Afraid that he wouldn't come home from school, afraid every time I saw an ambulance or heard sirens in the distance. I don't know why, I don't know where my fear came from. Suddenly, the world seemed so menacing. Or ... I guess maybe it's not so hard to understand why. But it wasn't just that stuff with Göran, I was a new parent, too. Claes was good, he calmed me, he was so much more level-headed. And now with Hanna it's totally different, now I'm able to enjoy motherhood in a completely different way.

I can just picture Jonatan in front of me, pale and weak with a runny nose and those big round eyes filled with wonder as he contemplated the world, and his hair like a disheveled cloud around his head. Jonatan as a seven-year-old. I only worked three-quarters time for those years after we moved to Falsterbo.

And then Jonatan started school, sometimes I would stand and watch him secretly while he and the other kids were out on the playground at school. Constantly afraid, with my maternal heart constantly in my throat. Would he be alone? Would he be teased and picked on because he was wearing the wrong clothes or saying the wrong things? I stood there hidden behind some trees, scanning the playground for him, feeling like an idiot, but I wanted to know, I had to know, that everything was as it should be.

Actually all my fear was wasted. Jonatan had a safe, peaceful childhood. He wasn't one of the most popular boys, of course, but he had two pals throughout his school years, Alexander and Benjamin, they always stuck together, Jonatan was the one who withdrew sometimes, it was like he needed his solitude sometimes.

Yes, actually, I was scared and anxious completely unnecessarily. Those early years I was so careful to buy him the same clothes the other kids had, and let him watch the same movies and listen to the same music, I wanted him to be a completely normal, average child, I couldn't stand the thought of his being excluded, but later I understood that Jonatan had the strength to be himself, and that he didn't care what the other kids thought, and then I was able to relax a little.

It's not easy being a mother.

There's an anxiety and a fear that can break your heart.

There's a sadness. A sadness that's always ready to come out.

17

One day, I knew that I wanted to have a child with Claes. Before it was too late. When I turn forty, it will be too late, I decided.

Jonatan was my child, even though Claes was there as a father. His two daughters lived with their mom, his separation from them had also been terribly painful, like his divorce, lots of bitterness and tears. We had two awful separations behind us. But now I wanted us to have a baby together.

Hanna was born in August 1995, and Jonatan loved his little sister from the first time he saw her. He was eleven, I'd been a little worried about sibling rivalry, I mean, he'd been an only child for so long, but he loved her from the moment he sat on my bed in the hospital, his mouth hanging open, almost reverentially poking at her tiny toes and fingers. Yes, you know yourself how much he still cares about her, I don't think that's so common.

Well, it was much easier being a mother this time. I was much calmer with Hanna. But when it came to Jonatan, I still had my fear and my anxiety.

And new fears came all the time. There was so much that could happen. Once those first six years at elementary school were out of the way, then junior high and a big new school with fifteen-year-old mini-gangsters to welcome the new seventh graders by shoving their heads down into the toilets and urinating on them and terrorizing them and forcing them into submission and obedience. In my imagination, I mean.

Although … true, it got tougher in reality, too. A harder phase. I was home with Hanna when Jonatan started middle school, I watched Jonatan change, he'd always liked school, he'd been curious and wanted to learn stuff; in middle school all of that got so much harder for him, the vast majority of the class just didn't care, they devoted all their time to trying to win points by being cool, by picking on the weak ones, by acting up, by fighting. And the teachers were such … cowards. Yes, it was like they didn't even dare to fight for what they believed, didn't dare talk to the kids about the importance of a good education. I don't know. But Jonatan suffered from that.

If there'd been a decent private school nearby I wouldn't have hesitated, yes, it's true, I wouldn't have cared about my old ideals, I wouldn't have cared about what my fellow party members thought.

I don't think he was ever picked on, but it got harder and harder for him to do his own thing. And he didn't want to hang out with Alex anymore. At first we didn't understand why, I even tried to convince him to keep up with his old friend, but in the end Jonatan told me why. That Alex had done a lot of stupid stuff, that he drank and caused trouble, and that he started hanging out with racists. Not like a rabid skinhead, of course, we don't have any of those in our neighborhood, here we have a different and probably more dangerous sort, well dressed and well spoken and polite and charmingly seductive young racists who picked up many of their opinions around the breakfast table at home.

But of course Benjamin was still around, yes, he's still around, obviously you know that, he went in the other direction, went all goth with wild green hair, at one time he really spiked his hair and had a black jacket with studs and spiked wrist cuffs, I would probably have been afraid if I'd run into him in town, but there he was sitting at our kitchen table in the evenings and he was the same sweet Benjamin who'd been Jonatan's buddy since they were six years old, who played with Legos and built a fort in the yard.

That's how it is. You have to look beyond the external. You forget that. Of course, that's exactly what the goths and the skinheads want, but we grown-ups mustn't forget to look beyond the exterior. There's a young person there, a person who was a little kid not very long ago. We shouldn't be so quick to be afraid of young people.

Sorry. I'm sorry, now I'm sounding awfully preachy and self-righteous, aren't I? But I've been thinking about all this so much. Sorry if I'm lecturing.

What was I talking about? About being a mother, right.

Actually, I was supposed to tell the story of Jonatan, and here I go just talking about myself. About how afraid I was.

18

It's strange, Göran and I really thought the same way about having kids. Never, we'd said. There's an important battle to be fought, if you have kids you get weak and cowardly and vulnerable, you become just a mother or just a father, and forget about being a person. That's what we said. We were right in a way, and yet we were so totally wrong. Because part of the point to life is having children, I understand that now. Maybe that is the point.

I was reminded of the time that Jonatan almost died. We were hiking in the mountains the summer Jonatan was thirteen. It was me and Jonatan and Claes and his two daughters, Sofie and Emma, they're three and four years older than Jonatan. Hanna was staying with my parents. And we were hiking in the mountains in Jämtland, we went from Storulvån to Blåhammaren and then over to the Norwegian side and then back via Sylarna, those first couple days the girls had whined the whole time, they complained about the heavy packs and the mosquitoes and the food, I was going crazy, everything was just going wrong, and I got blisters on my heels and my back hurt, but then ... then that night came ... I have to tell the story of that night first.

We'd left the trail and were walking over the moors up on a hill, we'd set up the tent, we'd made some food on the camp stove and eaten a freeze-dried meal. The girls were whiny and tired and irritable as usual, and Jonatan wanted to go home, I'm sure he mainly thought it seemed pointless to walk around carrying a big, heavy backpack day in and day out. But then suddenly, as we were sitting there outside the tent, we saw how the sky darkened, we were pretty high up, we could see quite far off, we saw the storm coming from a long way off, we saw the lightning over the mountain peaks, we heard the thunder, we sat there and couldn't do anything but wait.

I remember the feeling exactly. Of being so exposed, so powerless. We saw the storm approaching, and we couldn't do anything about it. There wasn't anywhere for us to take refuge or hide. Claes anchored the tent down with rocks, and we piled inside when the first heavy raindrops started to fall. Then we huddled together in there, we pressed in against each other, the rain pelted against the canvas, the lightning came closer and closer, booming thunderclaps rumbled, the girls whimpered with fright, we were definitely all just as scared, but both Claes and I felt that we should display some adult courage and we tried to soothe and comfort them. We counted the time between the lightning and the thunder, one two three four five six ... two kilometers, one two three ... one kilometer, one ... a thunderclap boomed right over us, like an explosion, and then ... then the storm moved on, farther and farther by our calculations, the rain let up, finally it was quiet, we held onto each other's hands tightly, we were shaking, we looked at each other without saying a word. We were still alive.

As the fear slowly subsided, we sat there in the tent in silence, speechless and dazed. That was when light filled the tent. At first we didn't get what was happening, at first we thought there was a fire outside, but then we pulled down the zipper and peeked out. The whole world outside the tent was radiant in this incredible gleam. If I were religious, I would've said the world was radiant with God's light. Yes, it's true. It's true, it was that kind of moment.

We crawled out and just stood there in the sunshine, we hadn't said a single word since the rain forced us into the tent, and we were still standing there in silence and holding each other's hands. No, I've never had anything closer to a religious experience.

I've never believed in God. I've always thought it was man who created God, not the other way around. Man created God out of fear. I've always believed in scientific explanations. I don't mean that I was saved or anything that night, I just mean that I was reminded that sometimes man is just a tiny, helpless little thing, a little worm, a little ant, that there are forces in the world that can crush us as easy as all get-out.

And after that, everything changed. The rest of our hiking trip was a delight, we enjoyed the vastness of nature, we enjoyed each other's companionship, we were so happy that we had each other. That we were alive. We never said a single word about what happened that stormy night, yet I'm sure we all had the same experience. That we were reminded that we should make sure to live before we die. Ugh, it just sounds silly now that I'm trying to put words to that feeling. It sounds banal. But I'll carry that memory with me forever, and I think about it from time to time.

I got another reminder of life's fragility on that trip to the mountains. And it was what happened on our very last night in the mountains that I really wanted to tell you about.

It was a nice night. We'd set up the tent by a bubbling mountain stream that emptied out into a little lake. We were feeling good. I remember I was sitting outside the tent, feeling good. I was thinking, *I'm almost happy now.* Maybe happiness is possible after all. After everything that's happened. After Göran. After all my anxiety for Jonatan. I was sitting there feeling good, a big bird of prey was circling way up above, it was probably a hawk, you could smell the bog myrtle, I heard the children playing and laughing, Jonatan and the girls were having a competition with their drinking cups in the creek, they would launch them upstream and let them sail down between the rocks and through little rapids while they ran alongside, each rooting for his own cup. Claes came and sat down next to me, I leaned my head against his shoulder and felt good; he asked if we should take a little evening stroll, and I nodded.

Exactly then I was reminded again, reminded of how thin the thread is between joy and despair, between life and death. And reminded of what's actually important.

Because suddenly Sofie and Emma started shrieking and yelling, we jumped to our feet, Claes and I, ran down to the lake where the girls were standing at the edge of the water, and we got there and ... and then I saw Jonatan down there in the water. That image will never be erased from my brain. Jonatan's hair was billowing like seaweed under the surface of the water, air bubbles were rising from his mouth, it was like a picture out of a horror movie or a nightmare. My first thought was that he was dead, but Claes took a step out into the water, he swore as he sank down into the muck, but then he found his footing on a rock and pulled Jonatan up.

We laid him on the ground, he was breathing, his eyes were open, I'll never forget the look in his eyes. Never.

"I wanted to get the cup," he whispered. "I sank in. And got stuck."

It was that close.

That's how thin the thread is.

If we hadn't been sitting there by the tent, if we'd gone for our little evening stroll, then Jonatan would have died. The girls wouldn't have been able to pull him up, he would have drowned in a little mountain lake at the age of thirteen.

What I was actually going to say was: That's when I understood what was most important to me, in my life and in the world. My child. My children. More important than anything else, more important than everything I believe in and fight for. Does that seem paltry? Cowardly? Bourgeois, maybe? I don't care, I know what I feel, I learned something on that trip to the mountains. And we were wrong, Göran and I, the children are the most important thing, the battle is being fought for the children's sake.

19

Yes. There's a joy and a sorrow. And anxiety.

And now I'm sitting here in the emergency ward and looking at my son who drank way too much. I feel stupid. It feels … cheap. A little humiliating. But sure, sure, sure, it could've been worse, it could've been much worse, sure.

I've been fooling myself for a long time, believing that Jonatan wasn't drinking. I know that kids start drinking as early as thirteen or fourteen, but I thought he was different, more mature, or more timid, maybe. There was this one time when Jonatan was in eighth grade, it was in the spring, he asked if he could have a party at our house, and I thought sure, of course, good that he feels like one of the gang, and Claes and I and Hanna cleared out so he could have the place to himself without any parents around and went to stay with some colleagues in Höllviken, we were invited to a barbecue, the first of the season.

I guess it was about ten or ten thirty when Jonatan called, I didn't recognize his voice, I couldn't understand what he was saying, but I could tell that something was wrong. You could hear that in the background, too, there was angry yelling and music and glass breaking, and obviously we drove home right away. When we were almost home and turned onto the street into our neighborhood, we saw two guys carrying something between them. Only after the fact did we figure out that it was our VCR.

And then when we pulled up in front of the house there was complete pandemonium, the neighbors were all outside, throngs of teenagers were hanging out on the lawn and in front of the garage, some were fighting and yelling at each other, a girl was throwing up in the mailbox just as I got out of the car, and before we had a chance to do anything a police car came with its siren on, one of the neighbors had called them, and after a while all the teenagers left and the police took two of the worst troublemakers with them.

I just wanted to cry when I opened the front door. The living room floor was covered with shards of porcelain and bits of food and beer, the stereo was gone, all the drawers in the cabinet were pulled out, and Jonatan was lying on the sofa, as white as a sheet and as drunk as a skunk.

What can I say? We got some of the stolen stuff back, our homeowner's insurance covered some of it, the humiliation was

17

the worst part, that thirty drunken teenagers wrecked our home, smashed things up, rooted around in our drawers, looked through our cupboards and closets. And the worst thing of all was that whenever we talked to people about it they would just shrug their shoulders and say, "That's how it goes." Everyone seemed to have been through something similar, or knew someone who had.

Is that reasonable? Young people obviously call each other on their cell phones on the weekends, get some tip that there's a party somewhere, and then the whole gang swoops in, they eat up the food, drink up the alcohol, steal whatever's worth stealing and ruin the rest. Is that reasonable? Our own young people have become like a swarm of locusts, like grasshoppers, like termites or wild barbarians. Is that reasonable? Are we going to have to protect ourselves from our own children? Have their lives become so sad and meaningless that destruction and drunkenness are the only things left?

No, I'll never understand this.

I was still feeling sorry for Jonatan. It wasn't his fault, he'd tried to drive off the troublemakers. And he was so ashamed and so dejected afterward. But he had been drunk, even him.

For six months he did a paper route every Sunday to pay for and replace all the stuff that had been stolen or wrecked, in the end I felt almost sorry for him, but he never complained.

What am I trying to say? I suppose I wanted to give you a picture of Jonatan after his father disappeared, but maybe it turned out to be more a picture of myself. My fear and my joy. And a trip to the mountains and a vandalized home.

I feel more secure now. Jonatan has grown, he's so wise

sometimes that it brings tears to my eyes. Tonight of course, though, maybe he wasn't so wise. More secure, but sadder, too. More alone. He's growing away from me, my son. He doesn't let me into his life anymore, I envy you and your friends sometimes. Sometimes I feel like he thinks I'm stupid. I don't want that, for him to think that. So often we end up butting heads, it feels as if everything I say irritates him, as if he always has to contradict me. The conversations we have over the kitchen table are mostly rhetorical displays. He says stuff to provoke Claes and me. Usually Claes. And usually he succeeds.

I want to be close to Jonatan. I don't want to lose him.

20

I never talked to Jonatan about Göran during those first years in Falsterbo, and he never asked. After what happened, I was glad if he forgot, too. Because I did. I wanted to put all the old stuff behind me, I had such a great need to look toward the future then.

It was while I was still on maternity leave with Hanna that I saw Göran on TV one night.

It was a piece about my party leader, you know, for my political party, she had just gone public about her drinking problem and now she was being interviewed at Nämndemansgården where she was staying for a while. It's a treatment center for alcoholics here in Skåne, their treatment methods have proven effective. So anyway, I was sitting there watching that piece on the news, and suddenly I saw Göran. He was sitting there in an armchair chatting with some of the other alcoholics, he looked happy, he was laughing and gesticulating.

That's how I found out that Göran was being treated at Nämndemansgården. Later I found out that he'd checked himself in, and that his problem was very minor compared to most of the other people. Or of a different type.

I just shrugged my shoulders and thought, *Oh. Well, he's alive anyway.* It didn't make me happy or afraid, I'd outgrown him now. I was looking toward the future. He was part of another life, another world. That's how it felt.

When Jonatan turned twelve, a package came in the mail. Luckily, I wasn't home when he got home from school and found it in the mailbox, otherwise I would've been terrified and wouldn't have let him open it. But it was just a normal birthday present. A little hunting knife, a nice journal and a book. Jules Verne's *Twenty Thousand Leagues under the Sea.* And then a little card that said: "Best Wishes on Your Twelfth Birthday from Dad."

At first I was mad. How dare he? After everything he did to us. And what the heck kind of way was that to get in touch with his son after seven years? But then one night a few days later, when I came into Jonatan's room to say good night, he was lying there reading the book he'd gotten, and he looked so ashamed, as if he were caught doing something forbidden. I went in and sat on the edge of his bed. It was a good book, he said. It was exciting, he said. I turned away so that he wouldn't see the tears in my eyes.

After that, I decided to try to find Göran. Don't get me wrong, I didn't want to see him, didn't want to talk to him, I just wanted to know where he was and maybe … maybe in some way keep kind of a watchful eye over him. For Jonatan's sake, just for Jonatan's sake.

It wasn't hard to find him. Sweden's personal identity numbers were a good invention in that sense.

It turned out that he'd moved to Göteborg, he was living in an apartment in the Majorna neighborhood and working in a photography group that shared a studio nearby.

"I thought ..."

Josefin looks a little confused, confusion wrinkles her forehead. "I thought ... when he said ... I pictured him being totally ... being outside ... that he was drinking and ... yes, I mean you said it yourself, how he looked when you saw him there by the sandbox. He told me that he's been sober for a year and ten months now, I thought that ..."

I shake my head. "No. Göran has never been an alcoholic. Maybe he made an attempt at becoming one, but ... that's just one of those mythic images in his world. I've finally understood him, I'm the one who knows him best. He wanted to play the alcoholic, the derelict. Just like he played hippie and drug addict at one time. He's been playing games the whole time, trying out different roles. That's how it is. He's never grown up, he's never gotten any older than seventeen. He's been living in his myths. The whole time he's been trying to emulate his own heroes and idols, and his heroes have been poets and philosophers, drug prophets and hippie leaders, drunken artists and authors and I don't know who all. His heroes have been the kind of people who demonstrated their sensitivity and their honesty by failing to live in this dishonest world. People who scorned the little life. The normal life. The everyday life. And Göran imitated their lives, without ever really daring to let go. Or being able to. That's how it is. He hasn't lived, he's imitated living. It sounds like an awful thing to say, but it's true. I don't know if he has grown up by now, I can only hope.

"But ..."

"That time when he was sitting by the sandbox, that was just acting, he was in costume, my first impression was right. He was living at home with his mother then, when he left the apartment by Möllevången he moved back in with his mommy. The whole time he was persecuting us he was living in that bitch's house, no doubt she knew what he was up to, and she lied as pleasant as can be to the police and to me. He was at Nämndemansgården for two weeks, he underwent treatment, but he was never an alcoholic, no matter how you define the term, I know that. It was all just acting ..."

Now I'm crying.

I'm crying for Göran's sake.

For what I said. I said that his whole life is a lie. Who has the right to say that about another person?

And I'm crying for my sake.

I cry when I hear my own words, because I know that Göran is still with me.

I hear Göran's voice every day. I see him every day, see his smile, his gestures, his way of walking ... I mean: I see Göran in Jonatan, and hear him.

21

Do you remember the other evening, Josefin? When we were talking politics at the kitchen table, well, of course we almost always do that when you're over, but that was the night Claes got so irritated. Do you remember what Jonatan said?

"The way we choose to live is a political act, right? We have a personal responsibility, right? We have a choice, right?"

Jonatan said it, but I heard Göran. Göran is still sitting at our kitchen table. I don't mean that Jonatan is some kind of carbon copy of his father, but every year that goes by they get more and more alike.

It startles me sometimes when I hear Göran's voice in Jonatan's. When I recognize Göran's words. Or when I see a gesture or an expression that takes me back.

Does it make me happy or sad? Both. There's a sorrow and a joy. I can only hope that each generation gets a little wiser, that all the mistakes don't need to be repeated.

And then we talked about those demonstrations in Göteborg and the antiglobalization protests, and Claes pointed out that he and I were politically active when we were teenagers, and said that what happened during the EU meeting was just a riot, and that it didn't have anything to do with a political protest.

Then Jonatan said, "But you failed, didn't you? You marched and demonstrated and passed out flyers and sold newspapers and were conscientious, but what was the result? Maybe in the end a few rocks through a few storefront windows is a more effective method. I mean, now everyone's discussing globalization."

That was when Claes got so irritated.

"You're wrong. No one's discussing globalization," he said. "Everyone's discussing rock throwing. And you have to learn from history. What you're saying about the battle we fought and are still fighting is just childish nonsense. And they ought to prohibit mask wearing in demonstrations. That's just chicken. Demonstrating means showing that you're standing up for your opinions."

17

"You don't get it," Jonatan said. "You don't get the world we live in. You don't get that the cops and the neo-Nazis are taking pictures of us. Maybe you think the Schengen Agreement is some kind of delightful little innovation so tourists won't have to fuss with passports. You don't get that I can be stopped at any border in Europe because I marched in a demonstration in Göteborg or Malmö. That's what the Schengen Agreement means. And you don't get that the neo-Nazis keep a list, too, someday they may knock on the door here. And they'll be armed. That's why we wear masks. You don't get the world we're living in."

Then Claes said something about how the demonstrators in Göteborg seemed to have forgotten that there won't be any revolution if the people are against you, and Jonatan said something about how the people are sitting dazed in front of "Survivor" and need to be woken up, and Claes said something about how if you fight a battle with violence without the support of the people then you're a terrorist, and living with childish illusions of becoming a hero or a martyr, and then Jonatan asked if Claes thought you could compare young people who threw rocks after having been provoked by the police with fundamentalist airplane hijackers and murderers.

Then Claes got up from the table and left.

Still, usually I think it's good that you care, that you're engaged. I don't always think you're wrong, either. But I don't understand those animal-rights discussions at all. If it's those animal factories that are the problem, then surely you could eat fish anyway. And game. But I'm glad you drink milk.

"I'm thinking about giving it up," Josefin mumbles.

I look at her and sigh.

"And the stuff about game, if only you knew how many elk are wounded every year and die excruciating deaths in the woods. Hunters aren't decent outdoorsy people, they're murderers," she says and I see how she starts arming herself with arguments to continue the debate.

But that's not why we're here, and I silence her by turning away.

Tears are still running down my cheeks.

I think about what Jonatan said, something I heard Göran say so often. The way we choose to live is a political act.

Well, we live in a house in Falsterbo surrounded by a bunch of conservative wackos. I earn a lot of money, my husband earns a lot of money. And we pay a lot of taxes, too, of course. We have two cars. Our daughter has the same clothes and the same gadgets and is in the same equestrian club as her conservative classmates. We don't need to scrimp and save. We can afford to buy organic milk and organic vegetables with their KRAV certification labels. And I still have faith, I haven't given everything up, I work on behalf of people who can't plead their own cases, there are hundreds of families whose lives are affected by my commitment, and I'm still an active member of the Left Party, and although Jonatan is right about a number of his criticisms, that's where the smartest people are. I was involved in the No campaign before the referendum on whether Sweden should join the EU, although I'm not so sure about that issue anymore. I belong to an amnesty group. I'm a member of the Swedish Society for Nature Conservation, we sort our trash and donate clothes to Emmaus.

The way we choose to live is a political act. Sure. But he made it so easy for himself, Göran did. He never got a driver's license, for example. I mean, that was convenient, then he could just say that he wasn't contributing any greenhouse gases or air pollution or big-city problems. But then when we moved out to Riseberga when Jonatan was little we needed a car, and then I was the one who had to drive and shuttle everyone around all the time. And Göran got out of it because he didn't have a driver's license. It was just the easy way out.

Why am I sitting here defending myself?

Of course it's because I'm not one hundred percent sure that Jonatan is wrong. Jonatan and Göran. Even the total failure that Göran has made of his own life doesn't prove that he's wrong.

But that's not why I'm crying.

I'm crying because I hear Göran's voice at my own kitchen table in my own home, I'm crying because of everything I've said about him tonight.

I'm crying. My tears are falling down onto Jonatan's shirt. It's only now that I realize that it's bloody. I rub the tears from my eyes and nod toward Jonatan.

"Blood," I snuffle. "His shirt is bloody."

"No need to worry," Josefin whispers. "It's my blood."

When I see that she's not planning to say any more, I proceed. I mean, I did promise to finish my story before she'll let me hear hers.

But there's almost nothing left to say.

We lived our family life, we lived in the house in Falsterbo and the children grew. Every birthday and Christmas, a package came from Göran, every year it made Jonatan happy. The accompanying letters got longer and longer, he wouldn't let me read them and I didn't snoop.

I honestly don't know if Jonatan has had any more contact with his father. I could tell that he was thinking more and more about Göran, I saw how he'd put Göran's pictures up in his room, and that picture over his bed. But the times I tried to talk to him about it he was just evasive, and I've almost been satisfied with that since it was hard for me, too.

In all those years I saw Göran just one time. I mean aside from that time on TV. It was while he was still living in Göteborg.

22

Yes, for Jonatan's sake I tried to keep track of Göran a little, I don't mean that I watched him, just that I checked from time to time that he was still alive, that he was working and that kind of thing. I mean, of course I had no idea what his life was like or how he was doing. And I didn't care, either, just wanted to know for Jonatan's sake that his father was still out there somewhere living a normal life. All the same, I was glad when I saw a little announcement in the paper that Göran was going to be part of a joint exhibit at the Hasselblad Center, and when I had to go to Göteborg for work a few weeks later, of course I took the time to go see the exhibit.

Then, as I was walking up the stairs there at Götaplatsen, a thought occurred to me: What if Göran's exhibit is of pictures of us? The pictures he took when he was following Claes and me that winter.

But no, of course they weren't. It was a kind of photography

I'd never seen before, black-and-white pictures of bodies in clay, bodies smeared with clay, bodies that had almost become one with the earth, and ... very suggestive pictures, I ... I was almost a little proud, it's true. And happy. This was still something he could do, he was good here, he was at home here.

It was on my way out of the exhibit that I saw Göran. He was standing by the ticket windows talking to an older man with a white beard and two teenagers. I felt as if I recognized the bearded man from TV. A beautiful, well-dressed woman was standing at Göran's side. Dark eyes and raven black hair, makeup, she looked feminine in that old-school way, like women from Eastern Europe or Greece. Strange to see a woman like her holding onto Göran's arm, and pressing herself in against him. The way she was standing there said she was in love.

Göran was wearing a black suit and a dark T-shirt. An artist's uniform. He'd gotten a little chubby, had a bit of a belly.

They looked happy, all five of them, they were chatting eagerly and gesticulating, and I heard Göran's laugh.

I stood there in the doorway, and felt like I was caught in a trap. In order to leave the museum I would have to walk right by them, and just the thought of that made my legs wobbly.

I stood there like a stupid cow, staring. Yes, that's what I felt like. And I was irritated, Göran's happiness annoyed me, I mean, fine, I wanted him to be doing all right, for Jonatan's sake, but he didn't need to seem so fucking happy. And surely that whole happy little group with all those interesting cultured people was uncalled for. And surely that woman didn't have to be standing so close to him, she didn't need to be making ridiculous lovey-dovey goo-goo eyes at Göran.

Yup. I'd turned into a teenage girl again. A stupid cow and a teenage girl. Not jealous. No no no. No, never. Not reminded of an old flame or overcome by happy memories. No. Just excluded. My loneliness humiliated me.

And I would be even more humiliated, because the woman at Göran's side noticed me, she felt me looking at them, and she went up on her tiptoes and whispered something in Göran's ear. Before I could escape, he turned to face me. For a few seconds, we looked straight into each other's eyes. He recognized me right away. And you know what? He smiled. That bastard smiled at me. As if we were two old friends who'd run into each other. He smiled as if he were happy. As if he couldn't help it. As if he thought he would get a smile in return. As if nothing had happened. Do you get it? He smiled, and I saw how his lips formed my name. He smiled as if he thought I would go over to him, as if he thought I would introduce myself to his friends. "This is Karin, my ex-wife, and this is …"

I scurried back into the gallery. Up a flight of stairs. Into the bathroom. I sat there for an hour. Stupid cow. Humiliated teenage girl. Then I washed my face and left without catching another glimpse of Göran or his friends.

That was the last time I saw him. About six months later I found out that he'd moved back to Malmö, now he lives in an old house in Klågerup, it's not clear to me if he lives there alone. He's part of a photography group with a studio in Limhamn. I see his name under pictures in various magazines from time to time, and I suspect he has some kind of little grant. He seems to be getting by. He's had a few exhibits, too. Yes, I have his address and phone number, but I haven't gotten in touch with him. I don't know if Jonatan has talked to him.

Josefin doesn't seem to understand that my story is over now, she seems to be waiting for a continuation, or at least a conclusion, so I say, "Then I saw him today. On the mattress here with you and Jonatan. You heard yourself what he said to me."

She tilts her head slightly. "I think he still loves you," she whispers.

Stupid little Josefin. I forget how young you are. Love, what does that mean? What good does that do me, even if what you say is true? Are you such a bad listener …?

Little Josefin, who knows more about my life than anyone else in the whole world. The part of my life that included Göran, at any rate. How little you've understood, after all.

Stupid little Josefin. You have a lot to learn.

"Now you were going to tell your part of the story," I remind her. "About what happened last night. About why we ended up here, why … Jonatan is lying here."

She nods again, but doesn't make any effort to say anything.

I wait.

A fan whirs.

The sun has found its way into the room, it casts a spotlight in the corner where the little desk is, I'm able to watch the sunspot grow and conquer more and more of the floor, a shadow sweeps past, it must've been a seagull flying past the window, the sun has crept almost all the way to the mattress before Josefin clears her throat and says, "Yes. Now I'll tell my part of the story."

Then the door opens.

the father

1

I don't know why I stayed there, sitting in the waiting room.

Everything that had happened overnight was dancing around in my head. First, all the memories that I stirred up in myself to give to Jonatan. I got to relive my whole life in a few hours. Then, meeting the wise and beautiful Josefin, and her story. And then she got scared, I can't understand why I frightened her. If … if I hadn't found my way back to her, then everything would've been wasted, my life would've been wasted. But then we lay there on the mattress and I was so happy, I felt how close I got to you tonight. Nothing can ever hurt me again, I thought. And just then Karin arrived. And I escaped. I can't run into her, not now.

There's a limit, the words "I'm sorry" can only bear so much. I'm a thousand tons over the limit. My guilt is so heavy. Maybe she doesn't think I realize that, but I no longer have a need to explain myself.

And time has dug an ocean between us, we're living on separate continents now, all our shared memories and all the plans we had for the future have drowned. I understand that. I'm not mourning. I don't have any secret plans to try to reach her again, I can't, and I don't want to. But she is the mother of my son. Always.

She stayed in there with him. Maybe she took my spot on the

mattress. Or maybe they left the hospital some other way.

Why did I say that to her? That she wasn't wearing any under-wear. It just slipped out, I couldn't stop my own foolish words. Fuck, I can't believe I can still be such a stupid teenager. But prob-ably it doesn't matter.

All the bitterness is gone now. Nothing can hurt me anymore. Not now that I've told you the story, Jon.

I've been sitting here for so long that my pants are stuck to the green vinyl upholstery of the waiting-room chair. I've seen a few accident victims come in, a girl who OD'd on something, an old lady who seemed to have broken something, a man about my age who'd been beaten up, and some women in shock who'd been in a car accident. But I think it was a calm Saturday night in the emergency room.

I'm still sitting here.

I don't want to do anything else. I'm not waiting for anyone or anything.

A great peacefulness has come over me.

This is where I've ended up, I think. I'm here now.

I'm not thinking about the past anymore.

I'm not making any plans for the future.

I'm just sitting here with my pants stuck to the chair thinking, *I'm here now. Here is the turning point, here the threads come together.*

Was I sitting here, in this same room, one Saturday in 1972? Was I sitting here with a blanket around my shoulders, waiting while Karin got stitches in her forehead? Was it precisely, exactly here that my story began?

I peer around, trying to remember. No. No, I don't remember

it like this at all. Not even if they redecorated, it must've been a different room, I didn't recognize the outside, either, although of course it would've been almost poetic to wrap up a whole life like that. Well, *your* life, to be precise.

Wait a minute now. Something just occurred to me.

Were you the one who called last night? My phone rang, and when I answered no one said anything. Was that you, Jon?

Was that your breathing I heard against my ear? Didn't I hear a sob, too? Was that your sadness I heard?

If only it had occurred to me earlier. I mean, you had my phone number on a slip of paper in your pocket. Surely you were the one who called yesterday?

Now I see a man and a little girl come in and walk over to the reception desk. I don't recognize him until I hear his voice:

"Is Jonatan Persson still here? I'm his father."

No you're not, Claes, you old scoundrel, I think. *Jonatan Persson's father is sitting right here.*

But I'm completely calm, nothing can hurt me anymore.

The nurse talks to him for a while, then he and the girl head straight toward me.

"You wait here a little while, Hanna," he says, showing her that there are magazines she can read while she waits. "I'm just going to go check first how things are with Jonatan, then I'll come back out and get you."

He casts a quick look my way, but doesn't recognize me. Then, he leaves the girl behind and disappears quickly through the doors.

"Hi," I say as soon as I hear the doors click shut behind him.

The girl looks up from her Donald Duck comic book.

Karin's eyes, Karin's hair, Karin's soft little chin. I can't see if she has Karin's earlobes, the girl's hair is long and falls down over her narrow shoulders.

"Hi," she says.

No distrustfulness, just the accepting gaze of a child looking directly into my eyes. Didn't her parents warn her about dirty old men?

"Is your name Hanna?" I ask.

"How'd you know that?" she asks, nodding contentedly.

"Oh, I heard your dad say it," I explain. "That was your dad, wasn't it?"

She nods again, sneaking a glance at the comic book, which is lying open in her lap.

"My name is Göran," I say.

She nods, but now Donald Duck seems to be more interesting than our little conversation.

"When my boy was little he liked to tell knock-knock jokes. Want to hear one?"

She nods, and now our little conversation seems like it might be more interesting than Donald Duck.

"Knock knock," I say.

"Who's there?" she says.

"Hawaii."

"Hawaii who?"

"I'm fine. Hawaii you?" I say, grinning.

Once she gets the joke she giggles and gives me a cute look. She peers at me with the tip of her tongue between her lips.

You're so adorable when I see the tip of your tongue, I think.

"What's your boy's name, then?" she asks.

"Jonatan."

"Weird," she says, and her eyes get big and round. "My big brother's name is Jonatan, too. He's back there."

With a little nod she indicates the doors her father walked through.

"Weird," I say.

"Sometimes I call him Yesnatan. And sometimes I call him Nonatan," she says, giggling.

"Huh?"

"Nonatan. No-natan and Yes-natan. Do you get it?"

"Now I get it," I say, laughing.

"But my mom's name is just Karin," Hanna says. "I don't call her anything."

"No?" I say. "Well, don't you call her Mom?"

"Well, duh," Hanna says.

Then we sit there in silence, but when I see her eyes drifting back toward the comic book again, I quickly ask, "So how old are you, Hanna?"

"Five," she answers. "But I'm gonna be six. How old is Jonatan? Your Jonatan, I mean?"

I hesitate. How far can I go before she gets suspicious? But I can't lie, I can't.

"Seventeen," I answer.

"Super weird," Hanna says, making such a funny face that I can't help but giggle. "My Jonatan is seventeen, too. Hey, what does your Jonatan look like?"

"He's very tall. And thin. And has really short hair."

17

"Super weird," Hanna says, and now she's totally giggling. "He looks exactly like mine. My Jonatan has a girlfriend named Josefin. Does your Jonatan have a girlfriend?"

I just nod. I have to stop here.

"My Jonatan is so crazy sometimes," Hanna continues, and a memory makes her laugh. "You know what, on my birthday, he made these treasure maps so everyone could hunt for their little sacks of candy and he'd hidden one in the washing machine. And one in the toilet, under the lid, and Leonora wouldn't eat her candy then because she thought that was gross, and then Jonatan and Josefin put on a puppet show, one with a policeman who was chasing a prince and a princess and was going to hurt them."

She falls silent, contemplating something, then leans forward as if she's going to tell me a secret that only I can hear.

"Do you know what?" she whispers.

"No, what?" I whisper, and almost can't help giggling from pure happiness.

"One time the police got Jonatan for real," whispers little Hanna. "But it wasn't his fault. It was the police who were being dumb."

"Uh-oh," I say. "Well what did he do? When the police got him?"

"Nothing," Hanna says, pursing her lips and enthusiastically shaking her head. "Not a thing. The police were dumb, they got him even though he hadn't done anything."

"Uh-oh," I say. "How dumb."

She pouts with her lips and nods enthusiastically.

But she doesn't tell me any more, and we sit there in silence in the waiting room. Hanna has forgotten about her comic book, she's just looking out the window with a thoughtful expression.

Her face is an open book, now I see how the sadness grabs hold of her, how it starts to tug at the corners of her mouth.

"Hey, Hanna, can I ask you something?" I say.

"Mmm."

She doesn't turn to look at me.

"What's your last name?"

"Hoff-Hansson," she mumbles.

Hanna Hoff-Hansson, poor girl, I think, but I say, "What a nice last name. Mine's just Persson. Hoff-Hansson is much nicer. Not as common."

"My Jonatan's name is Persson, too," Hanna mumbles.

We sit there in silence for several more long minutes, I watch Hanna and she sits there staring out at nothing, but then she turns toward me, revealing her watery eyes.

"I want to go to my Jonatan now," she says, and her voice reveals that she's on the verge of tears.

She gives me no choice.

"Come on," I say, and there's a crackling and a crunching as I stand up from the chair. "I know where he is. I'll show you."

"You know? Really?"

I nod and hold out my hand to her.

"Come on," I say.

And she stands up and puts her soft little hand in mine and follows me in through the doors and down along the corridor.

The Father, The Son, The Young Woman, The Mother, The Little Girl and The New Husband

Malmö General Hospital, a room in the emergency ward, a Sunday morning in May in the year 2001.

In the room there's a little desk, a cupboard attached to the wall, some hospital equipment and tubes, a simple upholstered desk chair and a stainless steel stool. On the floor there's a mattress. On the ceiling there's a fluorescent light that's still on. Outside the window, the sun is shining in a cloudless sky.

In the room there are also six people.

Jonatan Persson, 17, is lying on the mattress.

Josefin Modigh, 17, is sitting next to him.

Karin Hoff-Hansson, 45, is sitting in the desk chair next to the mattress.

Claes Hansson, 49, is standing to the right of the window.

In through the door walks Hanna Hoff-Hansson, 5.

In the doorway stands Göran Persson, 46.

Six completely ordinary people.

It looks like a scene in a movie is about to take place, a closing scene, the dénouement of a drama.

And what happens is that Hanna rushes right in and flings herself on top of her big brother, she starts kissing him on the cheek and throws her arms around him.

Karin looks at Hanna. Then she looks at Göran. Then she looks at Hanna and Jonatan.

Claes looks at Göran the whole time.

Josefin looks at Jonatan and strokes Hanna's back.

Göran lets his gaze wander over them all, he hesitates before entering the room and closing the door behind him. He stands there, just inside the door.

And Jonatan, what is he doing? Jonatan opens his eyes, carefully pushes Hanna away, blinks, looks around, tries to raise his head but groans from the pain, and grimaces.

Now, everyone in the room is looking at Jonatan. Now, he's definitely the main character. And Göran over there by the door laughs and says, "You woke him with a kiss, Hanna. Just like Sleeping Beauty. Only the other way around."

Jonatan moves his eyes around with difficulty until they land on the person whose voice he just heard.

"Dad," he says. "Hi, Dad. You're still around?"

We could end there. The credits could start rolling there, the music could start, the lights could come on, and the theater could slowly empty out. Only candy wrappers and drink cups and popcorn containers left when the words The End illuminate the screen.

But that's not the ending. It's not the beginning of something new, either.

It's just where we've ended up.

And Josefin still hasn't gotten to tell her part of the story.

Now Jonatan turns to Josefin.

"I'm sorry."

Obviously, he doesn't know that the words "I'm sorry" have been worn out tonight, that they've lost their power.

"How do you feel?" Josefin whispers.

"Like I deserve. Isn't that what people say?"

Now he looks at Göran again, as if the question were meant for him.

"I woke you with a kiss," Hanna says contentedly. "Although I almost didn't want to kiss you. You smell like a dead rat."

17

"You're the dead rat, Hannabanana."

"Bonatan, Jonatan," Hanna sings.

"Ugh, you're right. I definitely smell like a dead rat. My mouth tastes like dead rat, too."

"Gross," Hanna says, making a face.

"Hmm. I think I got turned into a dead rat."

"Why?" Hanna wonders.

Jonatan turns to look at Josefin. She shakes her head.

"I got turned into a dead rat because I was so … stupid," Jonatan says, and a seriousness and a sadness have crept into his voice. "Because I was so stupid and … cruel. Haven't you told them?"

Josefin shakes her head again.

"I … So much happened here tonight while you were lying there and …" She laughs. "And being lazy."

Jonatan groans and sinks back into the mattress.

"Oh, my head," he groans. "But it serves me right."

Mother Karin and her husbands, the current one and the ex, have become the audience, they're playing walk-on roles. But when Jonatan stopped talking their thoughts start to fill the room, their thoughts rise toward the ceiling and make the air thick and heavy.

Karin thinks: *I want to go home now I'm tired I just want this to be over now I can't take any more I don't want to hear any more I don't care what happened and I'm not wearing any underwear it all started on the kitchen table at home it feels like forever ago or everything also started at a crosswalk on Södergata almost thirty years ago and Göran is just standing there and Claes is pissed of course he doesn't understand any of this poor guy imagine the two of you both standing here I've known you for so long but now I want to go home and shower and Hanna has horseback riding at eleven and then there was some party this afternoon or am I mixing up the days it's Saturday today isn't it or is it Sunday I want to go home and shower and sleep and I have to get ahold of a locksmith right away even though it's the weekend and then I have to cancel Jonatan's debit card because even if there isn't any money in the account I mean someone could use it and maybe Jonatan would be stuck later with a bunch of debt and why doesn't the nurse ever come why isn't Claes doing anything you're the one I love Claes but tonight you've been a minor character what if my period starts now I mean it feels like it's time yes it must be what if the blood starts running down my legs I want to go home.*

Claes thinks: *What is he doing here, that bastard? When he came in he was holding Hanna's hand, how dare he that pig, after everything he did to us. And now he's just standing there grinning, I hate him, why don't I walk over there and punch him, I want to kick him in the balls, I want to hear him whimpering in pain, why don't I do that? He's a creep, a worthless creep, I fucking hate him.*

Göran thinks: *Here's where we ended up, all the threads come together here. The turning point is here. Dad, he said. "Dad, you're still around?" he said. He did hear everything. Nothing can hurt me anymore, never again. I see that Karin is someone else now. I want the best for her, I want her to be happy. And Jonatan, happy. And clever Josefin and cute Hanna, just happy. And Claes, you ugly stupid bastard, I just want you to be happy, too, for Karin's sake and Jonatan's. I am Jesus, I am Buddha. You have my blessing. And Jonatan, Jonatan, you're my boy, dead rat, ha ...*

"Speaking of dead rats ..."

Everyone turns to look at Göran by the door.

"Speaking of dead rats, do you remember when we were in

Greece when you were little, Jonatan? On Lesbos, we were staying in an inn there. You were probably only three. There were so many cats there, do you remember? Skinny miserable cats begging for food all over the place. You were so enchanted with the cats, but Karin didn't want you to pet them, she was scared you would get fleas or something, or that they would scratch you. And there was that really cute yellow cat that always managed to get onto our balcony, and then one morning we heard a cat howling from the balcony and so we rushed out there, Karin and I, and there you were fighting with the cat over a dead rat it had dragged up there, you were pulling on the tail and the cat was fighting and struggling to keep its prey. Do you remember that?"

Karin thinks: *I want to go home, I want to sleep.*

Claes thinks: *Is he drunk, that bastard?*

Jonatan thinks about it and says, "Nope. But I remember that balcony. I think. We used to hang up our beach towel as protection from the sun. I remember that. Was that where I went swimming so much? No, that must've been in the Canary Islands, where I learned to swim. And that was with … with Claes."

Göran nods and smiles, and Claes watches him, giving him the evil eye, thinking: *You're standing there grinning, you bastard, but you know why we were in the Canary Islands, don't you? You know what we were trying to get away from, don't you? You're standing there now looking all fucking saintly, thinking that everything will be forgotten and forgiven. Never. I hope I never have to see you again, you pig. And if you ever touch Hanna again or talk to her, then I'll make sure you're locked up somewhere, the statute of limitations will never be up on what you did to us, you got that?*

But Jonatan has raised himself up on his elbows and the look he's giving father Göran is full of sunshine.

"But do you know what I do remember, Dad? I remember the seagulls. When we were standing on that boat. You were holding me in your arms, I was feeding the seagulls bread, they were swooping around and the sky was so blue and they were so shimmering white and beautiful, and they were taking the bread right out of my hand. And I wasn't scared."

Göran looks at him and nods. His smile is as sunny as a Greek summer day.

"I dream about those seagulls sometimes," Jonatan continues. "That's my best dream. I'm always so happy when I wake up from that dream. Happy and sad."

He turns toward Josefin now and looks almost surprised, as if what he has just said surprises him.

Nothing else is going to happen now. Nothing important.

Jonatan will apologize to Josefin one more time, he will ask her to tell the story of what happened the night before. Josefin will hesitate, Jonatan will say, "No, really. I want everyone to know."

Josefin will sigh and nod, but just as she's about to start telling the story the door will open. A nurse will come in. Not the same one as during the night, not Sister Anna, no, a new one. She will say a few words to Jonatan, ask a few questions, and then she will say, "Now you can all go home. This adventure is over now. It turned out well this time."

Yes, that's all that will happen.